RED-HEADED STEPCHILD

The demon came forward without warning and jerked the arrow from my body. The damned thing had lodged itself so deep it took a couple of good pulls to get it loose. I grunted against the pain, and cold sweat broke out on my forehead. The tip of the arrow finally came free with a disgusting sucking noise. I collapsed to the floor and curled up in the fetal position in the puddle of spilled beer.

From the corner of my eye, I saw the demon hold the arrow up to the light. He lifted the tip to his mouth and his forked tongue darted out to taste the blood. My blood. I groaned and squeezed my eyes shut. At that point, I almost hoped he'd stake me. No words exist to describe the pain.

"Well, I guess that's that." The demon's hooves click-clacked against the hardwoods. I felt him hovering close. "You okay?"

My eyes snapped open. Already, my heightened healing powers were making quick work of the wounds. "Am I okay?" I barked. "You just shot me through the heart with an arrow!"

"Hey, it's nothing personal."

BY JAYE WELLS

Sabina Kane Novels

Red-Headed Stepchild

The Mage in Black

RED-HEADED STEPCHILD

Jaye Wells

orbit

www.orbitbooks.net

ORBIT

First published in Great Britain in 2009 by Orbit

A CIP catalogue record for this book
is available from the British Library.

ISBN 978-1-84149-756-3

Typeset in Times by Palimpsest Book Production Limited,
Grangemouth, Stirlingshire
Printed in the UK by
CPI Mackays, Chatham ME5 8TD

Papers used by Orbit are natural, renewable and recyclable
products sourced from well-managed forests and certified in
accordance with the rules of the Forest Stewardship Council.

Mixed Sources

Product group from well-managed
forests and other controlled sources
www.fsc.org Cert no. SGS-COC-004081
© 1996 Forest Stewardship Council

Orbit
An imprint of
Little, Brown Book Group
100 Victoria Embankment
London EC4Y 0DY

An Hachette UK Company
www.hachette.co.uk

www.orbitbooks.net

For Zach:
No take-backs needed.

1

Digging graves is hell on a manicure, but I was taught good vampires clean up after every meal. So I ignored the chipped onyx polish. I ignored the dirt caked under my nails. I ignored my palms, rubbed raw and blistering. And when a snapping twig announced David's arrival, I ignored him too.

He said nothing, just stood off behind a thicket of trees waiting for me to acknowledge him. Despite his silence, I could feel hot waves of disapproval flying in my direction.

At last, the final scoop of earth fell onto the grave. Stalling, I leaned on the shovel handle and restored order to my hair. Next I brushed flecks of dirt from my cashmere sweater. Not the first choice of digging attire for some, but I always believed manual labor was no excuse for sloppiness. Besides, the sweater was black, so it went well with the haphazard funerary rites.

The Harvest Moon, a glowing orange sphere, still loomed in the sky. Plenty of time before sunrise. In the distance, traffic hummed like white noise in the City of Angels. I took a moment to appreciate the calm.

Memory of the phone call from my grandmother intruded. When she told me the target of my latest assignment, an icy chill spread through my veins. I'd almost hung up, unable to believe what she was asking me to do. But when she told me David was working with Clovis Trakiya, white-hot anger replaced the chill. I called up that anger now to spur my resolve. I clenched my teeth and ignored the cold stone sitting in my stomach. My own feelings about David were irrelevant now. The minute he decided to work with one of the Dominae's enemies—a glorified cult leader who wanted to overthrow their power—he'd signed his death warrant.

Unable to put it off any longer, I turned to him. "What's up?"

David stalked out of his hiding place, a frown marring the perfect planes of his face. "Do you want to tell me why you're burying a body?"

"Who, me?" I asked, tossing the shovel to the ground. My palms were already healing. I wish I could say the same for my guilty conscience. If David thought I should apologize for feeding from a human, I didn't want to know what he was going to say in about five minutes.

"Cut the shit, Sabina. You've been hunting again." His eyes glowed with accusation. "What happened to the synthetic blood I gave you?"

"That stuff tastes like shit," I said. "It's like nonalcoholic beer. What's the point?"

"Regardless, it's wrong to feed from humans."

It's also wrong to betray your race, I thought. If there

was one thing about David that always got my back up, it was his holier-than-thou attitude. Where were his morals when he made the decision to sell out?

Keep it together, Sabina. It will all be over in a few minutes.

"Oh, come on. It was just a stupid drug dealer," I said, forcing myself to keep up the banter. "If it makes you feel any better, he was selling to kids."

David crossed his arms and said nothing.

"Though I have to say nothing beats Type O mixed with a little cannabis."

A muscle worked in David's jaw. "You're stoned?"

"Not really," I said. "Though I do have a strange craving for pizza. Extra garlic."

He took a deep breath. "What am I going to do with you?" His lips quirked despite his harsh tone.

"First of all, no more lectures. We're vampires, David. Mortal codes of good and evil don't apply to us."

He arched a brow. "Don't they?"

"Whatever," I said. "Can we just skip the philosophical debates for once?"

He shook his head. "Okay then, why don't you tell me why we're meeting way out here?"

Heaving a deep sigh, I pulled my weapon. David's eyes widened as I aimed the custom-made pistol between them.

His eyes pivoted from the gun to me. I hoped he didn't notice the slight tremor in my hands.

"I should have known when you called me," he said. "You never do that."

"Aren't you going to ask me why?" His calm unsettled me.

"I know why." He crossed his arms and regarded me closely. "The question is, do you?"

My eye twitched. "I know enough. How could you betray the Dominae?"

He didn't flinch. "One of these days your blind obedience to the Dominae is going to be your downfall."

I rolled my eyes. "Don't waste your final words on another lecture."

He lunged before the last word left my lips. He plowed into me, knocking the breath out of my chest and the gun from my hand. We landed in a tangle of limbs on the fresh grave. Dirt and fists flew as we each struggled to gain advantage. He grabbed my hair and whacked my head into the dirt. Soil tunneled up my nose and rage blurred my vision.

My hands curled into claws and dug into his eyes. Distracted by pain, he covered them with his palms. Gaining the advantage fueled my adrenaline as I flipped him onto his back. My knees straddled his hips, and I belted him in the nose with the base of my hand. Blood spurted from his nostrils, streaking his lips and chin.

"Bitch!" Like an animal, he sank his fangs into the fleshy part of my palm. I shrieked, backhanding him across the cheek with my uninjured hand. He growled and shoved me. I flew back several feet, landing on my ass with a thud.

Before I could catch my breath, his weight pinned me down again. Only this time, my gun stared back at me with its unblinking eye.

"How does it feel, Sabina?" His face was close to mine as he whispered. His breath stunk of blood and fury. "How does it feel to be on the other end of the gun?"

"It sucks, actually." Despite my tough talk, my heart hammered against my ribs. I glanced to the right and saw the shovel I'd used earlier lying about five feet away. "Listen—"

"Shut up." His eyes were wild. "You know what the worst part is? I came here tonight to come clean with you. Was going to warn you about the Dominae and Clovis—"

"Warn me?"

David jammed the cold steel into my skull—tattooing me with his rage. "That's the irony isn't it? Do you even know what's at stake here?" He cocked the hammer. Obviously, the question had been rhetorical.

One second, two, ticked by before the sound of flapping wings and a loud hoot filled the clearing. David glanced away, distracted. I punched him in the throat. He fell back, gasping and sputtering. I hauled ass to the shovel.

Time slowed. Spinning, I slashed the shovel in a wide arc. A bullet ricocheted off the metal, causing a spark. David pulled himself up to shoot again, but I lunged forward, swinging like Babe Ruth. The metal hit David's skull with a sickening thud. He collapsed in a heap.

He wouldn't stay down long. I grabbed the gun from his limp hand and aimed it at his chest.

I was about to pull the trigger when his eyes crept open. "Sabina."

He lay on the ground, covered in blood and dirt. The goose egg on his forehead was already losing its mass. Knowledge of the inevitable filled his gaze. I paused, watching him.

At one time, I'd looked up to this male, counted him as

a friend. And now he'd betrayed everything I held sacred by selling out to the enemy. I hated him for his treachery. I hated the Dominae for choosing me as executioner. But most of all, I hated myself for what I was about to do.

He raised a hand toward me—imploring me to listen. My insides felt coated in acid as I watched him struggle to sit up.

"Don't trust—"

His final words were lost in the gun's blast. David's body exploded into flames, caused by the metaphysical friction of his soul leaving his flesh.

My whole body spasmed. The heat from the fire couldn't stop the shaking in my limbs. Collapsing to the dirt, I wiped a quivering hand down my face.

The gun felt like a branding iron in my hand. I dropped it, but my hand still throbbed. A moment later, I changed my mind and picked it up again. Pulling out the clip, I removed one of the bullets. Holding one up for inspection, I wondered what David felt when the casing exploded and a dose of the toxic juice robbed him of his immortality.

I glanced over at the smoldering pile that was once my friend. Had he suffered? Or did death bring instant relief from the burdens of immortality? Or had I just damned his soul to a worse fate? I shook myself. His work here was done. Mine wasn't.

My shirt was caked with smears of soot, dirt, and drying blood—David's blood mixed with mine. I sucked in a lungful of air, hoping to ease the tightness in my chest.

The fire had died, leaving a charred, smoking mass of ash and bone. *Great,* I thought, *now I have to dig another grave.*

I used the shovel to pull myself up. A blur of white

flew through the clearing. The owl called out again before flying over the trees. I stilled, wondering if I was hearing things. It called again and this time I was sure it screeched, "Sabina."

Maybe the smoke and fatigue were playing tricks on me. Maybe it had really said my name. I wasn't sure, but I didn't have time to worry about that. I had a body to bury.

As I dug in, my eyes started to sting. I tried to convince myself it was merely a reaction to the smoke, but a voice in my head whispered "guilt." With ruthless determination, I shoved my conscience down, compressing it into a tiny knot and shoving it into a dark corner of myself. Maybe later I'd pull it out and examine it. Or maybe not.

Good assassins dispose of problems without remorse. Even if the problem was a friend.

2

*S*epulcher was my next stop after burying David. Located in Silverlake, near Sunset, it catered to hipster mortal clientele on the front. In the back, however, was one of the best vampire clubs in L.A.

I'd never seen the bouncer before. He had a thick neck and his mullet was not an ironic statement. He wore a black wife beater with the word "asshole" written on it in white. I assumed this was his name.

"Sorry, girlie, no ID, no entry."

"Look, " I said, "You're new so I'll forgive your ignorance. Ewan knows me."

Asshole smiled, his crooked teeth yellow from the cigarette dangling from his lips. "You're the tenth chick tonight who's claimed to know Ewan. No dice. Next!" He dismissed me, looking at the couple in line behind me. "ID?"

I pushed the guy who stepped forward out of my way.

"Hey!" he said, puffing up like a blowfish.

"Fuck off," I said without looking at him.

"Now, listen," I said to the bouncer, who sighed heavily. "I'm going in. You can try to stop me, but I wouldn't recommend it."

He laughed and flexed a bicep. "Bring it."

When I moved forward, his hand shot out and grabbed my left arm. With a quick twist toward his thumb, I extricated myself from his hold. Crushing his metatarsals crossed my mind, but I didn't want to make more of a scene than necessary. I kept walking, only to have him grab me around the waist from behind. He lifted my feet off the ground and hugged me hard to his body.

So much for avoiding a scene.

"You like it rough, huh?" he whispered in my ear. I was about to show him just how rough I liked it when Ewan appeared.

"Put her down, Tank," he ordered.

"She ain't got no ID, boss."

"It's all right," Ewan said.

"But, you said—"

"I said, put her down!"

As soon as my feet hit the floor, I spun around, ready to throw down. Before I could swing, Ewan grabbed my hand and pulled me roughly toward him.

"Stop," he said. "Or I'll personally kick your ass to the curb."

Our stare-off lasted only a few moments. Tension hung over us like a cloud, as the rest of the people in line held their collective breath. In the end, though, I knew my anger had nothing to do with the bouncer. Fighting him wouldn't erase the last two hours of my life. Taking a deep breath, I stood down and settled for glaring over Ewan's shoulder at the Neanderthal. Ewan placated Tank and sent him back to the door. With a jerk of his head, he indicated I should follow him to the back.

The place was wall-to-wall mortals. Many were crowded on the small dance floor in front of the stage, but the area around the bar was equally packed as people fought for the bartenders' attention. On the stage, an all-girl punk group thrashed their instruments. They sounded like a bunch of cats in heat. Above the stage, small lights spelled out "Salvation."

The whole scene felt claustrophobic. The smog of cigarette smoke mixed with the scent of sweat and stale beer, not to mention the overpowering aroma of blood pumping through all those mortal bodies.

As we passed, the women's bathroom door opened. Two bleached blondes in miniskirts were snorting lines of coke from the counter. Their blood would offer an amazing high were I to feed from them. But I knew better than to go there. First, Ewan would kill me if I sucked on his customers. Second, while the occasional pothead was a harmless snack, making meals out of drug addicts was bad news. Others before me had found the secondhand high too hard to resist, only to find themselves junkies for eternity.

Another bouncer stood about ten feet past the restrooms. This one was smaller than the guy out front, but far deadlier. Sebastian's auburn hair was shaved on the sides and rose into a Mohawk in the center. He had a bullring in his nose and a dragon half-sleeve tattoo on his left arm.

"What's up, Sabina?" he said over the heads of the mortal couple he'd been talking to.

"Hey!" The woman swayed as she spoke. I wasn't sure

if it was her massive silicone tits throwing off her balance or if too much alcohol was to blame. "We were here first."

"I already told you to get lost," Sebastian said calmly.

"There a problem?" Ewan stepped forward.

"Yes, there's a problem," the drunk chick's boyfriend said. He was a muscle-bound Hollywood type, probably an actor. Silverlake's alternative rock scene didn't usually draw his kind. Perhaps he felt hanging out there made him edgy. "He won't let us into the VIP lounge."

Ewan played it cool, looking back at Sebastian. "Are their names on the list?"

Sebastian didn't miss a beat. "No, sir."

"But he isn't holding a list," the girl whined.

The guy stepped in front of her and puffed up. "Do you have any idea who I am?"

"Yes, sir, I'm a big fan," Ewan said. "Unfortunately, there's a private party tonight."

"This is ridiculous," the guy said.

Ewan put a hand on the guy's shoulder and deftly maneuvered him back in the direction of the bar. Over his shoulder he mouthed, "I'll be back." As they moved away, I heard him promise the couple drinks on the house.

"Is my name on the list?" I teased Sebastian.

"What list?" he said, deadpan. "Go on back."

I walked through the door marked "private," which opened onto a dark staircase. As I descended the steps, the sounds of the club upstairs became muted, almost as if I'd ducked my head below water. At the bottom, I knocked on another door. A small panel opened and two eyes squinted at me through the slit. A bright beam from overhead illuminated me like an inquisitor's light.

"Password?"

"Fuck you."

"Very funny," said Dirk, another bouncer. "You know I can't let you in without the password, Sabina."

"Come on, Dirk,"

"Sorry, babe. Gotta say the words."

"Fine." I sighed. "Count Chocula." One of these days I was going to have to tell Ewan his sense of humor sucked.

"Atta girl," Dirk said. The panel closed and the sound of several locks clicking open filled the small space. Dirk closed the door behind me.

This room held a coat rack and a stool for Dirk. Yet another door waited ahead. I understood the need for security. Ewan had had problems in the past with mortals stumbling into the vampire-only section of the club, but it was a pain in the ass jumping through all these hoops.

"Hey, babe." Dirk smiled flirtatiously.

"What's up?" I said, not really caring.

"Oh you know, this and that." He unlocked the next door as he spoke. Pulling it open with a flourish, he motioned for me to go on in.

In comparison to the mortal area, the vamp section was relatively mellow. No flashing lights or strobes interrupted the darkness. The only light came from strategically placed candles, which sat in recessed shelves all over the exposed-brick walls and on the tables. The only other light was from the sign over the bar. This one read "Damnation."

Here and there, vamps lounged on purple velvet settees, smoking blood from long hoses attached to red-and-gold hookahs. Some used simple tobacco blends, which added a spicy scent to the air. Others sprinkled a little opium into the mix. The sweet smoke mixed with the ferric aroma of blood to create an intoxicating perfume.

A few familiar faces turned in my direction as I made my way to the bar. It was only ten o'clock, so the crowd was light. Soon enough, other vamps would filter in, their cheeks ruddy from recent feedings.

I leaned on the mahogany bar and waved to Ivan, the bartender. He strolled over with a grin on his freckled face. His hair, the color of rust, was pulled into a ponytail that hung down his back. A small golden hoop twinkled from his left ear.

"What'll it be, Sabina?"

"I'll take a pint of O-neg with a vodka chaser."

Ivan raised his eyebrows. "Tough night?"

"Just get the drinks." I was being a bitch, and I knew it. Maybe a few drinks would dilute the acid gnawing at my gut.

"Yes, ma'am," he said with a mocking salute.

As I waited, I scanned the bar again, tapping my fingers in time with the rhythmic drums of Godsmack's "Voodoo." A guy at the end of the bar caught my eye, not because he was trying to be noticed, but because he was trying so hard not to be. His head was down and he wore dark sunglasses. His black leather jacket hung on wide shoulders, which hunched over his drink. But the thing that really got my attention was his hair.

All vampires have red hair—ranging from the young strawberry blondes to the ancient mahogany reds. The darker the shade, the older the vamp. My own hair, since I was half vampire and half mage, was a streaky combination of bright red and black. We owed this telltale sign to Cain, whom God had marked with a shock of red hair after the infamous murder of Abel. After he was cast out, he met up with Lilith, who'd left Eden after she grew bored with Adam. Cain's affair with Lilith resulted in the creation of the vampire race. We got our blood thirst and immortality from Lilith, and our inability to go into the sun and our red hair from Cain. No amount of plant dye or salon work can disguise the Mark of Cain. Like a scar, it's the ultimate proof of our lineage. Luckily, since so many humans also have red hair, it's easy to blend in. Little do those humans know, their own red shades indicate some link to the vampire bloodline in their ancestry.

The guy at the end of the bar had dirty blond hair— not a streak of red to be found. He could be a mortal, I mused, but Ewan never let "worm food" in this part of the club. That left only one option: a mage. And a brave one at that, if he came to the vampire club alone.

As I was thinking this, he looked up. I couldn't see his eyes through the dark glasses, but it was obvious he was looking at me, too. A brief but intense jolt of déjà vu passed along my spine before he looked away.

What the hell? I started to move in his direction, but Ewan intercepted me.

"Freaking actors." He signaled to Ivan and then leaned next to me at the bar. "I had to give him a bottle of Cristal to shut him up."

"You should have kicked his ass out," I said. My gaze strayed back to the mage. He'd turned his head to watch a pair of female vamps on a divan. Red smoke escaped from between their lips as they kissed, sharing a hit from the hookah at their feet.

Ewan sighed beside me, drawing my attention from

the Sapphic display. "Believe it or not, I don't like to alienate my mortal clientele."

"Sell out."

"Mortals are good tippers," he said. "Unlike some immortals I know."

Ivan reappeared with my drink. I tipped him a twenty, with a pointed look at Ewan.

"Great, now I can afford that mansion in Bel Air," Ivan said, pocketing the money. I ignored him and gulped down some blood, followed by the shot.

Ewan watched me as he sipped on his own pint. "Have you talked to David tonight?"

Here's the thing about Ewan: His expertly mussed hair and designer clothes gave the impression he was just another party boy. However, nothing happened in the L.A. vamp scene without his knowledge. Information was his currency. Plus, Ewan also had an uncanny ability to read people.

I shrugged and looked at my glass. "Nope."

"Interesting." He took another drink, watching me over the rim. "He called here earlier and said he was on his way to meet up with you."

Shit. Forcing a casual shrug, I said, "Never showed."

"Maybe he'll stop by here then." I could tell from his voice he didn't expect that any more than I did. "Though he hasn't quite been himself lately."

"Oh?" Glancing up, I noticed that the mage at the other end of the bar seemed to be watching us. If he hadn't been so far away, I would have thought from the tilt of his head he was eavesdropping. When he saw me catch him, he looked away quickly.

Ewan leaned in. "Word on the street is he's got himself mixed up in a power struggle between the Dominae and Clovis Trakiya."

"Power struggle?" I asked, playing dumb. "From what I've heard Clovis Trakiya is nothing but a nuisance for the Dominae."

Ewan shook his head. "He's bad news. Mixed-blood."

My head jerked up. "Really?" Interesting, I thought. My grandmother failed to mention the mixed-blood tidbit when she gave me the rundown on Clovis earlier. She'd just said he was a fringe nut job up north who was trying to recruit vamps.

"Yeah. Rumor is he's half demon, if you can believe it. Anyway, he's building some kind of army in San Francisco. But get this, he claims it's a religious sect."

"A cult, you mean."

He nodded. "Apparently, Clovis is preaching unity among the races or some shit. He's recruiting young vamps, fae, and even some mages."

"He'd have to be insane to think he can overthrow the Dominae," I said.

"Maybe. All I know is his numbers are growing. And I have it on good authority our friend David might be considering defecting to Clovis's camp."

Here's where things were going to get tricky. Obviously, I couldn't confirm Ewan's hunch, but denying it too passionately might also make him suspicious.

"Come on," I said. "David wouldn't be that dumb."

Ewan raised an eyebrow. "Wouldn't he? You know damned well he's had problems with the Dominae's policies in the past. Remember when they decided not to ban feeding from humans? He threw a fit. If I have to hear him preach the gospel of synthetic blood one more time—"

Ewan shook his head. "Anyway, I'm just telling you what the rumors are. You might want to talk to him before he does something stupid. Like get himself killed."

I took a long drink to hide my reaction that that little gem. If I didn't know any better, I'd think he was goading me into admitting my crime. But there was no way even Ewan would have heard so soon.

"I'm just sayin', Sabina. Because you know if your grandmother catches wind of the slightest hint he might be in bed with Clovis, she'll have David killed."

I raised the glass in one sweaty palm and gestured to Ivan for another. "I'll handle it," I snapped. The irony of this statement wasn't lost on me. But at the moment, I just wanted another fucking drink.

Ewan's eyes took on an assessing slant. "You know, there's something I've always wanted to ask you."

"Oh?" I said, praying he was going to change the subject.

"Have you and David ever . . ." Ewan made an obscene gesture with his hands.

"What? No! David's been like a brother to me since we went through assassin school together."

Ewan toyed with his glass. "But you two always argue. I just thought maybe it was more of a sexual tension thing."

"Absolutely not. It's more like a he's-an-annoying-big-brother thing." Or he was, I silently amended. I took the glass Ivan delivered and took a long gulp.

Ewan shrugged. "My mistake."

Dirk appeared at Ewan's side and whispered something I couldn't hear. "There's an issue that needs my attention up front. If you'll excuse me?" Ewan said, standing.

I nodded. "Sure." The interruption was a relief. All this talk of David made me feel itchy, like my skin was too tight.

"Don't repeat anything I told you. I try hard to be the Switzerland of the vampire world, if you know what I mean."

"No problem," I said, forcing a smile.

As he walked away, I thought about what would happen once word got out I'd smoked David. Most likely Ewan would be pissed I hadn't told him so he'd have been the first to know. Despite their casual friendship, Ewan wouldn't mourn David's passing. It would just be another bit of information he would stash away in his mental savings account, ready to withdraw should it prove valuable.

From the corner of my eye, I saw an auburn-haired male move toward me. The scowl on his face didn't give me hope he just wanted to buy me a drink. His two buddies, both over six feet tall and almost as wide, had his back. I almost laughed, loving the fact that the guy felt he needed two friends to help him confront little old me. I subtly checked my rear waistband for the gun I always kept there.

"You're Sabina Kane." He filled out his leather pants nicely, and would have been hot if he hadn't looked like he wanted to spit at me.

"In the flesh." I took a slow sip from the pint.

He leaned in, crowding my space. "You killed my brother."

I turned slowly and looked up at him. "And? I've killed a lot of people's brothers."

My lack of fear seemed to confuse him for a second.

He looked at his friends. The one on the left nodded his head encouragingly. The other cracked the knuckles of his ham-hock hands.

"He was my only brother," he continued.

"Okay," I said, looking past him. My apathy seemed to agitate him further, which is exactly what I'd hoped it would do. This guy needed to be taught a lesson. If I let him get away with his bravado in public, it would make me appear weak to the other vamps. Word would spread, and next thing you know my reputation for being a heart-less bitch would be ruined. What good is an assassin if no one fears them?

"Listen, bitch, you need to pay for what you did."

I rolled my eyes. "Look, dude, I'll save you some time here. What was your brother's name?"

"Zeke Calebow."

I snorted. "You mean the Zeke Calebow who threat-ened to expose our existence to the mortal media if the Dominae didn't give him a billion dollars?"

The guy nodded curtly.

"That asshole was too stupid to live."

Zeke's brother hauled back a meaty fist. Dirk, who'd been approaching our little party from behind, grabbed the guy. His fist made a loud crunching sound as Dirk crushed it. The two friends moved in to help, but stopped at the telltale sound of a pump-action shotgun.

"Don't even think about it," Ivan said calmly. He stood behind the bar with the weapon pointed at their heads. Even if Ivan didn't have cider shells in the gun, a shotgun blast could blow their heads clean off, making them very dead.

"Didn't your mama ever teach you it's rude to hit a

lady?" Dirk asked Zeke's brother, whom he had in a headlock.

"Fuck off," the guy said, struggling.

I leaned against the bar, sipping on my drink, happy to let the staff handle the situation for the moment. If it'd been me, three dead vamps would already be on the floor.

"Apologize," Dirk said. He winked at me, and I toasted him with my drink.

The friends and Ivan were holding a stare-off. The rest of the bar had stopped to watch. No one rose to help, nor did they look especially excited. Vampire life tended to make one a bit numb to confrontation.

"Apologize," Dirk said again, tightening his hold.

"The bitch is gonna die."

I laughed out loud. After tossing a Ben Franklin on the bar, I approached him. He struggled against Dirk's hold while his eyes shot white heat in my direction.

"That's okay. I was leaving anyway." I lifted his chin with my index finger. Leaning close, I whispered, "Your brother screamed like a girl when I staked him."

As I swaggered away, the guy growled. Ewan rushed in, looking worried as he took in the scene. He moved toward me, holding up a hand. "Sabina, watch out!"

I turned just in time to see Dirk hit the floor and Zeke's brother come after me. He growled like an animal, showing a flash of fangs. I grabbed my gun and spun into a crouch, pulling the trigger as I rounded. He ignited midair—a brief, intense burst of heat—and then his ashes rained to the floor.

I turned and pointed the gun at his friends. Their mouths gaped stupidly as they eyed the pile of cinders and ashes on the varnished concrete floor. "Do we still have a problem?" I asked. They shook their heads frantically and backed away with palms held up in surrender.

Ewan stood over the mass of ash on the floor. He shook his head. "Someone's going to have to clean this up, you know."

"Put it on my tab."

Over Ewan's shoulder, I noticed the mage watching the scene without expression. This surprised me. I figured at the first sign of vamp violence he would have blinked his way out of there. Instead, he looked almost bored as he sipped on his beer.

"Hey, Ivan." I leaned on the bar to talk.

"Yeah?" he asked, sounding distracted as he watched the vamp's two friends get escorted from the bar.

"Who's the mage?"

We both turned to look where the mage was sitting, but to my surprise, he was gone. Poof.

"That's weird. He was just there," I said.

Ivan shook his head. "Freakin' mancies. They give me the willies."

"Do you know who he was?" I asked.

"Nah. But he was asking questions before you got here."

"What kind of questions?" I didn't know why I was so intrigued about some random mage, but something about him set off my warning sensors.

Ivan looked at me and said, "About you."

Well, if that wasn't the perfect end to a perfectly craptacular evening. Why in the hell would a mage be stalking me?

3

A guard holding a large semiautomatic rifle greeted me at the front door.

"Follow me." He had to turn sideways to get through the doorframe as he led me inside the Dominae compound. His hair was coppery red, indicating that, like me, he was less than a century old.

He lumbered up one wing of the double staircase. My boots scuffed the limestone steps, the sound unnaturally loud in the cavernous room. When we reached the top, he motioned me to follow him to the right, down a long carpeted corridor. At various intervals, we passed guards standing still as statues next to priceless artwork set in niches along the blood-red walls.

Finally, we reached the doors to the antechamber. A handful of other vamps littered the room. Most of them were young strawberry blonds; only a few had darker shades. These were hangers-on, hoping to curry favor. A pair of older vampires, members of the Undercouncil, stood in the corner whispering to each other.

As usual, all conversation ceased when I walked in.

More art hung here—landscapes mostly, depicting Tuscan hillsides. Flowing crimson sheers hung over arched windows, which reached from floor to ceiling. Beyond the panes lay the well-lit grounds of the estate. Past that, the ocean sparkled in the moonlight.

At the back of the room stood two doors, each emblazoned with a bronze relief. The left panel showed Lilith seducing Cain, which resulted in the creation of the vampire race. The right depicted her coronation as the Queen of Irkalla following her marriage to Asmodeus. On either side of these, torches sat in brackets, illuminating the raised images.

The sound of static from a walkie-talkie broke the silence. One of the guards spoke into it in low tones.

"Sabina Kane," he announced finally.

In unison, the guards each grabbed a handle, sweeping the large panels open with a flourish. I could feel the stares of the others as I moved. The words "killer" and "mixed-blood" were muttered in hushed tones. Once I passed the portal, the doors closed, locking out their judgment.

I had an impression of candlelight in my peripheral vision, but my eyes were focused on the middle of the room. Softly lit by recessed lights, the Dominae sat behind a long wooden table in the center of the chamber.

Lavinia, with her dark carmine hair, sat at the center with one female to either side. Her position as Alpha among the three was secured by her age. Some vampires, the bold ones, joked that she pre-dated the discovery of fire. In reality, no one really knew for sure when she was born. Hell, she was my grandmother and even I didn't know how old she was. I guess, like everyone else, I was too afraid to ask.

"Sabina," she said as I approached. Her voice was a seduction, husky and infused with quiet authority. "Welcome, child."

Kneeling before them, I kept my eyes lowered and touched my forehead with my right hand—a sign of respect.

"Protectors of all Lilim, the blessings of the Great Mother upon each of you."

"And to you, child," Lavinia said. "You may rise."

I stood and cleared my throat, which suddenly felt dry despite the quick feeding on the way here. Lavinia clapped her milky white hands once, bringing my gaze back to her. The sound of shuffling feet came from my right. A pale, slender male came forward bearing a tray. He opened a bottle of wine and poured a burgundy liquid into four stemmed glasses before handing them out.

I lifted the cool glass to my lips. The smell of oaky wine and metallic blood tickled my nose. The first sip exploded onto my taste buds like a liquid orgasm.

"Wow," I said, momentarily forgetting my esteemed audience.

"You like it?" Persephone said with an indulgent smile.

"Yes, Domina." I took another lingering sip. "Where did you find this?"

Her low chuckle sounded like dark chocolate. "It's ours. Tanith invested in a small winery upstate a few years ago," Persephone said, gesturing to the third Domina. "What you're drinking is from our first successful crop. It took us a while to find the perfect blend of grape varietals and blood type."

"I'd say you've succeeded." I drained my glass. A slight tingle reverberated through me. "It's some of the best blood-wine I've ever tasted."

"I think it will be quite popular among the elite Lilim classes," said Tanith. She was the second in command and handled most of the Dominae's business interests. She was also the least attractive of the Dominae, with her large Roman nose and kinky auburn hair. "Of course, we'll also be selling regular wine to the mortals in order to raise funds for our various interests."

I nodded, not really caring about anything besides getting a second glass. Tanith nodded to the servant, who promptly gave me a refill.

"Now," said Lavinia, leaning back, "you may tell us about your mission."

It looked like cocktail hour was over.

"The target was neutralized," I said.

"Were there any complications?" As usual, Lavinia's blue eyes watched me closely for signs of weakness.

Normally, I wouldn't have mentioned the fight leading up to David's death, but I knew any prevarication on my part would be detected immediately.

"The subject put up a struggle, but was ultimately unsuccessful."

The three nodded their approval in unison.

"You called him 'the subject,'" said Persephone, the youngest of the three. "Why do you not say David's name?"

"Forgive me, Domina, but it is standard protocol when discussing missions."

"Yet David has been your friend for many years, correct?" she continued. "Thus this was not a standard mission."

"A mission is a mission," I replied. Why were they making me talk about this? It was bad enough they asked me to do it. They had a whole stable of assassins who could have handled it. I longed to ask why they chose me, but no one questioned the Dominae.

"You did not have any qualms about killing your friend?" Lavinia asked finally.

"No," I said, looking straight into her eyes. "He ceased being my friend when he decided to become a traitor."

I took the last swig of wine and handed the glass to the hovering servant. Why was she pressing the issue? Admitting that I had any reservations about taking out a friend wasn't an option. Missions were never personal— Lavinia herself had taught me that.

The three seemed to exchange some unspoken communication I couldn't begin to decipher. Then Lavinia leaned forward. "We are pleased with your success in this matter."

Warmth that had nothing to do with the blood-wine spread through my midsection. "Thank you, Domina."

"However, it has come to our attention that in addition to the authorized killing last evening, there was another, unauthorized one at the bar called Sepulcher."

The warmth turned to chill as I took in the expression on her face. It was the same one she always got just before she reminded me of my many and varied shortcomings. I'd seen that look more times than I could count, and each time I felt shame for not being able to overcome the flaws I'd inherited from my mage father.

My first instinct was to lower my eyes and apologize. But, frankly, I felt ambushed. Here I thought I was summoned to receive praise for carrying out their orders, when in fact I was really being called to the carpet for defending myself.

"Well, Sabina? Is this true? Did you kill a Lilim without permission?"

My neck was tight as I nodded. "It's true I didn't have permission. However, your own laws make it clear that self-defense falls under justifiable homicide."

"Do not quote our own laws back to us, girl," Lavinia's voice cut through the air like a slap. I cringed, knowing I'd overstepped the line.

"I apologize."

Lavinia took a deep breath and motioned for the servant to hand her the pipe connected to an unseen hookah at her feet. She lifted it to her lips and inhaled a deep drag of red smoke. The sickly sweet aroma drifted to me.

Tanith jumped in, reading from a sheaf of papers on the table. "The accounts show one Billy Dan Calebow— brother of Zeke—threatened you more than once. However, our source also states you were heard taunting the victim prior to his attack."

Lavinia, whose eyes now looked glassy under the overhead lights, slammed her hand on the table. "Dammit, Sabina, you should know better."

"So I was just supposed to let him kill me?"

Her eyes narrowed. "Curb your tongue."

My jaw clenched and I crossed my arms, my posture saying what my mouth couldn't.

"Sabina, you are one of our best assassins. But you can't go around killing everyone who threatens you. We expect you to be able to subdue those who threaten you without deadly force." Persephone's voice was soft, as she tried to play mediator. I heard her but my eyes were locked with my grandmother's. "You have to understand, the Lilim community trusts us to use your skills to dispense justice to those who break the laws. If they have to worry about you losing your temper and taking it out on the public, it will undermine our authority."

"This is especially true for you, Sabina," said Tanith. "Given the circumstances of your birth, many of our followers already worry you're a loose cannon. You have to be above reproach."

I took a deep breath, trying to tamp down my frustration. How many times had I heard that lecture over the years? Like I didn't know I was different. Like I hadn't spent my entire life trying to be the perfect vampire so everyone would overlook my mage heritage. If I had to hear one more lecture about how the standards were higher for me because of my parent's sins, I was going to puke.

"You will apologize now." Lavinia's voice didn't leave any doubt this wasn't a request but an order.

I swallowed down the knot of resentment clogging my throat. It didn't help, but it's not like I had a choice about apologizing. "I'm sorry. I should have tried to defuse the situation before it got out of hand."

Tanith and Persephone eased back in their chairs a bit, but my grandmother's face was cold and her shoulders stiff. Her eyes held mine, communicating her disappointment and anger more than any words could have.

"In light of this development, we were tempted to suspend your duties until further notice."

My heart dropped into my stomach. "What?"

She held up a finger. "However, after some discussion, we decided this transgression might actually work in our favor. We have another mission for you, beginning immediately."

I so was not following her, but if it meant I wasn't going to be suspended, I was all ears. "Okay?"

"Your target is Clovis Trakiya."

I almost said a very naughty word. Actually, I might have said it aloud if the shocked looks on their faces were any indication. I wasn't really paying attention because I was too busy trying not to piss myself.

"We have it on good authority he is trying to form an alliance with the Hekate Council."

I'd recovered enough from my shock that I'd begun analyzing the situation. "But we have a truce with them. Why would the Hekate do something so foolish? Surely they'd refuse, knowing it could lead to another war."

Mages and vampires had been enemies for centuries, resulting in several wars. The conflict boiled down to vamps believing we were the true descendants of Lilith, while mages were a bastard race spawned by the goddess Hekate. The sympathy mages have for humans didn't help matters. However, after the War of Blood, which lasted for a couple of centuries, the two races had agreed to sign a treaty of sorts, called the Black Covenant. Among other things, the agreement banned interracial breeding, as well as requiring vamps to feed only from humans. To say the peace was tenuous would be understating things. Some felt another war was inevitable, but thus far it had been avoided. If the mages sided with the Dominae's enemy, it would be seen as a declaration of war by many vampires.

Tanith broke into my thoughts. "At this point, we believe he is merely recruiting mancies off the street and has yet to approach their Council. However, his numbers of Lilim are rapidly growing. We want to stop him before he becomes a real threat."

"How is he managing to recruit our own?" I asked.

Lavinia spoke up. "His church, called the Temple of the Moon, preaches unity among all of Lilith's descendants. Some misguided vampires believe all of us—vampires, mancies, faeries, and demons—should band together."

I remembered what Ewan said about Clovis being half-demon. If he could use his mixed heritage to unite the vampires and demons, he would have a real chance of overthrowing the Dominae. Add mancies to that mix and he'd be almost unstoppable.

"Obviously, the situation is quite troubling," said Lavinia. "He must be stopped. And we want you to do it."

"You want me to assassinate him." Already, I was reviewing my knowledge about killing demons, which I hated to admit was slim.

"No, my dear, we want you to infiltrate his organization, find out his plans, root out his spies, and then kill him."

My stomach dropped. I might be talented at killing people, but I certainly wasn't a spy.

"How?" I asked.

"We believe Clovis has spies high up in our organization. Perhaps high-ranking members of the Undercouncil. We will take advantage of this unauthorized killing last night and suspend you—at least this will be our public position. Meanwhile, you will do everything you can to bolster the belief that you are in the midst of questioning your allegiance to us."

"However," Tanith cut in, "you'll have to convince him you're serious. You'll be tested."

I didn't care about tests or even the inevitable fallout once the vampire community believed the Dominae suspended me. I suppose part of me saw killing Clovis as a way to lessen my own guilt about killing David. Another part of me hoped by disposing of the Dominae's enemy, I'd finally prove to my grandmother that I wasn't just some fuckup.

"I'm in," I blurted.

"Excellent." Lavinia smiled, an expression so rare on her pale face, I expected her skin to crack.

"Sabina, there is one small matter we must discuss before you begin this task," said Tanith. "No one must know that you have not actually broken from us. Clovis may have several operatives planted within our ranks. No one outside this room can be trusted."

What she wasn't saying was that once word spread that I'd broken from the Dominae, some of their followers might decide to punish me for my disloyalty. "And what are my instructions should one of your people decide to come after me?"

Lavinia looked at Tanith and Persephone, who both nodded. "You will have total amnesty. In addition, you have our permission to do whatever it takes to succeed. As far as Clovis or anyone else is concerned, it is to appear as if you have abandoned our ways entirely."

The irony of the situation wasn't lost on me. They'd just ripped me a new asshole for killing someone without their permission, but now they were almost encouraging it to further their own plans. My mind started to race as I considered the ramifications. Not only would Dominae-loyal vamps come after me, I'd also have to do some unsavory things to prove I'd broken from the Dominae's laws. Because I was raised within the confines of the Temple of Lilith with my grandmother, the sacred laws were as much a part of me as my bloodlust.

"Sabina?" The room throbbed with tension as they waited for my answer.

It occurred to me that this might be a test. Did they expect me to back down?

Screw it, I thought.

"I'll do it."

4

$\mathcal{M}$y purse hit the side table door with a thump. I dropped my motorcycle helmet on the cluttered dining room table. My blouse landed on the floor in a heap, leaving me clad in a white camisole and jeans. I discarded my black stiletto Mary Janes in the hallway on my way to the kitchen.

I grabbed a beer from the fridge and chugged it as I started the water in the bathroom. In the shower, the water scalded the stress of meeting with the Dominae from my skin. Afterwards, I wrapped myself in my favorite robe. The short silk hem tickled my thighs as I walked back into the kitchen to grab another beer.

As I closed the fridge door, the air suddenly crackled with electricity. Through the breakfast bar, I saw a flash of green light and a puff of smoke. I grabbed my gun from the kitchen counter and ran into the room with my heart palpitating. When I saw what waited for me, the bottle crashed to the floor. Broken glass and cold beer coated my stinging shins.

The demon stared down at me with a fierce scowl. His eyes had horizontal pupils, and black horns jutted from his temples. Two wicked-looking black claws rested on scaly green hips. My stomach felt like I'd swallowed frozen stones. My mind screamed for me to move, but the message got lost in translation on the way to my limbs.

"Sabina Kane." His voice had this odd echo effect, as if it came from another dimension. A reptilian smile hovered on his black lips. This wasn't a social call. I crouched low, ready for battle. I'd never fought a demon, but damned if I was going to stand there like some B-movie actress waiting for him to kill me.

"Get out." I pointed the gun at his chest.

"I'm afraid I can't do that," he said—at least I thought it was a he. The black leather codpiece kind of hinted in that direction. A wooden stake appeared in his claw, the tip whittled down to a single spear-like point.

That didn't bode well. "Who sent you?" I slowly stepped to the right, trying to find a way to the exit. The demon's eyes tracked me.

He didn't answer, just moved a couple of steps forward. I held my ground, but tightened my grip on the gun. I didn't know if the apple bullets worked on demons, but they might slow it down. I glanced at the stake. The demon would have to get in close range to use it, whereas I had the gun. I pulled back the slide and squeezed the trigger twice.

The bullets ripped through the demon's chest. He blinked and looked down at the two rapidly healing holes. "That wasn't very nice." The stake disappeared and a crossbow took its place.

Panic froze me to the floor. My brain screamed at me

to move, move, move. Instead, I watched the demon lift
the crossbow as if in slow motion. I opened my mouth to
scream, but no sound came out. The arrow flew through
the air so fast I barely saw it before it slammed into my
chest. I flew back as the arrow went through my body
and speared me to the wall. I registered the impact on
some level, but my mind was too busy dealing with the
fact I was about to die. Any second my body would burst
into flames and I'd be gone. Poof. Nothing left but a pile
of ash.

Hot tears rolled down my cheeks as I closed my eyes
and waited. There was no pain. Just shock and a dull
sense of inevitability.

"Why haven't you exploded yet?" The demon was
closer now, only a few feet away. I opened one eye to
look at the arrow. Blood bloomed from the site of impact,
just over my left breast.

"I—I don't know." Holding myself up became diffi-
cult as the seconds passed.

"Hmm. I wonder if I should stake you just to be
sure."

"I'd really prefer it if you didn't," I said. "I'm sure I'll
ignite any second." I focused on the pain, which had just
started to register. It didn't feel like I was about to combust, though. It felt more like a freaking arrow had ripped
through my heart. Not the best feeling in the world, but I
had to imagine it paled in comparison to having my immortal soul sucked from my body in a fiery death.

The demon came forward without warning and jerked
the arrow from my body. The damned thing had lodged
itself so deep it took a couple of good pulls to get it loose.
I grunted against the pain, and cold sweat broke out on

my forehead. The tip of the arrow finally came free with a disgusting sucking noise. I collapsed to the floor and curled up in the fetal position in the puddle of spilled beer.

From the corner of my eye, I saw the demon hold the arrow up to the light. He lifted the tip to his mouth and his forked tongue darted out to taste the blood. My blood. I groaned and squeezed my eyes shut. At that point, I almost hoped he'd stake me. No words exist to describe the pain.

"Well, I guess that's that." The demon's hooves click-clacked against the hardwoods. I felt him hovering close. "You okay?"

My eyes snapped open. Already, my heightened heal-ing powers were making quick work of the wounds. "Am I okay?" I barked. "You just shot me through the heart with an arrow!"

"Hey, it's nothing personal."

I levered myself into a sitting position against the wall. The pain was fading but I felt drained. I'd need blood soon to make up for what I'd lost. "Here's a tip," I said. "Next time you want to kill a vampire you might try apple wood."

The demon frowned. "Hello? What do you take me for? An idiot? It was apple wood."

What little blood I had left in my head drained out. "You're wrong. If that was apple wood, why am I still alive?"

"That is the million-dollar question, isn't it?"

"Who sent you?"

He ignored my question and leaned forward, looking me over. "You should be incinerated." He sniffed the air.

"Wait a second, what the heck are you? Your scent is weird."

"Not that it's any of your business, but I'm Lilim."

"You don't smell like one," it said. "Vampires smell like blood. You've got that going for you, but there's something else. Sandalwood?"

"Geez, interrupt much?" I said. "I was about to say that I'm only half vamp. The other half is mage."

His eyes widened. "That's fucked up."

"You're telling me."

"So what now?"

I narrowed my eyes. "What do you mean? Since I obviously can't kill you, you're going to leave and I'm going to try to figure out who summoned you so I can kill them."

He crossed his arms and tapped his hoof on the hard-woods. "Jeez, you really don't know anything about this, do you? I can't just decide to go back to Irkalla. I have to be sent back."

"Well, go back to the person who summoned you. In fact, that works well for my plan too."

He shook his head. "Can't do that."

"Why not?" I huffed out a breath, annoyed by this entire scene.

"Duh. I didn't meet them. One minute I was lounging by a pool of lava in Irkalla and the next thing I know, I'm in your living room."

I felt my eyebrows squeeze together. "How did you know what you were supposed to do then?"

"Are you sure you're half-mage? I mean, I thought you guys learned all about how this demon summoning worked from birth."

"Humor me."

He sighed. "When a summoning occurs, the spell used is encoded with instructions. In this case, I knew my orders immediately."

"And they were?"

"To test you."

"And by test, you mean try to cremate me?"

"Something like that." He shuffled his cloven hooves on the floor. "Like I said, it was nothing personal."

"Right." I placed the heels of my palms against the wall to pull myself up. Two claws grabbed my shoulders to help me. I shied away, determined not to take help from someone who'd just tried to kill me. Call me ungrateful. "Okay so we don't know who sent you, which means we can't track him down and make him send you back. Any other ideas?"

He tapped a hoof as he thought. "Don't you have any mage friends who could help you?"

"I don't know any mages."

His goat eyes widened. "How can you not know any mages? You are one."

"I'm only half, remember? My mage father died before I was born and my vampire mother's family raised me." I didn't know why I was telling the demon about my family history. I needed to figure out how to get him the hell out of my house. Pronto.

I limped to the couch. The demon wandered around the room, checking the place out as I considered options. I couldn't call my grandmother because she'd freak. If I had to guess, the apple wood didn't kill me because of my half-mage blood. Let's just say Grandmother didn't exactly like to be reminded of my mage side. I glanced at the clock. Sunrise was in half an hour. There was no way I could do anything with the darkness I had left. I'd have to tackle this tomorrow.

"Look, as long as you're stuck here, you might as well tell me your name." The demon turned from where he'd been nosing through my mail.

"I'm Giguhl."

"Sabina." I shook his claw, but withdrew my hand quickly, totally icked out by the cold feel of his scaly skin.

"Charmed."

"I promise I'll find out how to send you back as soon as I can. But until then, I'm afraid you're stuck here."

He sighed and shook his head. "That sucks."

"Look, it's not like I asked you to come here, you know. The last thing I need is a demon sleeping on my sofa. I've got bigger problems to deal with right now." Like finding out who would summon a demon to try to kill me. And figuring out why I wasn't dead from that apple wood arrow. Oh, and that whole infiltrating-Clovis's-sect-so-I-could-assassinate-him thing. My temples started to throb in time to the pain radiating from my chest. "Don't you have anyone you can go to for help?"

"No, I do not. This is my first time in this realm, if you must know. And don't give me that attitude." He crossed his massive arms and frowned at me. "I didn't exactly ask for this either. I was minding my own business and the next thing I know I'm here in this godsforsaken place." He looked around my house with the same expression I imagine I'd use if I was trapped in Irkalla.

"Okay, fine. We're both screwed. As long as you prom-

ise not to try to kill me again, I promise I'll find out how
to get you home. Deal?"

"Deal," he said. "Now about sleeping on the couch."
He turned and raised his shaggy green eyebrows at me.
"You were kidding, right?"

5

*W*hen I woke up the next evening, Giguhl sat in the same spot I'd left him the morning before. His eyes were bloodshot and slightly unfocused from watching TV for hours.

"Tell me you haven't been watching TV all day?" I shouldn't have bothered asking. From the beer bottles strewn about like passed out drunks, and the cheese doodle dust coating his chest and face, it was pretty clear what he'd been up to.

"Humans are weird." He pointed to the TV, where MTV was running a *Real World* marathon.

"Uh, yeah, I guess they are." That's when I spotted my wallet open on the coffee table next to the phone. I walked over and picked up my credit card, which had telling orange smudges all over it. "What have you been doing with my credit card?"

"Oh. I just ordered a couple of things from the infomercial channel."

I paused and counted to ten, trying to remind myself that he was new to this world. "You what?"

He sat up. "You wouldn't believe the amazing products they offer."

"How much?"

"What?" His attention had strayed back to the TV, where some co-ed was throwing up in bushes. "Eww."

I grabbed the remote and turned off the TV.

"Hey! Give it back."

I stepped back, putting the remote behind my back. "I said, how much of my money did you spend?"

"Oh, Sabina, relax. The Ab Blaster is only ten easy payments of nine-ninety-nine."

I stared at him for a moment. "What the hell do you need Ab Blaster for?"

"I bought it for you." He sent a pointed look to my midsection.

"My abs are just fine, thanks. Now call them back and cancel it."

"No can do. All sales final."

"Is that all you bought?"

His eyes shot to the left. "Um."

I clenched my teeth. "What else?"

"A Super Mega Juicer," he said quickly. "But, Sabina, seriously that juicer is a miracle machine."

"I'm a vampire, Giguhl. The only liquids I drink are blood and alcohol. I don't do juice."

"You might want to consider a little roughage in your diet. According to the commercial, an increase in fiber will help you be more regular."

The last thing I wanted was to discuss my fiber intake with a freaking demon. I grabbed my credit card and shoved it back into my wallet. *Too bad I can't just kill him.* "I have to go out, and I'm taking this with me so you can't buy anything else."

He tapped his head with one talon-like finger. "Already memorized."

"Shit." As annoyed as I was, I needed to get some things done. If letting him fill my house with infomercial crap kept him out of my hair, it might be worth the debt. "Okay, just keep it to a minimum. And don't leave the house. I don't think L.A.'s ready for you."

"Where are you going?"

"I've got to meet someone who might be able to help me figure out how to send you back home."

"Cool. Can you get some more beer while you're out?"

"I had a twelve pack in there last night!"

"What can I say? Shopping makes me thirsty."

I turned on my heel and walked to the door before I popped a blood vessel. Like I didn't have enough on my plate without a demon racking up debt on my credit card and drinking all my beer. Just before I closed the door, he yelled, "And get more cheese doodles!"

Freakin' demons.

Sepulcher didn't open until nine, so when I pulled up in front of the building, the lights were out. I knew Ewan would be back in his office, doing whatever it was he did to get ready for opening. I looked in the window and didn't see any movement. After knocking for a couple of minutes, I decided to try around back.

The metal door in the alley stood ajar. I grabbed the

edge and opened it, pulling out my gun just in case there was trouble. I crept down the hallway, my boots sticking to the floor. Ewan's office door was closed, but a light spilled from under it into the dark hallway. I heard shuffling followed by a grunt. I grabbed the doorknob and threw the door open.

I'm not sure my eyes will ever recover from the sight that greeted them. Ewan's bare ass was like a beacon in the dim light. He had one hand on his hip and the other on top of someone's head. His own head was thrown back. The person kneeling before him wore a gray pinstripe suit and black wingtips. Realizing what I'd walked in on, I gasped. Ewan turned, his face morphing from ecstasy to shock.

"Get the fuck out of here!"

I backed up quickly and shut the door. My mouth hung open as I leaned against the wall. I wasn't shocked to find out Ewan was gay. Instead, I was surprised he had a sex life at all. Ewan seemed to get off on strategically gathering and spreading information. But I guess even gossips have needs.

Hushed voices came from inside the office. I considered leaving, but, despite my embarrassment, I needed Ewan's help. Since I needed everyone to think I was breaking from the Dominae, Ewan was the perfect person to go to. All I had to do was convince him I was sick of the Dominae's shit, and he'd take care of the rest by telling everyone he knew. Hopefully, once word got out, it would reach Clovis and he'd come find me.

A few moments later, the door opened. I'm not sure who I expected Ewan's blower to be, but it sure as hell wasn't who walked out that door.

"Councilman Vera." I tried to keep the shock out of my voice, but it wasn't easy. With his perfectly combed executive haircut—a bit disheveled at present—and his strict adherence to the letter of the Dominae's laws, he'd always seemed to have such a stick up his ass. I guess I wasn't too far off on that assessment, after all. I almost smiled, but stifled it. No sense making the man more embarrassed—his cheeks already burned.

"Sabina," he said with an awkward nod. "I don't think I have to tell you how damaging it would be if word of this—indiscretion—became public."

"Say no more." I mimed turning a key at my lips. "They're sealed."

The tension in his shoulders relaxed a bit. "Thanks."

I nodded, not sure what else to say. The situation definitely called for some off-color jokes, but I restrained myself. He scurried away toward the back door. I watched him go, wondering how in the world Ewan had managed to seduce the most conservative member of the Undercouncil. With a shrug, I decided it wasn't my business—unless I could use the knowledge as leverage against Ewan.

I took a deep breath and headed into Ewan's office. His pants no longer sagged around his ankles. Instead, he leaned fully dressed against his desk, smoking a post-b.j. cigarette like some bad cliché.

He looked up and exhaled a puff of smoke. "I thought I told you to leave."

I walked forward with a small smile pulling at the corners of my mouth. "Oh, you meant the building? I thought you wanted me to get out of the office so he could finish."

"You're a pain in the ass, you know that?"

"So I've been told." I leaned on the desk next to him. "So . . . Nicolo Vera, huh?"

He took another drag and held it. "Yes, and . . ." He blew the smoke at my face.

"What?" I scrunched my nose up and waved away the smoke. "I'm just surprised is all. Not about the gay part," I said quickly. Ewan cocked an eyebrow. "Just he's so, I don't know, conservative."

Ewan crossed his arms and pinned me with a stare. "I'm surprised, too."

"You are?"

"Yeah, I'm surprised you have the balls to show up here after you lied to me the other night."

I pursed my lips and considered how to play this. If I wasn't careful he'd know I was using him. "I wasn't ready to talk about it. I had some shit to work through."

"What kind of shit?"

I crossed my arms. "Can I be honest with you?"

He stubbed out the cigarette in an ashtray and nodded. I had his full attention now that he thought I had secrets to share.

"I'm sure you've heard about my suspension."

"Yeah. Thanks for killing that asshole in my club, by the way. The Dominae's task force showed up to snoop around later that night."

I cringed. "Sorry." He shrugged and waved a hand at me to continue. "Anyway, this suspension is total bullshit. The more I think about it, the more I wonder if maybe I should just walk away."

"Walk away? What do you mean?"

"I think maybe it's time for me to go out on my own. Get out from under the Dominae's thumbs."

"Like a mercenary?"

"Something like that," I said, inwardly smiling that he was taking the bait. "Look, I had major reservations about the David thing. I didn't tell you about it the other night because guilt was eating at me big time. Then, on top of all that, they punish me for defending myself?" I shook my head, playing it up. "It got me thinking that maybe it's time for me to strike out on my own."

"Sabina, you shouldn't talk like this. If the Dominae— if your grandmother—finds out you're thinking about quitting them, they'll freak."

I stood and started pacing. "I don't care anymore. I've gritted my teeth and taken their shit my whole life. I'm tired of being reminded how much of an embarrassment my mixed blood is to her. I'm tired of doing the Dominae's dirty work. I'm tired of not having a life of my own."

"Holy shit, you're serious, aren't you?" He lit another cigarette and inhaled deeply.

I mentally pumped my fist, amazed at how easily he was buying my story. Maybe if he hadn't just gotten off, he'd have been harder to convince. Or maybe I was a better actress than I thought. Either way, it was working. I schooled my features into a frown and continued, "I know it won't be easy. As it is, once they find out I'm going solo, I'll probably have to disappear for a while."

"Who else have you told?" he asked on an exhale. This question wasn't asked out of concern for my welfare, instead he wanted to be sure he had the scoop.

"No one," I said. "My suspension was for a month, but

I'll probably start looking for work before then. Word will spread pretty quickly once that happens."

Ewan glanced at his watch. "Look, I've got to get the bar open in half an hour. Do you want to hang out and we can come up with a plan?"

I shook my head. "I need to figure this out on my own. But I do need a favor."

"Name it."

"What do you know about demons?"

Ewan hadn't been able to shed much light on my little demon issue. Of course, it's not like I could tell him the whole story. I'd just said a friend of mine needed to get rid of a demon. He'd given me directions to the Red Moon because he'd heard the mage who owned it specialized in demon issues.

I couldn't believe he'd bought the lie about "my friend," let alone the one I'd fed him about wanting to break from the Dominae. I wasn't sure if I was just a good actress or if his gullibility stemmed from his post-fellatio glow, but I wasn't going to argue with success. He'd probably started spreading the word the minute I left. Half the vamps in California were probably talking about my little epiphany by the time I pulled up to the Red Moon.

The sign for the store hung from an archway between two buildings. The tunnel led to an ivy-draped courtyard filled with statuary, small stone benches, and a bubbling fountain. The hidden garden smelled of rosemary, sage, and other herbs I couldn't identify. Small twinkling lights draped over more ivy, which hung over the open front door. I ducked inside, wondering what other surprises this shop offered.

Inside, pipe music drifted through the space, which smelled of incense and candle wax. In the far corner, a fire crackled in a small stone hearth. Two rocking chairs stood to either side of the fire. Every inch of the place was filled with treasures, from magical implements to candles and essential oils to books. Dried roses and herbs hung in tidy bundles from the ceiling. I should have felt claustrophobic from all the clutter, but instead I found the place charming. It was as if I'd entered the home of a hobbit instead of a place of business. I certainly didn't feel like I was still in L.A.

I walked to the front desk and rang the little bell next to the cash register. A voice called from behind a purple curtain near the back of the store. "Be right with you!"

I leaned against the counter, wondering if I was making a mistake. Vampires and mages didn't exactly hang out, and I wasn't sure how helpful one would be when I told him about my current predicament.

The curtain parted, revealing a raven-haired man who appeared to be in his early forties. His welcoming smile faded when he saw me.

"Can I help you?" His brusque tone verified my suspicions.

He was closer now, so I took a deep breath. Sure enough, the telltale scent of sandalwood overpowered the mingling scents of herbs and elixirs. His eyes narrowed as he took stock of me.

"You're a mage?" This was really just making conversation. Besides the distinctive sandalwood scent, something about the way he carried himself told me he was powerful. Maybe it was his aura or his posture. I couldn't put my finger on it, but I knew he wasn't someone to mess with.

He nodded curtly. "Yes, and vampires are not welcome in this shop." He turned to go, but stopped short. He turned his head and sniffed the air. "Wait a second. What the hell are you?"

"I'm mixed-blood," I said.

His eyes widened. "Impossible."

I crossed my arms. "Actually, it's quite possible."

He seemed to consider it and let it slide for a moment. "What do you want?"

"I have a demon issue." Oh boy, did I. In spades.

"What sort?"

"Well," I fidgeted with a statue of Isis. His eyes shot to my hand disapprovingly. I set it down and cleared my throat. "Someone summoned a demon to kill me. I survived and now I'm stuck with him."

"You said you're half-mage, right?"

I looked away. "Yeah, but I've never had any training."

"Do you know who summoned the demon?"

"No."

"Sorry, lady, you're screwed." He started to walk away again, but I held out a hand.

"Wait! What do you mean?"

He turned slowly, obviously annoyed. "Only the summoner or the target can return the demon." He shrugged his bony shoulders. "Good night!" He moved to go again, as if he couldn't stand to be in the same room as me.

"Hold on." My temples began to throb. "You're telling me there's no way to send this demon back to Irkalla?"

He crossed his arms. "Did I stutter?"

My heart sank. I looked around at the shelves full of dusty, leather-bound books, as if one of the spines would offer an answer.

"Look, you want my advice? Get used to having that demon around. Because without the summoner you're up shit creek."

I slumped against the counter. Giguhl was going to freak when I told him I couldn't get him home. "Can't you tell me how to send him back?

The mage snorted. "The art of summoning demons takes years to learn."

"Isn't there a *Demon Summoning for Dummies* book or something?"

He frowned at me, obviously insulted. "Goodnight."

I turned to go, but something shiny caught my eye from a shelf behind the counter.

"Wait. What's that?" I pointed at an amulet.

He trudged over to the counter with a deep sigh. When he saw where I was pointing, his eyes widened. "You can see that?"

I looked at him as if he was one can short of a six pack. "Uh, yeah. What is it?"

His mouth dropped open, his shock evident. "You're not supposed to be able to see it."

"Obviously I can."

He stared at me for a moment, a new expression in his eyes. Intrigue? "That," he said, taking it down, "is the Lilith amulet."

The item in question was made from solid gold. It shone in the dim light as if lit from inside. The metal was formed into the shape of an eight-pointed star—a symbol I knew very well.

"The Lilith amulet?"

He cleared his throat and looked around nervously. I looked around, too, wondering about his sanity since we were completely alone in the store. He waved his hand for me to lean in closer.

"The Lilith amulet," he whispered, "is worn by members of the Caste of Nod." He said this last with a dramatic flair. When I merely blinked back at him, he continued. "The Caste is a secret society rumored to be the protectors of the *Preascarium Lilitu*."

I snorted, remembering melodramatic stories about the Caste traded among the fledglings in school. "That's a myth."

He raised a challenging eyebrow. "Oh, I assure you, it's very real." He raised the amulet so it spun over a lit candle on the desk. "This came to me from a faery whose mother was a member of the Caste."

"How much do you want for it?" I had no idea why I wanted it. Maybe I felt it might give me some clue about the birthmark on my back. Maybe I just thought it was pretty. All I knew was that I felt oddly compelled to own it.

He jerked the amulet back. "Not for sale. That's why I placed a cloaking ward on it." His eyes narrowed. "Which brings me back to the question, how did you see it?"

I shrugged. "Maybe your ward was bogus."

He frowned. "My wards never fail. Are you sure you're not a member of the Caste?"

I laughed. "If they exist, do you honestly think they'd choose a mixed-blood to be a member?"

"You have a point," he said. "Still, it's odd."

"Whatever," I said, feeling uncomfortable with his scrutiny. "Are you sure you won't sell it to me?"

He put the amulet in the pocket of his jacket. "Yes."

I briefly considered stealing the amulet from him, but I didn't want to tangle with his magic. "Well, thanks for nothing."

"Bye now. And listen, don't tell anyone about the amulet. I can't have every vamp, faery, and mage coming in here asking about it."

I nodded and walked toward the door, confused. I'd come in wanting to know how to get rid of my demon problem, and left with more questions. The mage's talk about the Caste made me uneasy. I'd heard of it, of course. Vampire fledglings were warned about the Caste by their parents. They were like the dark race version of the Boogeyman. Break the Sacred Laws and the Caste would punish you. But the mage in the shop had seemed convinced of their existence. I thought about the mark on my back and a shiver passed down my spine. Could the birthmark have some connection to the fact I could see the amulet despite the cloaking ward?

There was only one place to go with these questions, but I had to put off meeting with my grandmother until I'd made contact with Clovis' people. For that to happen, I could only hope Ewan was busy working his own brand of magic.

6

A couple of nights later, I pulled into the parking lot of Phantasmagoria, a club located in a renovated theater off Wilshire. I'd left Giguhl on the couch at home watching TV. His most recent purchases were a Kitchen Ninja knife set and something called Venus Cream, which he explained would transform my sex life. As much as I appreciated his concern for the quality of my orgasms, I really needed to get rid of him before he maxed out my credit cards. In the meantime, I let him be, hoping his shopping would keep him out of trouble.

As I walked past the line toward the entrance of the club, a movement on the neon marquee caught my eye. A white owl seemed to be watching me with unblinking red eyes. I stopped and looked at it. What were the chances of seeing two white owls in the same week? Something told me they were pretty slim. As I watched, the owl spread its wings and swooped away from the building. It flew over me and disappeared into the night.

I shook my head, wondering what I'd done to deserve

the complication that was my life. Over the last two nights, I'd hit several vamp bars in the greater Los Angeles area. In each, I'd had two goals. First, I needed to confirm the rumors that I'd planted with Ewan. Second, I tried to gather information on Clovis and make contact with his people. Thus far Ewan had come through, but the second goal was a complete wash. If I didn't make contact with Clovis soon, I'd have to come up with another plan. Lilith only knew what that would be.

What I'd gotten instead was a lot of grief. Apparently, as the news got out about my suspension, every vamp with something to prove had decided I needed to be taken down a peg. It was a pain in the ass.

As I approached the front doors, I thought about how my to-do list was growing and I wasn't making much progress. The bouncer waved me in, much to the dismay of the people who stood behind metal barriers. All I'd wanted to do was my job, and instead I ended up killing two more vamps and injuring a few others. In addition, I'd gotten myself banned from at least two clubs because the owners were worried the Dominae might punish them for allowing me entrance.

And now I had some freaking red-eyed owl following me around—not to mention a demon roommate sent by some weirdo mage stalker. In other words, I had a plate full of crap to worry about.

I continued into what used to be the lobby of the theater. Now it served as the main bar area. The art deco design of the old building had been preserved. The walls were the color of dried blood with amber glass sconces scattered to give the room a warm glow. The lobby reverberated with the bass coming from the ballroom. Several patrons loitered in the lobby, taking a break from dancing, their sweat-soaked bodies lazing on settees along the walls.

Instead of going into the ballroom, I opted for the elevator leading directly to the VIP lounge. Another bouncer sat on a stool in front of the elevator doors.

"Name?" he asked without looking up from his magazine.

"Sabina Kane."

His head snapped up and his eyes squinted in the dim light. He was obviously a vamp, since the VIP area was reserved for our kind.

"Password?" he clipped, still eyeing me.

"Rasputin," I said. It was common for these vamp clubs to use the names of historic vampires as passwords. Since most humans didn't know these famous figures were vamps it was unlikely they'd guess the word.

The bouncer nodded and pushed a button on the wall. The doors opened immediately. I started to enter the elevator, but he stalled me with a calloused hand on my arm.

"You'll have to check your weapons."

I eyed him with my best "make me" expression, but he didn't seem impressed. Finally, with a sigh, I retrieved the gun from my waistband, where it had been hidden by my leather vest. Handing over my weapon made me feel naked, but I still had a stake in my boot.

He took it and handed me a ticket stub, so I could get it when I left. The bouncer picked up his magazine and dismissed me with a wave of his hand.

When the doors reopened, the deep bass of techno music buffeted my body. The occasional red laser punctuated the darkness and a cloud hovered from the over-worked smoke machines. The VIP area was a large balcony overlooking the dance floor. Below, a mass of writhing bodies danced under two massive chandeliers.

I walked past the railing to the bar on the far wall. Most of the vamps waiting for drinks were young. They tended to like Goth clubs like this one because the patrons were easily seduced.

I eased my way into an open space and waited for service. A few of the vamps cast curious glances my way. I didn't see any familiar faces, so I ignored them.

After a few minutes, the bartender finally deigned to notice me. "What'll it be?"

"A-pos with a shot of vodka," I said.

He paused. "What?"

"A-positive," I enunciated, "with a shot of vodka."

"We don't serve blood here." He said it like it was the most obvious thing is the world.

"Why not?" I asked. "You used to."

"Some mortals are getting the passwords somehow, so we have to be more careful," he said.

Freaking mortals. "Fine," I sighed. "Just the vodka then."

When the drink finally arrived, I spotted a couple of free chairs near the railing. I settled back into one, which gave me a good view of both the VIP area and the dance floor below. A few other vamps lined the balcony railing, scoping out potential meals below.

It didn't take long for company to arrive.

"So you're the notorious Sabina Kane." Despite the concussive music, I heard him clearly, taking note of the slight accent. He wore a silk shirt open at the throat to reveal a thin gold chain. A matching hoop winked from his right earlobe. Combined with the accent, the full effect screamed Eurotrash.

I took a sip from my vodka. "Look, if I killed one of your family members, you're going to have to take a number."

He smiled. "No, nothing like that. Allow me to introduce myself. Franco Allegheri, at your service," he said with a slight bow. The movement caused a cloud of cologne to drift in my direction. I grimaced, overcome by the scent of musk.

I crossed one booted foot over my jean-clad knee. "Sorry, Frank, but I'm not looking to get serviced tonight."

He grimaced at my use of the Americanized version of his name, but didn't correct me. "You misunderstand. I represent a certain party who would like to contract your services." He motioned to the chair next to mine. "May I sit?"

I shrugged. Inside, I did a little happy dance. If my hunch was correct, Frankie Boy worked for Clovis.

He sat in the club chair across from me. I waited as a waitress came to take his drink order. He asked for a martini, which left me in serious doubt about his character. After she left, I sipped on my drink and waited.

"My employer—" he began.

"And who would that be?"

He smiled again, a tight expression totally lacking in friendliness. "I am not at liberty to divulge his identity at this time."

I leaned forward, finishing off my drink before speaking. "Well, Frank, I am not at liberty to discuss my activities with strangers."

He nodded. "Would it help if I mentioned my employer and you shared a friend in common?"

"Depends on the friend."

"David Duchamp."

My stomach dropped. I'd managed to avoid thinking about David until now. I didn't enjoy the reminder.

"My employer would like to extend his condolences on Mr. Duchamp's recent passing."

I nodded slowly, wondering how much Clovis knew about the circumstances surrounding David's death.

"My employer would also like you to know that he is aware that you were merely carrying out orders. He does not hold you responsible for Mr. Duchamp's death."

Well, that answered that question.

"Boy, that's a relief," I said. "But I didn't kill David."

Frank sent me a look, clearly indicating we both knew that was bullshit. "Nevertheless, my employer would like to offer you his friendship."

"How does your employer know I would be a good friend to have?" Normally, this kind of verbal poker made me impatient. But I found myself enjoying the game. If I played my cards right, I'd be on my way to San Francisco to kill Clovis in no time.

The waitress came back then with Frank's martini. I ordered a beer before she took off again.

"Sabina, might we speak candidly?" When I nodded, he continued. "Word on the street is you're looking to become an independent contractor. My employer believes you and he might be able to form a mutually beneficial arrangement."

"Mutually beneficial?"

"Indeed." He nodded. "My employer would like to

offer you protection from the Dominae and other unsavory elements in return for your services."

I laughed then. "And what makes him think I am in need of protection?"

"Didn't you just imply you have a line of angry vamps waiting to seek revenge for your past deeds?"

"True," I said. "But remember those skills you mentioned?"

He shifted in his seat. "Please understand. I do not mean to suggest you cannot take care of yourself. However, given your circumstances plus your . . . shall we say questionable heritage, my employer feels you would benefit from an alliance with his cause."

My eyes narrowed. "Listen, asshole, my 'questionable heritage' is none of your employer's business. This meeting is over." I rose to leave. As expected, Frank stood quickly and grabbed my arm.

"Wait," he said. "Forgive me if I've offended you. Please sit. There's more."

I paused as if weighing my options. Finally, I pretended to be reluctant as I sat, nodding for him to continue.

"I had a reason for bringing up your mixed lineage," he began. "You see my employer is trying to end the ongoing tension between the vampire and mage populations. He believes we can all coexist peacefully."

The waitress brought my beer. I nodded for him to continue after she'd gone. I'd need the drink if I was going to have to sit through a speech about how all the dark races should hold hands and sing "Joy to the World."

"Seeing as you are of both races, my employer thought you might be open to his ideas."

"He was mistaken."

Frank smiled. "Perhaps you'll consider meeting with my employer anyway. I think you'll find his ideas quite revolutionary."

I sipped on my beer, pretending to think it over. Inside, I was mentally creating my packing list. Perhaps I'd buy a new black Burberry trench for all that foggy San Francisco weather.

"I don't know," I said. "I'd feel better if I knew who your employer was."

Frank's jaw clenched. I could tell he was losing patience. He sighed and said, "I'm really not supposed to tell you." The tone he used indicated he was lying. Surely, Clovis had known I would demand to know this information.

"But, as long as you promise not to tell him I told you?" He looked at me expectantly.

I nodded solemnly.

"Clovis Trakiya," he said dramatically.

I pursed my lips. "Hmm, never heard of him."

Frank looked shocked. I smiled on the inside, hoping the little dig would make its way back to Clovis. Frank opened his mouth to speak, but I held up a hand.

"But if what you say is true, I'd agree to at least meet with him. What could it hurt, right?"

Frank's smile was genuine this time. Obviously, he'd been worried about going back to Clovis with bad news.

"How soon can you make it to San Francisco for the meeting?"

I leaned back in my chair and took another swig from my beer. "Well, Frank, I tell ya, it just so happens I have some room in my schedule day after tomorrow."

7

I left Phantasmagoria feeling better than I had in days. Things were finally coming together. I'd meet with Clovis in a couple of days and hopefully in a week or so he'd be dead.

It wasn't lost on me that my eagerness to do this job had a lot to do with David. The rational part of me knew that killing Clovis wouldn't bring David back or erase the fact he'd betrayed the Dominae. But the other side, the one that made me irrational, wanted to punish Clovis for his role in leading David in the wrong direction. Sure, I knew David made the choice to work with Clovis, but that didn't matter. In my mind, this whole mess was Clovis' fault for thinking he could threaten the Dominae's power. Now that I was on my way to see the job done, I felt more at ease.

Humans filled the sidewalk as they spilled out of the clubs on Wilshire. Music, car horns, and laughter created the usual Friday night soundtrack. I dodged a few drunken co-eds and turned on a side street. I'd parked my Ducati about a block away in an underground parking lot beneath an office tower. The beauty of motorcycles is how easy they are to get around those pesky wooden arms at garage entrances.

I ducked into the lot and walked down the ramp to the level below. My footsteps echoed against the gray concrete walls. I'd just turned the corner when I heard the footsteps following me. I turned slowly, ready to scare off any drunken frat boys who might have mistaken me for easy pickings. Instead, a group of nasty-looking male vamps came around the bend. Something told me they weren't lost.

I recognized two males at the front from Ewan's bar—Dumb and Dumber. They were the friends of the guy I'd smoked. Behind those two, stood four other huge males. If you put all six of them together, you'd probably get a cumulative IQ of 100. However, it doesn't take much smarts when you have fangs, muscles, and guns to do your talking.

I held my hands up, trying to buy some time. "Evening, boys. What's up?" As I talked, I scanned the area for exits. Besides the ramp, a door marked "stairs" stood at the opposite end of the parking lot. The Ducati stood about six feet behind me and was the only vehicle in the lot.

"What's up is you're going down, bitch." Dumber had no neck and his biceps were like barrels. Obviously, he also felt he had a great sense of humor. It was sad, really.

"Look, I know you're probably upset about the other night, but you can't blame a girl for defending herself, can you?"

5

64 Jaye Wells

"Billy Dan didn't deserve to get smoked by no bitch," said Dumb. He was leaner than his partner, but had a feral gleam in his eye that told me he was the more dangerous of the pair. "And this time you don't have your bodyguards holding us off with no shotguns."

The group spread out, forming a semicircle to block my escape. The time for talking was over. I reached back to grab my gun. When my hand touched nothing but the waistband of my jeans, a cold sweat broke out on my scalp. I cursed myself seven ways to Sunday as I realized I'd forgotten to get it back from the bouncer on my way out. I'd been so excited about the upcoming meeting with Clovis, I'd lost my head.

The group was closing in slowly, obviously expecting some spectacular move on my part. They would be disappointed. My mind scrambled for a solution as I leaned down and pulled the stake from my boot. As far as weapons went, an apple wood stake was quite effective. However, one stake versus six massive male vamps was pitiful. My only hope was to reduce their numbers by at least one to make the odds more sporting.

I crouched down, ready for the inevitable first wave. In fights like these, usually one or two macho assholes decide to show off. For some reason, it never occurs to them that if they all attacked at once I'd not stand a chance. Not that I was complaining.

A few seconds later, two came at me. I noticed that the leaders fell back, ready to have their friends do the dirty work. Turning sideways, I tripped one with a leg sweep. He fell down hard and fast, giving me enough time to spin and catch his buddy in the heart with the stake. The stake made a sickening sucking noise as I pulled it out before he ignited.

Before anyone could react, I jumped on top of the first guy and stabbed him in the chest too. This time, the bloody stake was too slippery to remove, so I jumped back just as it and he went up in flames.

I turned my back on the two smoldering piles and faced the rest. I was barely winded, but panic made my heart race as I realized I still had four vamps to kill and no weapons. The odds were better, but I'd have to do some serious maiming in order to escape.

I lifted an eyebrow at Dumb and Dumber. They traded glances and then both ran at me. I managed to fell Dumber with a stomping knee-joint kick. He fell instantly, grabbing his broken knee. It wouldn't slow him down long, but it bought me a few seconds. I turned to Dumb, who flashed his fangs with a snarl.

"I'm going to enjoy this," he said. His body fell back into a classic martial arts pose. I felt my lips curl into a smile.

"Bring it on, asshole." I swiveled my body sideways and went at him with a roundhouse aimed at his ribs. He grabbed my ankle before it made contact. He jerked my leg toward him. My arms windmilled as I tried to keep my balance. I managed to grab his free hand and take him down with me. He might have been bigger, but I had speed on my side. I straddled him quickly, making sure to land high up on his chest to pin his arms.

His facial bones were like steel, and after a few punches my hands felt like tenderized meat. He used his massive body to buck me off. In a flash, he had me. His arms snaked under mine and he locked his fingers together

behind my head, pulling me up. I scraped his shin with
my boot heel. He jerked his hips back, out of range. Then
he laughed in my ear. "Not so tough now, are you?"

His breath felt hot in my ear and his voice caused my
spine to shrivel. His friends came forward, laughing like
demented hyenas. I fought like a wildcat, trying to break
free. At best, they would stake me. At worst, they'd rape
me, drain me, and then stake me. As they surrounded
their friend, they hurled insults and groped me with their
paws.

I knew if I didn't keep my head, I'd never make it
out alive. My training kicked in and I took a slow, deep
cleansing breath. I refocused my rage and let it fill my
limbs like steel. They might have me trapped, but I'd be
damned if I was going down without leaving at least a
few scars.

The male in front of me leered. "Hey, boys, I think she
likes being manhandled."

I leaned back into Dumb and used the leverage to kick
up with my legs. My boot heels caught two of them in
the face. They fell back with howls. My face snapped to
the side as I received a slap for my impertinence from
Dumber. Pain bloomed in my cheekbone and I tasted my
own blood. That was all right. Pain was my friend. It
meant I was still alive.

"Okay, enough horsing around," Dumb said. He tightened his arms and held me closer to him. Another one
crouched and grabbed my legs. I struggled against them
as Dumber came at me with fangs extended. I reared my
head back, trying to evade him, but it was no use. His
hot breath on my neck made my skin crawl. When he
scraped his fangs over my artery, my eyes stung with

revulsion. I didn't close them. That would be a sign of acceptance. The idea of this cretin vein-raping me made me want to vomit, but I'd never give him the satisfaction of showing my fear.

Before he could break the skin, his body flew backward. I heard a loud thump and then a shriek. I tried to look up, but the one holding me threw me behind him. My head smashed into the floor. Stars of pain exploded behind my eyes, but I shook it off quickly. Behind me, the lot filled the sounds of crunching bones and male grunts. I turned and my mouth fell open in shock.

The mage from Ewan's bar stood several feet in front of me. As I watched open-mouthed, one of his boots made contact with a vampire's face. I jumped up, confused but determined to put an end to this. I ran toward Dumb, who was coming at the mage from the side. The air crackled, making the hair on my neck tingle. I tackled the male from behind, and on my way down, I saw a spark of blue light shoot through the air like a missile. A wave of heat followed as another vamp bit the dust.

I didn't have time to ponder what kind of spell the mage was using. Instead, I whacked the leader's forehead into the concrete. He went limp, but not for long. My eyes scanned the area for something I could use as a weapon, but found nothing.

A whistle caught my attention. I looked up to see the mage holding up a knife. "Catch," he said. He threw the knife to me, and I caught it by the apple wood handle. Without hesitation, I jabbed the blade down through the leader's back and straight through his heart. When the handle made contact with his blood, his body exploded, throwing me back a couple of feet. I lay stunned for a moment, before jumping back up to rejoin the fight.

Only the fight was over. The mage leaned against my bike with his arms crossed. Six piles of ash in various stages of smolder littered the floor.

I brushed off my jeans and walked toward him. He wasn't winded. I gasped for breath. He didn't even look dirty. I felt as if I'd been dragged through a dumpster.

"Thanks," I said, panting. "But I didn't really need your help."

He chuckled. "Liar."

I stopped a couple of feet away and eyed him. His sandy hair and goatee shouldn't have made him look danger-ous, but they did. He wore a white tank that displayed his nicely muscled arms and chest. His chinos hung low on his slender hips, and battered brown boots filled out the urban commando look.

"So are you going to tell me why you've been follow-ing me?"

His full lips quirked into a lopsided smile. "Let's just say I'm a friend. By the way, how's your new roommate?" Before I could react, he waved a hand in the air. I blinked and he was gone. The Ducati stood alone where the mage had been only a second before.

"Well, that's just great!" I yelled, hoping he could still hear me. When no answer came, I ran a hand through my tangled hair and sighed.

"Asshole." The insult lacked heat because he'd saved my ass. The idea was unsettling. I made my living with my wits and my fists. The idea that those bastards had almost bested me didn't sit well. Not to mention the fact

I still had no idea who the mage was other than the one who'd summoned Giguhl.

At least I now knew who sent the demon. What I couldn't figure out was why. It didn't add up. Why would he summon a demon to try to kill me and then turn around and help me in a fight? It was just one more mystery to solve in the riddle my life had become.

8

*O*ne benefit of growing up in the Temple was my knowledge of its complex floor plan, which included several hidden passages meant for quick escapes. They worked equally well for sneaking in if you knew where to look.

The chapel still smelled of myrrh. The heady scent reminded me of my childhood and watching my grandmother perform the sacred ceremonies. I used to watch the secret incantations and breathe in the mysterious aromas with childish awe. Those days, my grandmother was a goddess—the breathing embodiment of the Great Mother, Lilith. Back then, before I knew better, I dreamed of following in her footsteps.

I ran my hands lightly over the red velvet covering the altar, lost in thought. Now she was more like a benevolent dictator—light on the benevolence, if truth be told. I knew part of her hardness had nothing to do with me. After my mother's ill-fated love affair with a mage, which resulted in both their deaths, my grandmother turned all her focus on me. It was as if she wanted me to be everything my mother wasn't and couldn't be. But my mixed blood prevented me from ever really being accepted into mainstream vamp society. So she raised me to be the best vampire I could be, despite the limitations of my birth.

Honestly? Sometimes, I resented being blamed for something I had no control over. And my grandmother's constant expectations and pressure ate at me. But I believed she'd done the best by me she could.

I tried not to think about why she asked me to kill David. Going there in my head led to questions I wasn't quite ready to face. Surely, I reasoned, she had a plan. Maybe I didn't understand it or like it, but sometimes loyalty asks things of us we don't quite understand. At least, that's what my grandmother had taught me.

As if summoned by my thoughts, she walked in. She glanced at me and then closed the door quickly.

"We don't have much time to talk," she said. "The acolytes will arrive shortly for prayer."

She moved forward toward the altar and knelt. As she touched her head to the floor, I stood silent. When she rose, candles around the altar sputtered to life without the aid of matches. Next, she lifted the golden lotus figurine and kissed it. That done, she turned to me.

"What news?"

I knew we didn't have much time, but part of me longed for some hint of warmth from her. Pushing the thought aside, I got down to business.

"I'm leaving tonight for San Francisco. The meeting is tomorrow."

"Excellent," she said. Her slender, milky hands rubbed together. "I'll alert Persephone and Tanith."

I nodded, but she didn't see it, lost in thought. "Are there any further instructions?"

She shook her head. "I'll be checking in with you via your secure phone. I'll remind you not to give the number out."

No shit, I thought. Resentment tickled my gut, but I knew she only wanted to be sure the mission went off without complications. She couldn't help herself.

"Yes, Grandmother," I said. "I'll be careful."

"Now, have you considered how you'll play the meeting with Clovis?"

"Yes, I feel it's important to feign reluctance. If he thinks I'm too eager to join him he'll be suspicious."

She nodded. "I expect he might also try to use your birth to lure you onto his side. Use it to your advantage."

Her mercurial attitude set my teeth on edge. One minute she treated my mixed blood like a shameful secret, and the next she wanted me to use it manipulate someone. I nodded anyway, hoping I could get to Clovis without having to share too many intimate details with him.

"You must remember that Clovis is half-demon. He can appear quite charming when he wants to be."

"You've met him?"

"Yes, his father was a trusted adviser to the Dominae when we were still in Rome. Clovis showed a lot of promise despite his father's unfortunate affair with the demon Akasha. However, his mixed blood lured him away from the Lilim early on. He's been a thorn in our side ever since."

"That certainly sheds some light on the matter."

She didn't acknowledge my sarcasm. Instead, she turned and seemed to dismiss me as she prepared the room for midnight prayers. I stood there for a moment, waiting for something. A good-bye. Anything.

"Grandmother," I said finally. "What do you know about the *Praescarium Lilitu?*"

She swung around, her eyes intense. "Why do you bring up that nonsense?"

I shrugged. "Someone mentioned it in connection with the Caste of Nod."

"Sabina, why are you wasting my time with questions about faery tales? The *Praescarium Lilitu* is a myth. There is no Caste."

I nodded. "So the birthmark on my shoulder blade isn't a symbol of the Caste?"

She went very still. "Whom have you been talking to?"

The anger in her voice gave me pause. "Just some guy. He said the symbol for the Caste is the eight-point star."

"Did you tell this person about your birthmark?" Her voice was intense and I got the sense the answer to this question was important.

"No."

"Good. What have I always told you?" she said, coming closer. "That birthmark is like a neon sign advertising your mixed blood to the world. You'd best keep it to yourself."

I still didn't understand how keeping the mark to myself was doing me any favors. After all, my mixed scents and hair were immediate signals to all the dark races that I was mixed-blood. But I could tell from her tone that Grandmother didn't want to talk about it any more.

"Like I said, I was just curious. Sorry to waste your time."

She nodded regally. "You should go."

I turned to leave through the door hidden by the tapestry hanging behind the altar. It depicted the first mating of Lilith and Cain, which resulted in the birth of the vampire race. For the first time, I noticed the serpent curled in the tree behind the lovers. The erotic picture had been a fixture in my life since I could remember, but as I looked at it now I wondered why I'd never noticed that detail before.

Shaking off the strange feeling, I lifted the panel.

"Sabina." Grandmother's quiet voice stopped me. I turned with my eyebrows raised. "I don't think I have to remind you of the critical nature of this mission. Do not fail me, child. It's shameful enough to me that your birth prevented you from entering service to the Temple."

I swallowed the argument that sprang to my lips, and the movement felt violent to my throat.

No sense in reminding her I'd not chosen this path. When I'd reached maturity, I was told that because of my mixed blood, I would not be allowed to become an acolyte at the Temple. Instead, the Dominae decided I would train for the only profession fit for a mixed-blood. So, I was sent away to train as an assassin, despite the fact half my blood was from one of the most noble vampire bloodlines. The job usually fell to lowborn vampires, who didn't mind the outcast status the profession required. Eventually, I accepted my role as pariah, because I was damn good at my job and it made me useful to the Dominae. At times, though, I still resented not having a choice in the matter.

"I understand." Somehow I managed to keep the lingering resentment out of my voice. She nodded once and returned to her task, dismissing me.

As I made my way through the corridor, dust filled my lungs, weighing them down. At least, I told myself it was the dust.

9

*W*hen I got home that night, I found Giguhl lying on my couch in my hot pink kimono.

"Nice robe," I said by way of greeting. He ignored me and continued watching Jerry Springer. I dropped my stuff on the kitchen table and plopped into the armchair.

"Mortals are silly," he said finally. "What's a 'baby daddy,' anyway?"

On the screen, a woman with serious dental hygiene issues was beating a man upside the head. "I guess you don't get to watch much TV in Irkalla."

He propped his head on one scaly bicep and turned to look at me. "Nah. We stayed busy torturing the souls of the damned and playing hide the hot poker. You know, the usual."

We watched the show for a few minutes. The scene onstage turned into an all-out brawl. "As amusing as this is, we need to talk." I grabbed the remote from the table and clicked it off. Giguhl sat up, careful to arrange the silk around his hips.

"What's up?"

"I'm going out of town for a little while."

"What?"

"I've got to go to San Francisco to take care of some business."

"What kind of business?"

"The kind that is none of yours."

"Very funny. So what? You're just going to leave me here?"

"That's the plan."

He stood up, looming over me. "No way, sister. If you're leaving town, then I'm coming with you."

I was already shaking my head before he finished speaking. "No way."

"Come on, Sabina. I've been trapped in your house for days—even shopping has lost its once-heady appeal. Plus, you're no closer to getting me home than you were when I arrived. And now you expect me to just sit here while you run off for Bael knows how long?"

"What do you want from me?" I asked, frustrated. "I can't put off this mission any longer."

"Give me one good reason why I can't come with you?"

I looked him over—from the tips of his horns to the cloven hooves. Not to mention the pink robe. "For one thing, you wouldn't exactly blend into the mortal world."

He rolled his goat eyes. "Is that all?" He snapped his fingers. A surge of energy tingled down my spine and a plume of violet smoke filled the room. When it cleared, instead of a seven-foot-tall demon standing over me, a black-and-white cat was looking up at me.

I blinked and shook my head. "What the hell?"

The cat spoke. "Someone played hooky the day they covered demon powers in school, huh?"

I wasn't sure what freaked me out more, the ease with which he changed himself into a cat or the fact I was having a conversation with a talking pussy.

"What's wrong?" he said. "Cat got your tongue?" The sound that came out of his tiny pink mouth was part laugh and part meow.

"Wait a second, all this time you've been able to change shape and you never told me?"

He sighed and twitched his whiskers. "Didn't come up. So when are we leaving?"

"You're not going." I stood and walked toward the kitchen. The cat tripped me up as he wound around my ankles, purring. I cursed and he sat back on his haunches and widened his little cat eyes at me. "Stop that."

"Come on, Sabina. Hey! Maybe I could help with your mission."

"I work alone." I started walking again, but a puff of smoke and the acrid smell of brimstone stopped me. I turned slowly, finding Giguhl back in demon form. Naked.

My eyes bulged out of my head as I saw what rested between his hips. "Good Lord!" I said without thinking. A forked penis will do that to a girl.

He glanced down at the appendage and smiled knowingly. "Once you go demon you never go back."

"Give me a break," I said. "And while you're at it, put on some clothes." I grabbed the robe from where it lay on the ground. Keeping my eyes averted, I tossed it to him.

"If I put this on, can I go with you?"

I crossed my arms and took a deep breath. Taking him

with me wasn't in the plan, but the more I thought about it, having a demon at my disposal might be a good thing. Surely he had other talents besides the shapeshifting. Besides, maybe he could teach me more about demons in general, which would definitely help me when it came to Clovis.

"Fine, but you have to promise to do whatever I say."

He snorted and pulled on the robe. "Deal."

"You will stay in cat form unless I give you permission to do otherwise, is that understood?"

He cursed under is breath and did the shapeshift thing again. Another puff of smoke and a disgruntled cat reappeared. "Fine."

"We're leaving in fifteen minutes."

He went still, his cat ears twitching. "Tell me we're not going on the Ducati."

I frowned. "Of course we are."

"Bael's breath, Sabina, you can't expect me to ride on that thing. My fur will get all mussed."

"Quit pouting," I told him. He didn't look at me, but he followed me into the bedroom. I grabbed an old cat crate from the closet. I'd bought it years ago for a stray I'd taken in. The damned ungrateful thing ran away before I could even name it. A hiss sounded behind me. Giguhl's back was arched and the hair on his neck stood up in spiky tufts.

"Chill, cat," I said. He hissed again, this time keeping his eyes on the crate. "I can still change my mind and leave you here, you know."

"You're a real bitch, you know that?"

"So I've heard. Get in." I set the crate on the bed and

opened the little gate. He shot off like a hairy bolt of lightning, heading toward the living room.

I breathed a martyred sigh and headed after him. The crate bumped against my shins as I dropped it to give chase. I caught him just before he disappeared under the couch. I held him by the scruff an arm's length away, which protected me from his swiping paws and bared teeth.

"You're not putting me in that cage!" he hissed.

"Quit being such a drama queen," I said as I marched back to the bedroom and the waiting crate. "You're the one who wanted to come with me."

"No!" His paws grabbed for the doorjamb just as I went through, leaving claw marks on the white paint.

"Nice," I said, pulling his nails free from the wood. "You'll be fixing that when we get back."

Just before I reached the crate, he did a crazy death roll maneuver and managed to break loose. He landed on his feet, momentarily stunned at getting free. My own surprise prevented me from grabbing him before he bolted under the bed.

I looked up at the ceiling and prayed to Lilith for patience. "Must not kill the demon cat. Must not kill the demon cat," I chanted.

The clock next to the bed said it was already eight o'clock. I'd hoped to get to the City by the Bay with enough time left to feed again before sunrise. I didn't have time for this shit.

"Fine," I said. His refusal to get in the crate had ignited my competitive impulses. That cat was getting in the crate if it killed me. Besides, now that I'd had a chance to think about it, taking him with me made perfect sense. In addition to Giguhl's helping me on the mission, I might be able to find someone in San Francisco to help me send him back to Irkalla.

I walked out of the room, only to return about two minutes later with a cat toy and a bottle of spray catnip—more leftovers from the stray. I scooted to the edge of the bed. A paw swiped out from under the bed at my foot. A muffled, angry yowl accompanied it. "Screw off!"

"Here, kitty, kitty." As I spoke, I waved the pink feather enticingly in front of the open space where I'd seen the paw. As I wiggled it, it occurred to me how ridiculous I must look.

Finally, a paw poked out from the bed and took a half-hearted swipe at the feather. I hid the bottle of catnip spray behind my back as I continued to wave the toy in front of the paw. Eventually, a pink nose appeared and sniffed at the toy.

I could tell he was trying to resist the siren call of the catnip. But nature won out and soon he pounced and buried his face into the feather. He rubbed it all over his head as he purred.

Within a few seconds, he lay on is back in a dreamlike trance, purring softly. I laughed softly in triumph, relieved the catnip spray hadn't expired. Wasting no time, I picked up his limp body and placed it carefully in the crate. I locked the gate, hooked a water bottle to it, and squeezed in a squeak toy.

Eight minutes later, I was strapping the duffle onto the back of the bike behind the crate when furious scratching and mewling noises started.

"Let me out, you misbegotten daughter of Lilith!"

"Shut it, cat." I said. "It's for your own good."

I swung my leg over the bike and threw on my helmet. We were burning nighttime and it was time to get the hell out of Dodge.

"Fasten your seatbelt."

He hissed in response, this time it sounded suspiciously like the word "bitch."

In no time, we were doing ninety on the 101. I usually preferred to take the Pacific Coast Highway, but I didn't have time to spare for the scenic route.

I lowered my body into the wind, feeling alive and full of purpose. But a weird feeling tingled at the base of my skull—like I was leaving more than L.A. behind. I shook the feeling off, trying to keep my mind on the road and on the challenges ahead. The next night I'd meet Clovis.

I gunned the engine, bringing my speed up to an even hundred. The sooner I could kill Clovis, the sooner I'd be back in L.A. Only then, I'd have finally earned my grandmother's respect.

It was about damned time.

10

The next night, I left Giguhl in the motel room I'd rented in a seedy section of town near the airport. He still wasn't acknowledging my presence, but I figured once his hair depuffed a bit, he'd come around. I thought about letting him shift back into demon form, but I couldn't risk a hotel worker walking in on him.

Of course, you were more likely to find a roach than a mint on your pillow at the rattrap Sleep Inn motel. The place smelled of mold, and the bodily fluid stains on the dingy carpet didn't suggest a high risk of a maid walking in on my demon. But I still didn't want to risk it. Until I got a feel for what we were facing with Clovis, I didn't want to take any chances. Giguhl would just have to make do for the time being.

Frank had called my cell phone with instructions. The meeting with Clovis would happen at midnight. It was only ten o'clock, but I wanted to feed before the meeting and still have enough time to scope out the scene before he arrived.

As I drove, the industrial spread of South San Francisco gave way to more scenic areas. A cool mist blanketed the city, making me glad I'd worn my leathers. I had guns strapped under my arms inside my coat, but I had no illusions I'd get within twenty feet of Clovis without a thorough pat-down. If shit went down I'd have to rely on my fists and my wits.

An hour later, I drove down Baker Street, which ran in front of the Palace of Fine Arts. My belly was full of fresh blood and my cheeks felt rosy and warm, despite the cool night air. I felt so good, I'd let the bum I fed from live. He'd be light-headed for a while, but the hundred-dollar bill I gave him for his time would buy him a nice warm meal to help raise his blood sugar.

As I cruised, I had a nice view of both the Palace Rotunda, which sat across a lagoon, and the lights of the Golden Gate Bridge in the distance. The fog in this section of the city was thicker, causing the bridge to rise like a glowing apparition. Unfortunately, I didn't have time to gaze at scenery all night.

Clovis deserved some credit for his choice of location. The Rotunda was situated with a lagoon on one side and a theater and museum complex behind it. In other words, there were no easy exits and not a lot of opportunities to sneak up on someone.

After pulling into the public parking lot on the north side of the complex, I prepared for the meeting. In deference to my helmet, I'd left my hair down. Now, however, I pulled two apple wood chopsticks from my saddlebags. A quick twist of my hair and I slid the sticks into the mass, careful not to stab myself in the scalp with the sharp points. In a pinch, the hand-whittled sticks would serve as makeshift stakes. Clovis's men would take away the guns and knife, without a doubt, but they'd never think to check my hair for weapons. Besides, the sticks did an excellent job of keeping my hair out of my face.

A few couples strolled through the grounds holding hands. Here and there, bums lounged on benches or sat between columns of the colonnade. Instead of using the concrete path leading to the Rotunda, I chose to stick to the shadows.

I skirted the Rotunda's perimeter. At the front, next to the lagoon, I took a seat on a bench, partially hidden by overhanging trees. From inside the octagonal structure, the sound of a guitar and a male voice singing "Stairway to Heaven" wafted toward me. I could see flashes of fire as jugglers wowed a handful of spectators with flying torches. A pair of white swans floated into view in the lagoon. The scene would have been peaceful under other circumstances. Taking a deep breath, I settled onto the bench to wait for Clovis to arrive.

The wind picked up, whipping a few pieces of trash around the base of the octagon. With it came the distinctive scent of male vampire—a mix of blood and musky pheromones, meant to disarm potential victims.

Frank strolled in from the back of the Rotunda. His relaxed gait gave the appearance of a man out alone enjoying the night air. But as he approached, I saw a handful of other males, new arrivals who awkwardly tried to fit in with the tourists. Clovis wasn't among them. Not sure how I knew this; I just did.

Frank stopped in front of me and nodded. "Glad you could make it."

I stretched my arms along the back of the bench, a

portrait of relaxation. "So is it just you and the welcoming committee tonight?" I asked, nodding in the direction of the other men.

Frank glanced over his shoulder with a smile. "Come now, Sabina. Surely you didn't think Clovis would come here himself."

I placed my hands on my thighs and pushed upright. "I don't appreciate being played, Frank. Games don't amuse me."

Frank moved in front of me, holding up his hands. "Not so fast. I'm sure you understand the obvious security issues involved with such a meeting. Let's not forget how recently you were on the Dominae's payroll."

My hands landed on my hips. "You need to check your memory there, Frank," I said. "You approached me, remember?"

"True," he said. "Which is why Clovis has instructed me to bring you to the temple."

Okay, now I was annoyed. Why didn't they just have me go there to begin with? My question must have been written on my face because Frank responded.

"Clovis wanted to be sure you came alone."

"Clovis sounds a little paranoid, if you ask me."

"You would be too, if you had the Dominae threatening your life," Frank said, watching me closely. "Then again, I guess you do know what that's like."

He was testing me. I silently cursed my big mouth. Of course, Clovis would want to be careful. And, for someone who supposedly had pissed off the Dominae, I was acting awfully unaffected.

"Look, I didn't mean to offend anyone. I'm just annoyed because I feel like I'm getting jerked around here."

He stared at me for a moment, then said, "Understandable, but also unavoidable. Now, if you'll follow me, I'll take you to meet Clovis."

I hesitated. I hadn't expected this. "Uh . . . where are you parked? I'll get my bike and pull around to follow you."

Frank walked away, expecting me to follow. "That won't be necessary. It's hard to drive wearing a blindfold."

He wasn't kidding. About the blindfold, that is. It chafed my face as I sat in the back of a limo, surrounded by guys with extremely broad shoulders.

Normally, I would never have gotten into the car, much less allowed myself to be rendered sightless by anyone. But I knew the only way I'd be able to meet Clovis was if I conceded. Frank had assured me it was merely a security measure, but it felt more like a test. If I agreed too readily then he'd suspect something. However, if I gave too much of a protest I'd also arouse suspicions. So I played the middle ground. After a few half-hearted complaints, I pretended to reluctantly agree.

The limo went over a bump, which lurched me in the direction of a hard body. I quickly righted myself, while trying to listen. Unfortunately, the men in the car kept up a steady stream of dull conversation, discussing everything from the weather to sports. I'd hoped they'd at least let a bit of information about Clovis' operation slip, but no dice. I took a deep breath and tried to mentally prepare myself for the upcoming meeting with Clovis.

I knew almost nothing about him other than his name and that he was part demon. My only exposure to demonkind was through Giguhl. I wasn't sure, but I highly doubted most demons watched *Oprah*.

Regardless, in a few moments I'd finally see the infamous Clovis Trakiya in the flesh. I took a deep breath to calm what felt like bats taking flight in my midsection. The car slowed and then finally stopped.

Show time.

11

Rough hands grabbed my shoulders and pulled me out. My feet hit the pavement and I stumbled. Someone reached to help me, brushing my right breast in the process.

"Oops, sorry," Frank said, sounding anything but. I gritted my teeth and focused on taking cautious steps. I held one hand in front of me, praying I wouldn't walk straight into a wall.

"Four steps." Frank said close to my ear. He placed a hand at my elbow to help me. I longed to shake him off, but knew I wouldn't get very far without his help. His cologne smelled like cheap drugstore aftershave and he'd applied it liberally. I held my breath and cautiously picked my way up the stairs with him guiding me. A loud creaking sound that could only signal a large door opening sounded in front of me. The moist coolness of the night quickly gave way to warmth. The air here was thick with the perfume of incense and candle wax.

Fingers at the back of my head untied the blindfold.

I blinked a few times as my eyes tried to regain focus. We were in what appeared to be a church vestibule. A smattering of candles flickered in the dim room. To my left, Frank stood, watching me closely. We were alone. Up ahead was another set of doors, large wooden panels etched with ancient symbols, resembling cuneiform.

"The service is about to begin," Frank said. "Go in and take a seat. Clovis will meet with you after."

When I hesitated, Frank nodded at the doors. I took a deep breath and walked forward. The sounds of chanting and voices raised in song filtered through the thick doors. The handles were made of gold and the metal felt cold for a moment before my grasp warmed them. Squeaking hinges announced my arrival in the chapel.

Here, the spicy scent of the incense was stronger. My sensitive nose detected notes of calming spikenard in the mix, as well as an undertone of something sickly sweet. Clovis would later tell me he sprinkled white powder heroine in the censers. No doubt about it, visitors to the Temple of the Moon were being primed for submission.

A tall male dressed in black robes stood upon a dais in front of the altar. His eyes found me, and my body jerked to a standstill. His eyes narrowed as he took me in, then a slow smile spread across his saturnine features.

"Clovis." The word floated into my head like a whisper. My stomach flipped. As his eyes did a lazy trip south, I felt his gaze like a caress. His hair shone like polished mahogany in the candlelight—proof of his advanced age. Flowing black and red robes accentuated the smooth paleness of his skin. The robes hid his physique, but power radiated off him in waves.

Our stare-off could have lasted seconds or days. I felt
spellbound by his eyes, which, from where I stood, resembled dark pools of sin. Part of me wanted to stay and
bask in his gaze forever, but the other part—the part in
charge of my survival—screamed at me to run.

He broke the connection first, turning to the congregation. A small smile hovered on his lush lips, as if he
sensed my discomfort. My breath puffed out, as if the
loss of his attention left me deflated.

"Children of Lilith, welcome," Clovis said. His dark
voice washed over the room, but I barely registered the
audience. I was too busy trying to regain my composure.
My body felt all tingly and my panties were wet. Oh yeah,
this guy was definitely going to be trouble.

I shook off the lingering haze, and, embarrassed, went
to sit in the back pew. The church was filled near capac-
ity. I was shocked to see mortals mixed in with a smattering of vamps, mancies, and a few faeries. The mortals
didn't seem the least bit nervous, which meant they either
didn't know they shared the room with beings that could
suck their life from them as easily as we breathed—or
they didn't care.

The altar behind Clovis was made of black marble and
gold. The two-story wall behind the altar was a combination of Byzantine design and Romanesque columns.
There was nothing especially menacing about the décor,
unless one had an aversion to gaudiness. I supposed if
any unsuspecting mortals stumbled in the place they'd
assume an eccentric mortal designed it. In fact, I'd seen
Christian churches and Jewish temples that made this one
look minimalist by comparison. The only thing different
here was the lack of Judeo-Christian symbolism. Instead

of crucifixes or Stars of David, golden eight-pointed lotuses appeared on both the altar and on the red velvet drapes, which hung on either side of the dais.

Clovis clapped his hands, the sound reverberated through the silent chapel, breaking me from my trance-like state.

"It is time." He signaled to the brothers of the Order of the Moon, who stood at the side of the altar. Two of the group disappeared behind a curtain.

A chant rose as the audience closed their eyes in spiritual bliss. I wondered what Clovis had promised to bring them here. There didn't seem to be one specific type. They wore everything from business suits to standard-issue BDSM latex. Of the mortals present, ages ranged from angry teen to midlife-crisis adult. I felt a little lost as the chants grew more intense and the tension in the room rose.

The two males, their hoods covering their faces, led a woman onto the altar. A mortal. Her long blonde hair fell in ropes around pert breasts, covered by a gossamer white robe. One delicate hand clutched the fabric together, an unusual show of modesty given the way she undulated her hips as she approached Clovis. It was as if her pelvis was trying to get to him first. I would have laughed if I wasn't so hypnotized by the pageantry of it all.

The chanting stopped abruptly, leaving the sanctuary in silence. Yet the scent of lust—both the sexual and the blood varieties—seemed palpable. Clovis approached the woman and stroked her cheek with his palm. With a flick of his wrist, he untied the thin rope that held her robe together. Her chin came up as her nude body was exposed. No one blinked. It was as if they saw naked chicks on altars every day. The scene made my fangs feel too large for my mouth.

The crowd held its collective breath as Clovis stroked the woman's long ivory neck. His tongue replaced his finger, causing her to moan in the silent sanctuary. She shivered—in anticipation or fear I didn't know.

Clovis brought his head up a fraction, just enough to see a flash of fangs. He bit savagely into the tender skin, causing the girl to gasp softly. Her eyes widened and then closed in bliss.

Conflicting feelings warred within me. I felt like both a voyeur and a participant. Even though feeding from humans was as natural to me as breathing, what was happening on the altar felt like a desecration. Perhaps it was the fact Clovis was taking something mortals feared and selling it as religion.

I felt an odd sensation that I couldn't quite define rising behind my eyes like a tickle. My rarely used conscience springing to life.

It was over quickly. The woman slumped in his arms, out cold. Clovis licked the wound closed with gentle care. The image of his tongue sliding over her skin was erotic as hell. Shaking off the feeling, I stood to leave. I needed a few minutes to compose myself before our meeting. If I saw him in my current aroused state, I was likely to fuck him first and introduce myself later.

While the brothers carried the woman off the altar, I made my way to the aisle. Clovis caught my eye. When he smiled, his fangs were tinged with blood and there was a thin streak of it next to his lush lips. Lifting a hand, he blew me a blood-soaked kiss.

At that moment I knew without a doubt it was a mistake to be there. He was going to consume me just like he had that girl—only he didn't want my blood. He wanted my soul.

Clovis walked into his office half an hour later with Frank hard on his heels. I stood facing the door with the floor-to-ceiling bookcases at my back, not wanting to be caught off guard.

"Sabina Kane." His voice drifted over me like a hot wind.

I nodded and took the hand he offered. His palm singed mine with a surge of power. Careful to keep my face expressionless, I absorbed the throb. Any show of weakness at this point would put him at an advantage. Of course, he had the advantage already, considering I was in his office with Frank guarding the door and a legion of goons no doubt standing sentry in the hall.

"It's a pleasure to meet you," he continued, finally releasing my hand. "Your reputation precedes you." He motioned to the chair on the other side of his massive ebony desk.

"Depending on your source it's either all true or not true at all."

"I assure you the reports have been positive."

"Then it's all true." I sat in the chair he'd offered with practiced ease.

The corner of his mouth quirked, but the half-smile didn't reach his eyes. Speaking of his eyes, they were even more intense up close. It was as if he had no irises to speak of, only large black pupils—like twin black holes.

I worried if I stared into them too long, I'd be sucked in. I lowered my eyes and crossed my legs.

"I understand you've . . . had a bit of a falling out with the Dominae," he said, leaning back into his black leather chair.

"Let's just say we've had a difference of opinion."

An eyebrow quirked. "Oh?"

"They expect me to follow their rules, and I try to break them whenever I can."

He looked pleased with my response, but I couldn't be sure. On the façade, he looked like a businessman, with his charcoal pinstripe suit, white shirt, and silver and black tie. But something lurked just below the surface. I couldn't put my finger on it; every time I tried to find the right adjective, my thoughts would shift like mercury.

"Let me ask you a question." His voice seemed to break me out of a trance. When I nodded, he continued, "What did you think of the mass?"

"It was certainly . . . interesting."

He chuckled then. "Sabina, I didn't know you were a diplomat as well as an assassin."

I smiled then. "Honestly? I'm not sure what I thought of it. I have a question, though. Why didn't the mortals freak out when you fed from the blonde?"

He nodded and leaned forward. "Our human congregants are thoroughly prepared for what we're about before they ever step foot in the Temple."

"But aren't you worried someone will go to the mortal authorities?"

"Not in the least. The woman signed consent forms. It's all aboveboard, I assure you."

"But—" I began, only to be cut off.

"Sabina, may I speak plainly?" he said. "You seem like someone who appreciates candor." He looked to me for confirmation.

"Sure," I said, trying to sound casual. Inside, I was worried he might call me on my bluff.

"As I said, your reputation as an assassin is well-known. In addition, your knowledge of the Dominae is an asset. I need you on my team."

Blinking, I hesitated, trying to figure out how to respond with the right mixture of hesitancy and interest. "I'm flattered. However, I'm sure you understand I need to know more about your operation before I can answer."

He stood. "Let's walk, shall we?"

When I rose, he held a hand out indicating I should precede him. Frank opened the door. As I passed, he winked at me with a leer. I ignored him and focused on Clovis, who dismissed Frank.

Clovis fell in beside me as we walked down the wood-paneled corridor. I would have wondered about why he felt himself safe enough to be alone with me, but then I saw the guards. They stood at intervals along the corridor, their eyes straight ahead and their bodies rigid as posts. Soon we came to a pair of glass doors. The guards on either side moved to open them for us. Clovis nodded and thanked them. The move surprised me. Most of the leaders I knew treated their staff like faceless slaves.

We walked out into a covered walkway, which extended on all four sides of a central courtyard. A fountain stood in the center with the paths spreading out in a starburst pattern around it. The fountain itself resembled an octagonal baptismal font with engravings circling the basin in a wide band. In the center was a female figure holding torches in each hand. Water bubbled up under her feet, creating a musical sound.

"Do you like it? I had it imported from Greece," Clovis said. He nodded at the figure. "She is the goddess Hekate."

I turned sharply to look at him.

"Surprised?" he asked.

"A little," I admitted.

"If you decide to join our group, you'll learn quickly that we honor all of Lilith's children here. The hostility between the Hekate and the Lilim has gone on too long. It's time we all came together to honor the Great Mother."

I kept quiet since I couldn't very well tell him I thought his philosophy was bullshit. Instead, I nodded thoughtfully, as if considering the possibility.

Clovis led on past the fountain and through another set of doors directly across the courtyard from the ones we'd used a few moments earlier.

"We're entering the school now," he said, pride evident in his voice. "This is where our members learn about our sacred history."

"Bible study from hell?" I joked.

Clovis stopped and pinned me with a stare that would have turned a lesser female to stone. "You'd do best to leave your mockery at the door. We take our teachings very seriously here."

Worried I'd ruined my chances, I tried to look chastened. "I'm sorry. It's just this is all new to me."

The hard planes of his face softened a bit. "Of course.

I apologize if I spoke too harshly. I'm sure you understand that we've had our fair share of detractors among the Lilim."

No shit, I thought. This guy sounded like some freaky mortal televangelist. It just didn't compute. My kind wasn't known for our goodwill toward the other dark races.

Clovis must have interpreted my silence for insightful reflection because he continued into the building. Down another corridor and a couple of turns later, we entered a classroom. It seemed your standard-issue desks-and-blackboard kind of place. The only thing odd about it was the class, which was made up of vampires, mancies, a few faeries, and a couple of mortals. If this group had been thrown together anyplace else, there'd be lots of fighting and even more blood. But here, they all behaved themselves as they watched the teacher. She appeared to be human, but didn't smell like one. Most humans smelled like dirt. This chick didn't smell like anything. Odd.

The teacher paused in midsentence when she saw us. "Brother Clovis, we're honored," she gushed.

"Please don't let us interrupt, Sister Gianna."

"Not at all," she said. "We were just discussing the Sacred Mother's creation of the Titans."

Clovis nodded. "Carry on; we'll continue with our tour."

Back in the hall, he talked as we passed more filled classrooms. "Most of our students are in the acolyte stage. They must go through hundreds of hours of training before they are allowed to go through the joining ritual."

"Joining ritual?"

He nodded. "Before anyone can be welcomed into the sect as a full-fledged member they must go through an initiation to prove their dedication to our path."

I noted his lack of specifics, but said nothing. "We'll continue on to the dormitories," he said, opening another door. We entered a large room. The walls were lined with bunk beds. It looked like military barracks.

"Who stays here?" I asked as we walked along the aisle formed in the middle of the room.

"The trainees," he said. "We have found that total immersion in our way of life nets the best results."

The more I saw and heard, the more this place sounded like a monastery . . . or a cult.

"Training for what?"

"For service to Lilith, of course."

I hesitated. "What exactly does service to Lilith entail? Like religious service?"

He paused. "Something like that. It is our belief that instead of warring against each other and the humans, the Lilim and mortals should band together to make the world a better place. After all, whether Lilim or Adamite, we are all children of God."

I almost gagged. Seriously, no one I knew ever said His name. Most vamps believe we were forsaken by Him. After all, Lilith had disobeyed the big guy in Eden and then—after sowing her wild oats—shacked up with Asmodeus in Irkalla. Not exactly a righteous path by biblical standards.

Besides all that, I didn't trust the line of bullshit Clovis was feeding me. His spiel seemed a little too polished. My guess was he was training his recruits to rise up against the Dominae. Although why he would use mancies and humans to do it was beyond me.

"Tell me something, Sabina," he said, leaning against one of the bunks. "Haven't you ever wished you weren't discriminated against because of your mixed ancestry?"

It was a low blow. I gritted my teeth to hold back my angry retort. "I'll admit it's been frustrating at times."

He looked into my eyes then, as if he was trying to see into my soul. Something told me he might just succeed. "Haven't you ever felt angry that you bear the burdens of your parent's sins? Haven't you longed to be at peace?"

He continued to stare into my eyes as he spoke. A sense of calm washed over me, almost as if he was hypnotizing me with those obsidian eyes. Suddenly, I felt a brush against my mind. The nudge rocked me out of my trance. The last thing I needed was Clovis busting through my mental barriers. I cleared my throat and focused my energy on keeping him out.

He smiled knowingly. "You don't trust me yet to see your secrets. I hope in time you'll let me in."

Don't hold your breath, buddy, I thought.

"If I were to agree to join your"—I'd almost said cult but stopped myself just in time—"group. What would it entail exactly?"

He started walking again, through another door and back out into the courtyard. As we walked, he seemed to be pondering my question, as if he hadn't given it thought before. *Riiight.*

Even though I didn't trust him any more than I would a snake, as we walked my body felt drawn to his. I literally had to force myself to keep a respectable distance between us. He stood about a head taller than me and the broadness of his shoulders was emphasized by the cut of his suit. And that face. Damn. A face like that would make a nun reconsider her vows.

So, yes, physically he was gorgeous in a hot villain kind of way. But it was more than that. He had some aura about him that was pure seduction. I'd do best to remember he was my enemy.

We'd reached the fountain again by the time he spoke. "Your initiation would happen fairly quickly. Just a formality, really."

Again, I noticed he failed to give specifics. "I don't mean to be rude here, but if I'm going to agree to join you, I'm going to need particulars. What is the project and exactly what does the initiation entail?"

He ran a hand across the surface of the water, almost as if he was stroking it. He lifted the hand and water dripped from his fingertips. With one finger, he reached up and rubbed the liquid on his full bottom lip. My mouth went dry and my crotch got wet.

He shrugged. "I'm afraid I can't reveal that until you agree to join me. However, I'm sure you'll have no problem."

"And the project?"

He rubbed the remaining water between his palms and watched me. "I'm afraid the details will have to wait until the initiation rites have been performed."

"You sure don't give a girl a lot to go on, do you?"

He smiled. "Unfortunately, the nature of the assignment is such that only those within my circle of trust can know the details."

He was a slippery one, I'd give him that.

"Say I decide against joining you," I said. "What then?"

He shrugged. "Then you go your way and I go mine. However, I'm sure that won't happen."

My eyes narrowed. "And why is that?"

"Because soon enough you're going to realize that the world is about to change for all the dark races. Those not aligned with a power will find themselves trampled."

"I can take care of myself," I said.

"I have no doubt on that account," he said. "However, I seriously doubt you want both the Dominae and me as your enemies."

Ah. There it was. A subtle threat, but a threat nonetheless.

He straightened from his slouch. "Forgive me. There's no need for that kind of talk now." His smile was friendly, but the threat hung in the air between us. "Where are you staying while you're in town?"

The change in subject caught me off guard. "In a hotel with my de—cat."

"If it wouldn't be too forward, I'd like to offer another suggestion."

I tilted my head, trying to figure out where he was going with this.

"The Temple owns a few apartment complexes around town. It just so happens a female member of the congregation has an extra room."

I was already shaking my head when he held a hand up to stall my protest.

"Vinca is one of my brightest followers. I think you two would get along splendidly," he said. "I'm sure she would be happy to answer any of your questions about the good work we do here."

"That's nice of you to offer," I lied. "However, I'd feel uncomfortable moving in with someone I've never met."

We had almost reached the front doors of the church again. Frank was standing sentinel in the hall.

"Oh, but I insist," Clovis said. "Unless you'd like to move into our dormitories here?"

That idea I liked even less than moving in with this Vinca chick. I quickly weighed my options. Arguing too much might make him suspicious. But I seriously didn't like the idea that someone would be able to track my movements. However, living with one of Clovis' people might give me an edge. If I could cozy up to this Vinca and pump her for details, the arrangement might work in my favor. I looked at Clovis, who smiled as if my acquiescence was guaranteed. I guess, in the end, I really didn't have a choice.

"Okay, I'll do it. I only ask that you give me a little time to consider your offer."

"Done," he said. "I'll have Frank call Vinca and tell her to expect you tonight."

12

Two hours later, I looked up at a pink stucco two-story apartment building about a mile from the Temple. Frank had taken me back to get my motorcycle at the Palace of Fine Arts and then waited for me to pack up Giguhl and my things so I could follow him to Vinca's place. Giguhl, Lilith love him, had remained silent throughout the ride over. I was sure I'd get an earful later, however.

As I stood in front of the cheery façade, my stomach rolled. Somehow Clovis had talked me into walking into this situation with absolutely no clue what was awaiting me.

Frank nudged me with Giguhl's crate, which he'd offered to carry for me because my hands were full with my bag and helmet. "It's through the courtyard," Frank said.

I took the hint and walked up the four concrete steps leading to the courtyard of the U-shaped building. It surrounded a central green space with a small pool in the center. The building and grounds were well-maintained and clean, and the neighborhood seemed fairly upscale. It was a definite upgrade from the no-tell motel by the airport. However, I couldn't shake the sense of unease I felt walking into this situation totally unprepared.

Frank walked in front of me, no doubt impatient to dump me in my new digs so he could return to the Temple. He walked to a door near the pool. A welcome mat sat in front of the door and wind chimes hung from a small hook. A window stood to the right of the door and someone had installed a flower box, which was filled with yellow and purple pansies.

Frank knocked with his free hand. Almost immediately, the door flew open and light flooded the dim walkway. A petite blonde with a halo of soft curls around her pixy face smiled at us.

"Omigod, hi!" She moved around Frank and hugged me before I could jump out of the way. "I'm so excited to meet you, roomie!"

My arms were too loaded down to shrug her off. I was engulfed by the scent of lavender. Freaking great. My new roommate was a faery.

I glanced at Frank, who cracked a smile, obviously delighted by my discomfort.

"Vinca, this is Sabina," he said. "Sabina, Vinca."

"Um, hi," I said, taking a step back to disengage the overly affectionate waif. "Nice to meet you."

Her 500-watt smile blinded me as she pulled back. "Come in and make yourself at home," she said. She took my helmet and walked in before I could respond.

Frank stopped me as I was about to walk past him. He shoved the cat crate in my hand. "I'm going to head out and let you two get acquainted. Call my cell if you need anything."

My mouth dropped open. "You're leaving?"

"Got things to do," he said. "Don't worry, Vinca will take good care of you."

Vinca's voice came from inside the kitchen causing me to look away from him. "Can I get you something to eat?"

By the time I looked back, Frank was already halfway across the courtyard. I thought about calling him back, but I knew it was silly. It's not like I was afraid of Vinca. I just wasn't used to being around someone so . . . peppy.

With a resigned sigh, I walked in and shut the door. I set down Giguhl's crate and took in the room. A floral armchair and a comfortable-looking moss-green couch filled the small space. On the trunk, which served as a coffee table, fresh flowers sat in a glass vase. The smell of lavender was stronger in here, and underneath it the scent of freshly baked brownies tickled my nose.

Vinca stuck her head out of the kitchen. "Roomie?"

I cringed. "Yeah?"

"I asked if you were hungry."

"Oh, no, I'm fine," I said. "Where's my room?"

She giggled. "Oh, silly me. I'll show you."

She moved toward me only to stop in her tracks about five feet from where I stood. Her eyes focused on the crate. Her smile vanished and she pointed an accusing finger at the crate.

"That's not a," she gulped, "a cat, is it?"

Her sudden change in mood confused me. I looked down, "Yeah, his name is Giguhl."

"Oh no, Clovis didn't tell me." She backed away a few steps.

"Oh. Are you allergic or something?"

She put a hand to her throat, as if at any moment Giguhl was going to bust through the crate and attack. "No." She dragged her fearful gaze from the crate to look at me. "I'm a nymph."

I didn't really see what one had to do with the other. "Yeah, and?"

"Geez, don't you know anything? Cats are the mortal enemies of all the faery species."

My lack of knowledge obviously had lowered her opinion of me. I wasn't sure why that bothered me.

"Sorry, I haven't known many faeries," I said. She snorted and muttered something about that being obvious. "But you don't need to worry. Giguhl isn't really a cat. He's a demon." I didn't really want to tell Vinca about Giguhl's demon status. But she seemed so anti-cat, I figured a demon might be the lesser of two evils, so to speak. Plus, since we'd be living in close quarters, it would be nearly impossible to hide his ability to talk.

Her eyes widened into big green disks. "A demon? I've never heard of a demon in cat form."

"It's a long story."

"Either way," she said. "I'm afraid if you want to stay here he'll have to stay in your room at all times."

Oh great. One more thing for Giguhl to give me shit about.

"Fine," I said. "Can I see the room now?"

She was looking at the cat crate with interest, her anxiety having given way to curiosity. "Follow me," she said.

She led the way to a short hallway to the right of the living room. She went through the only door, which led to the bedroom.

"Wow, this is certainly . . . floral," I said.

"If you like this you should see my room," she said. "I just love flowers."

That much was obvious. The place looked like a rose bush exploded. The white bedspread had a pink rose pattern that matched the drapes on the small window. The white dresser had a huge vase of yellow roses. There was even a rose wallpaper border along the ceiling.

"My room is across the living room from here, so you'll have plenty of privacy. Plus, most nights I'm busy outside tending to the grounds."

"Are you the landlord or something?" I asked.

"No, silly, I'm a faery, remember? Taking care of plants is kind of our thing."

"Oh, right."

"Anyway, I'll let you get settled," she said. "The bathroom is through that door. There are plenty of towels in there. Make yourself at home."

"Hey, Vinca?"

She turned as she was about to walk through the door. "Yes, roomie?"

Every time she said that word it was like someone running fingernails down a blackboard. "Thanks for putting me up for a few days."

Her smile lit up the garden-like room. "It's my pleasure." She stopped and put a hand to her forehead. She swayed and I stepped forward to help, worried she might be in pain. Then she seemed to recover completely, as if coming out of a trance. "Whoa, that was a strong one."

"What? Are you okay?"

"Oh yes," she waved a delicate hand through the air. "Just one of my visions."

"Do you have visions often?" I asked, trying not to sound too freaked out.

"Sometimes. It's a nymph thing."

I was almost afraid to ask, but I did anyway. "What did you see?"

"I saw the two of us laughing together under a mighty oak tree. You know what that means, don't you?" She looked at me expectantly. All I could do was shake my head. "We're totally going to be best friends!"

I felt my eyes widen. "Great," I said slowly and backed away a step.

She waited and smiled at me, like she was expecting more of a reaction. I hated to disappoint her, but I tended to avoid declaring my undying friendship to anyone, especially overly enthusiastic nymphs I'd just met.

"Okay, well, I really need to unpack now."

"Okay, roomie! Just call if you need anything."

As she shut the door, I dropped on the bed. Best friends? With a nymph? Not likely. At best, I was counting on her openness to work to my benefit as I grilled her for information about Clovis. At worst—well, at worst, I was going to have to figure out a way to put up with her perkiness. I don't do perky.

Shaking myself from my thoughts, I got busy unpacking. I only had about four hours until sunrise and I still needed to feed.

*   *   *

After unpacking my few belongings and a brief argument with a severely pissed-off Giguhl, I left my room. My plan was to get directions from Vinca to the nearest vamp bar, so I could grab a pint or three.

I found her in the kitchen. When I walked in she was humming a tune while she tended to a pot of some type of herb on the windowsill. She stopped and turned to me with a smile when she saw me.

"Hi there. All settled in?" she asked.

I nodded. "Yeah."

"So." She dusted dirt from her slender hands as she spoke. "I was thinking we could hang out and get to know one another."

I hesitated. I didn't want to be outright rude to her, especially when she looked so eager. But I desperately needed to feed.

"Err, actually, I kind of need to head out for a little while."

Her face fell. "Oh. Where are you going?"

"I was going to see if you could direct me to one of the local vamp clubs."

"Really?" The excitement in her voice set me on guard.

"Do you know where any are?"

"There's a place a few blocks away that I've heard about. It's supposed to be pretty cool. I've never been there. Or any vamp club for that matter."

The statement hung in the air between us for a few seconds. She didn't say it, but it was obvious she wanted to come with me.

"You wouldn't want to come with me, would you?" *Please say no.*

Her eyes lit up. "I thought you'd never ask! Let me just change. I'll just be a sec."

She ran off toward her room before I could call her back. The last thing I needed was a nymph with sunshine coming out of her ass tagging along with me. Now I'd have to find some way to sneak away from her a little bit so I could feed. On the bright side, it might be a good opportunity for me to get some info out of her.

Five minutes later, she came back into the living room. Gone were the faded jeans and soft green sweater. Now she wore a something straight out a of strip club. The skirt landed about an inch below her girly bits and the black scrap of lace across her breasts could only be called a blouse in the loosest sense. I stared at her in shock for a moment, but she only smiled back innocently. Then I looked down at my own black leather pants and black and red mesh halter, and decided I didn't have a lot of room to question her fashion choices.

Her cheeks were pink with excitement. "You ready?"

Ten minutes later, Vinca's gecko-green Volkswagen beetle pulled up in front of a dance club. I slumped down in my seat as vampires near the entrance eyed the car. No self-respecting vampire would choose to ride around in that hippiemobile. Especially one with a license plate reading "FLWRPWR."

A valet guy came forward immediately and handed Vinca a ticket as we left the car. I ignored the stares and led the way into the club.

The club itself was a soaring mass of concrete and steel. The two stories of windows rattled with the deep bass reverberating from inside. Two brawny bouncers wearing matching black T-shirts waved us in after a few salacious comments.

The din inside made my eardrums ache. The crowd seemed a mix of vamps and Gothed-up mortals. It always made me laugh that vampires usually dressed in modern clothes, while those who emulated them seemed stuck in some Goth time warp.

Vinca was nearly skipping with excitement as we approached the bar. I prayed she wouldn't do anything to embarrass me. The bartender, a skinny guy with a shock of orange hair, leered at Vinca before asking for our orders. Given the lack of security at the place, I settled for ordering a whiskey, while Vinca asked for a Shirley Temple. When I looked at her, she smiled back as if her drink order wasn't totally ridiculous.

"Don't you want something with a little kick?"

She shook her head. "Faeries don't need alcohol. Sugar is our intoxicant of choice."

We got our drinks and wound our way through the sweaty hordes to an unoccupied booth on the other side of the club. As we walked, I noticed more males looking at my new roommate as if she was dessert. She didn't seem to mind as she winked and smiled at them. Once we were settled, Vinca took a large gulp of her pink drink, while I watched the action out on the massive dance floor. From the corner of my eye, I saw Vinca watching me. She finally leaned into my field of vision to get my attention.

"So, Sabina, tell me everything."

"What do you mean?"

"About you, silly. Tell me about your life."

She waited with a patient smile while I tried to figure out how much to tell her. "There's not much to tell, really.

Up until recently I was an assassin for the Dominae, but that didn't really work out. So here I am."

"Oooh, an assassin! How interesting. How many beings have you killed?"

I was shocked she took the news in stride. "I'm not sure, really. A lot."

"Interesting. And now you want to join Clovis. I guess that makes sense if you had a falling out with the Dominae."

"I guess so. I'm not really sure about it, though."

"Well, why not? Clovis is amazing."

"How did you meet him?" I asked.

She shrugged and played with the little umbrella in her drink. "It's a long story, but the short version is the city is no place for a naive young nymph fresh from the forest. I fell on some hard times and ended up getting involved in a faery porn ring."

I choked on my drink, sputtering whiskey all over my pants. Vinca patted me on the back and handed me a napkin. Once I recovered, I said, "Faery porn?"

"Yeah. There's a big black market for it here. And since I'm a nymph, and my kind is known for our . . . skills, I was a big hit for a while." She paused to take a sip from her drink. "Anyway, Manroot, my manager, eventually moved on to a younger *ingénue*. I was left with no money and a bad case of crabs. Clovis heard about my problem from a friend who'd joined the Temple and offered to help me get back on my feet. The rest is history."

"Wow," I said. "How long ago was that?"

"Ten years next month," she said. "Anyway, when I met Clovis, I had a vision that told me I could trust him. I don't know where I would have ended up if Clovis hadn't helped me. And I'm not the only one. He's taken in dozens of vampires, mancies, and other beings since I've known him."

I let the vision comment slide. "What does he ask for in return?" I wasn't buying this touchy-feely crap. Clovis didn't strike me as the kind of guy who'd help someone without a little *quid pro quo*.

"Nothing much. I volunteer at the Temple a few nights a month, making sure the plants are healthy. And of course I let him feed from me sometimes."

My jaw dropped. "He feeds from you?"

She shrugged. "Sure. It's a small price to pay."

"Does he feed from all his followers?"

"I think so. Why?"

"Vinca, you're aware that when a vampire feeds they absorb some of the essence of the host, right?"

"Yeah, so?"

I shook my head, unable to understand why she didn't get it. "Don't you see? If he's feeding from all his followers then he's gaining whatever powers you possess for himself. He must be incredibly strong."

She frowned. "I am happy to share my powers with him, limited as they are. He needs all the strength he can get to overcome the oppressors."

I glanced at her drink. She'd barely touched it, which contradicted my theory she was suddenly drunk. "Oppressors?"

"You know, the Dominae, the Hekate Council, the Seelie Court, the Demon League?" she said. Her voice had risen with the fervor of the converted. "The institutions that have fostered enmity among all the races for untold centuries?"

"Oh right, them." Suddenly, I had a feeling I'd underestimated my new roommate. She seemed flighty, but hearing her talk just then I realized she was actually fully invested in Clovis' doctrine.

"Clovis only wants to save us from the tyranny we've all been living under. If donating some blood helps him do that, then so be it."

"Okay," I said slowly. "So how does he plan to unite everyone?"

She took another sip of her drink. "By spreading his message of love."

I almost choked again. "What does this message entail exactly?"

"Instead of answering you directly, let me ask you a question."

I leaned into the booth with my arms spread along the back of the seat. "Shoot."

"Do you ever get tired of being an outcast?"

I sat up straight, my arms falling to my sides. "What do you mean?"

"You—us—we've all been marginalized as mythology by the humans. We're forced to blend in or hide in the shadows, afraid of discovery. But, in fact, we're the superior beings."

I was beginning to understand. "Ah, so Clovis really wants us to unite against Adamites." Not with them, as he told me. Interesting.

"Exactly," she said. "Not to wipe them out, mind you, but to finally take our place as the leaders of the earth. As the sons and daughters of Lilith, it's our right to rule."

I rolled my glass between my palms, considering what

she'd said. It made some kind of sense, although I still wasn't sure how Clovis intended to accomplish any of it.

"When he called me, Clovis mentioned you were a bit reluctant to join our cause," she continued. "But Sabina, I can tell you without a doubt in my mind that Clovis's intentions are noble."

"I'm sure they are. But you have to understand that it's quite an adjustment for me to go from one master to another so quickly."

"Ask yourself this," she said. She leaned forward and placed a slender hand on my arm. "Did you ever feel loved by the Dominae? Did they ever promise to make your life better? Because that's what Clovis is offering you. It's a gift. I predict you'll thank him one day for offering it."

I shifted in my seat, away from the intensity in her gaze. It was time to change the subject. "Listen, I need to hit the bathroom. Do you need another drink while I'm gone?"

She chugged the rest of her Shirley Temple. A delicate burp erupted from her Cupid's-bow mouth. "Make it a double."

13

I wandered through the dense crowd, wondering where I could score a quick bite. Usually, clubs like this one had private rooms set aside for vamps. However, being an unknown in these parts, I wasn't sure how I'd be received, especially if the news I was *vampira non grata* with the Dominae had spread this far north.

I made my way back to the main bar and got the attention of the young vamp who'd served us earlier. He leaned on the bar in front of me. "What'll it be?"

I leaned in close, so as not to be overheard by the mortals surrounding the bar like thirsty wolves. "Do you have anything 'organic' back there?"

His eyebrows knitted. "Sorry, you have to buy your weed elsewhere." He started to go, but I grabbed his arm.

"Not weed. Blood."

His mouthed formed into an "oh" as the light dawned. "You mean a Bloody Magdalene?"

I nodded at the code word. "Yes, a double, hold the vodka."

He knelt down in front of a small fridge hidden under the bar. I couldn't see around his shoulders, but I knew he was pouring blood from a bag into the shaker in his hand. He made a show of adding spices and shaking it before pouring the blood into a highball glass. He even garnished it with a stalk of celery.

"That'll be fifty bucks," he said.

"What! That's highway robbery," I said.

"Listen, lady, we're the ones risking having the stuff in stock. You want cheap, you gotta hunt it yourself."

Glaring, I grabbed my wallet and plunked down a Benjamin. "I need another Shirley Temple. And change."

He smiled a toothy grin and went to fill the rest of the order. I took a sip and grimaced. Cheap well blood was the worst. Bars like these usually had a deal to get the bottom of the barrel from local blood banks. Luckily, the spices tempered the overly ferric taste of blood. I grumbled to myself about the high price of fast food while he made change.

The bartender slapped two twenties on the bar along with Vinca's drink. "Hey," I said. "Ten bucks for a Shirley Temple?"

"No, that was five bucks. The extra five was for the tip you were about to stiff me on."

"Asshole," I grumbled as I walked away sixty dollars poorer. It's not that I'm cheap. It's just that inflation hurts a lot more when you're immortal.

I had two choices for getting back to my seat. I could take the long way around and fight the crowd, thus risking spilled blood and grenadine all over my clothes. Or I could cut straight through the dance floor and risk spilled blood and grenadine all over my clothes. I chose the more direct route.

I'd not taken two steps onto the packed dance floor, when I felt a suspicious presence in the vicinity of my ass. A male mortal, decked out in gold lamé, leered at me while grinding his pelvis into my backside. He wore about four gold chains around his neck, an obvious bid to compensate for the tiny member he was jabbing at my ass. There was nothing worse than a horny mortal male.

I speared him with a glare. "Back off, asshole."

"Hey, baby, why you hatin'? Give a player some love."

"Not interested."

"Damn, girl, that's cold." His suburban-thug persona was ridiculous, but his inability to take a hint was downright suicidal.

An opening appeared just next to me in the crowd, so I scooted off before I was tempted to show the player some love in the form of my knee to his nuts. Now I remembered why I usually avoided dance floors.

About halfway through the gyrating mass of humanity, I felt a hand on my shoulder. Annoyed, I swung around ready to teach another asshole some manners. Vinca's drink sloshed all over the guy who'd grabbed me. Only, instead of another doughy mortal midsection clad in gold, I faced a nicely toned chest encased in a white tank with a rapidly spreading pink stain.

I looked up to see a familiar, yet annoyed, face. "Hey, don't you know it's rude to grab people?" I immediately went on the attack. This freaking mage had to quit following me.

"Don't you know it's rude to spill drinks on people?" He countered loud enough to be heard over the music.

"What do you want?" Bodies bumped into us from all sides. I cradled my drink to my chest. There was no way I was letting fifty bucks worth of blood go to waste.

The mage didn't look too happy to be jostled either. He grabbed my arm and started pulling me back toward the bar. When I dug in my heels, he looked over his shoulder with a frown. I thought about it for a second and shrugged. Time for the mage to answer some questions.

He led me to a door on the other side of the bar. Another bouncer stood here. He was a vamp, but merely nodded when he saw the mage. Not for the first time, I wondered how this guy seemed to move so effortlessly through vampire territory.

The mage led me to a private room. Low black leather couches and steel tables created conversation areas. The music from outside was being piped in through speakers, only at a much less deafening level.

Once he shut the door, I turned on him. "All right, who the hell are you?"

He chuckled. "You don't mince words, do you, Sabina? I'm Adam Lazarus." He held out a hand as he came forward. I looked at it as if he was offering me a snake.

I tilted my head and looked at him. "I think I'll pass."

He pulled back and frowned. "Do you really think I'd harm you after I saved your ass in L.A.?"

I placed a hand on my hip. "You didn't save my ass. You merely assisted me, and for that I owe you thanks. But that doesn't mean I trust you, far from it."

"Fair enough," he said. He wandered over to the small

bar at the side of the room. From a mini-fridge, he grabbed a beer. He held up the bottle, offering it to me. I ignored him and took a long gulp of my drink, which, thank the gods, had survived the trip from the dance floor.

"In the Bay Area on vacation?" I asked.

His lips twitched at my sarcasm. "Believe me, if I was on vacation, following a bitchy vampire wouldn't be my first choice," he said. "As for why I'm following you, the answer is simple. Your family sent me to check up on you."

I crossed my arms. "Right. Do you really expect me to believe the Dominae would hire a mage to follow me?"

He shook his head. "Not the Dominae. Your Hekate family."

My stomach dropped. "I don't have a Hekate family."

"On the contrary, you have a very large Hekate family." He sat in one of the armchairs, seeming totally at ease while I felt as tightly wound as concertina wire.

"Nice try. The Hekate side of my family disowned me at birth. So, who really sent you?"

Adam leaned toward me, his expression intense. "The Dominae told you that?"

I was getting a little annoyed with the subject. "Even if they hadn't, it was pretty obvious since the mages made no effort to contact me."

Resentment grew in my belly like a poisoned vine. Resentment toward my parents for breaking the rules, resentment toward the Dominae for blaming me for their actions, and resentment toward Adam for reminding me of my red-headed stepchild status.

"You weren't disowned, Sabina. Your existence was hidden from the Hekate Council until recently."

"Give me a break. Do you really expect me to believe that shit?" I said. "Look, I don't know who you're really working for, but I'd suggest you tell them I'm not buying it."

"And I'm not selling. The truth is your family sent me to make contact in the hopes you'd consider a meeting. I've been ordered to pursue this until you agree."

"Don't hold your breath, hemophobe."

He smiled at the insult. "You'll find I'm a patient man, Sabina Kane."

I grimaced. Names held power and this mage had just declared a challenge. "Look, dude, I don't have time for this shit. Now go away. And while you're at it, keep that freaking owl away from me. It's creepy."

I started to walk to the door but he reached me faster than any mage had a right to move. He placed a hand on my arm, causing me to jerk away and bare my fangs at him. He stepped back instantly with his hands up.

"Easy there," he said. "What owl?"

"Oh, please," I said. "Don't pretend you don't know what I'm talking about."

"Sabina, I don't know anything about an owl."

"Yes, you do. It's pretty hard to miss a huge white owl with red eyes."

His face blanched. "When did you see it? Tell me."

I sighed, sick of playing around. "The night I saw you at Sepulcher and then again at Phantasmagoria before the fight."

"Have you seen it since then?"

"Jeez, no. What's the deal?" I mocked him with a pout. "Don't tell me you lost your owl. What a shame."

"It is not my owl." His face was serious and I suddenly had a bad feeling in my stomach.

"Whose is it then?"

"You don't want to know."

"Yes, I do."

He sighed. "You said the owl has red eyes?" When I nodded, he continued. "According to the legends, Lilith has a red-eyed owl named Stryx. He's her spy."

I stared at him for a moment, dumbfounded he expected me to buy this crap. Next he'd probably tell me burning bushes spoke to him. "Whatever," I said finally. "I'm out of here, psycho."

I started for the door, ready to pretend this conversation never happened.

"How's Giguhl?"

That stopped me. I turned slowly, spearing him with a look that should have turned him to ash on the spot. "Oh, yeah. What the hell do you mean sending a demon to kill me?"

He held up his hands. "I had to be sure."

"Of what?"

"That you were her."

"Who her?" I asked losing patience.

He opened his mouth to speak and then closed it. His expression became shuttered as if he'd just decided to tell a lie. "I had to be sure you were really the daughter of Tristan Graecus."

"You're lying."

"No, I'm not." His eyes shifted to the left.

"Look, it doesn't really matter. I should kill you for sending that hell beast after me." I advanced on him, but he held up a hand to stop me.

"I wouldn't do that if I were you," he said quickly. "Think about it. If you kill me you'll be stuck with him forever."

I paused, thinking about the grim prospect of spending an eternity with Giguhl. A shudder passed through me. "Damn it!"

Adam smiled and crossed his arms.

"All right," I said. "What's it gonna take for you to send him back?"

He rocked back on his heels, thinking it over. "You have to agree to meet with your family."

I laughed in his face. "You're insane."

"No meeting, no spell."

"I should just kill you."

"You are welcome to try it, but you won't make it an inch in my direction before I blast your ass with a spell that will make Irkalla look like a week in Tahiti."

"You're a real pain in the ass, you know."

He pressed a business card into my hand. "Think it over," he said. "When you're ready to make a deal, call me."

"Not likely." I handed the card back but he refused it.

"Take it. Even if you're not ready to meet your family, call me if you have any questions about where you came from or your magic."

"I've done fine so far without using my magic, if I even have any."

"You have it," he said. "The question is why would you deny your birthright?"

I'd had enough of him. "Good-bye, Adam Lazarus. If that's even your real name."

"Good*night,* Sabina Kane. We'll be seeing each other again real soon."

"Oh, goody," I muttered to myself as I walked away. Funny thing was he didn't look crazy, despite his wild claims. I glanced at him over my shoulder, and he waved at me. I glared at him before going back into the club. I wasn't running from him, but instead toward Vinca who was probably worried about my disappearing act. I wasn't sure why, but I tucked Adam's card in my back pocket. Probably, I should have trashed it. Something told me to hang on to it, though.

When I finally reached the booth, Vinca was gone. I couldn't blame her for leaving when I'd been gone so long. I sat down to finish my drink, in no hurry to leave in case that mage was waiting for me outside. The thing was he seemed pretty convincing, or at least he seemed convinced what he was saying was true.

Lavinia had warned me from a very young age to distrust mancies. She claimed part of their magic was in their words, and that they never hesitated using lies to manipulate their victims. According to her, mancies lacked loyalty and integrity. To her my father's family rejecting me at birth proved this fact.

So, yeah, I found it hard to trust a mancy who sent demons after me and generally skulked around making outrageous claims. But who was he working for? And what did he think feeding me lies would accomplish?

With any luck, he'd leave me alone. But given the way my luck was going lately, I didn't put too much stock in it.

Taking another sip of blood, I pushed the mancy from my mind to focus on my Clovis project. I really needed to figure out my next steps there. Obviously, I'd have to undergo his initiation before he'd share any of his plans with me. After talking with Vinca, I had a pretty good idea of what that initiation entailed. The thought of letting him feed from me gave me the willies, but I didn't see that I had much of a choice.

I finished off the blood, which was now warm, and left. The cool night air washed over me as I left the club. I caught a taxi back to the apartment.

I paid the driver and got out, ready to close myself in my room and prepare for a long sleep. As I climbed the steps to the courtyard, I heard a screech echo through the quiet predawn sky.

I stopped and scowled at the owl. He was sitting on the roof of the building next to a TV antenna.

"Leave me alone," I said. I felt kind of stupid talking to an owl, but I was beyond caring. It was all too much to digest.

Once again, the owl's screech sounded like, "Sabina." A shiver passed down my spine. What if Adam was right and this owl was a spy for Lilith? I laughed at myself. Why would the Queen of Irkalla and mother of all the dark races be spying on little old me?

"I must be more tired than I thought," I said out loud. To the owl I said. "Go home."

I continued into the quiet apartment, where Vinca had left a light on for me. I collapsed in bed after pushing Giguhl off my pillow. I was out almost before my head hit the pillow.

That night I dreamed of vampire owls feeding on David's corpse.

14

I'm surprised you need guidance already, Sabina. Surely you haven't already run into problems." Lavinia's voice sounded shrill as it came through the receiver.

I shifted on the hard park bench, trying to relieve a pressure point. The park was empty this time of night, except for a few drug dealers and other lowlifes. They'd make a good midnight snack once I got off the phone. "It's not really a problem," I said quickly.

"Well, out with it," she said. I could hear chanting in the background as the acolytes prepared for midnight mass.

"He wants to feed from me," I blurted.

Grandmother sighed, a deep inhalation that clearly communicated her impatience. "You're wasting my time."

"Can't I just kill him?"

"Your mission is to infiltrate his inner circle and find out who is spying for him and what his plans are. You will not kill him until you are told to do so."

I rubbed my forehead. "So I'm supposed to prostitute myself out until then?"

Her voice came through the phone like a slap. "I did not raise you to be weak. Your loyalty to the Dominae supersedes your pride."

I looked down, ashamed I'd questioned her. But inside, my stomach was churning. Allowing another vampire to feed from you was the ultimate form of submission. All the Dominae's underlings went through it as a sign of fealty once they came of age. But I'd never allowed anyone else to do it. Some vamps got off on the master and servant aspect of sharing blood during sex, but not me. To me it represented vulnerability—weakness—something I tried to avoid whenever possible.

"If you can't handle this assignment, tell me now."

My head snapped up. Her words stung my pride, and I suspected that was her intention. "I can handle it."

"Excellent. Do not call again until you have real news to share."

"Yes, Grandmother," I said.

I pulled the phone away from my ear to disconnect, feeling confused by the emotions jockeying for position within me.

"Sabina?"

I put the phone back to my ear. "Yes, Domina?"

"Do not disappoint me, child. Is that clear?"

My teeth clashed, like my jaw had been wired shut. "Crystal."

I hung up and went to go take my frustration out on a few of my fellow park visitors.

*   *   *

When I opened the door to the apartment an hour later, a black streak ran past. I turned to see Giguhl's tail speeding toward the street.

"Hey! Come back here." Before I could catch up with him, Vinca ran by. She caught him by the scruff just before he ducked under some bushes.

"Gotcha!" she shouted. Giguhl spit and hissed at her as his paws swiped at the air.

"What the—" I began. Vinca brushed past me as she lectured the cat. The wild-eyed cat mouthed "help me" as he went by.

I followed them in, glad for the distraction from the little chat with my grandmother. "What the hell is going on?"

She turned on her heel and looked at me. She now had the cat under one arm.

"Let me go, you freak!" Giguhl struggled to break free, but Vinca subdued him with a glare.

"What's going on?" she repeated. "I'll tell you what's going on." Her tone sounded conversational, but I detected cold steel underlining the words. "Hmm, let's see. First, the demon cat escaped your room when I went in to leave fresh towels on your bed. Then the flea-ridden heap of fur decided to pee on my Maidenhair fern."

I almost laughed, but her scowl made me smother the urge. She continued to tick off Giguhl's sins on her fingers. "After that, he used my sofa as a scratching post. And if that wasn't bad enough, he started humping my heirloom needlework throw pillow!"

I cringed as she pointed out where Giguhl shredded the corner of the couch. "Vinca, I'm so sorry. I'll pay for the damage."

"This cat," she lifted him a little higher, eliciting a hiss from him, "is a menace. You're going to have to crate him while you're gone if you want to stay here."

I was about to respond when Giguhl wiggled free and ran. I watched him go, figuring he'd hide in there until things blew over.

"Again, I apologize. I think he doesn't like being cooped up in the room for so long."

"It's not just that," she said, crossing her arms. "You totally disappeared last night."

I sighed. If I wasn't careful she'd kick us out before I could get my mission done. "I'm sorry. It's just . . . well, I got waylaid by a mancy who's been following me."

"Still—" Her demeanor changed as she leaned forward with wide eyes. "Wait, a mancy?"

I nodded slowly, confused by her quicksilver change of mood.

"I had a vision about you and a mancy just last night. He has black hair, right?"

"Um, no. It's kind of sandy blond."

"Hmm. Was he wearing the color black?"

I thought about it for a second. "His boots."

"Yes, that must be it. Well, my intuition is telling me he's going to be very important in your life." She stopped and looked at me with a huge smile. "I'm getting a major love vibe here."

Not bloody likely, I thought. "Vinca, have you ever considered that your intuition might be a little off?"

She frowned. "Of course not. Nymphs are known for being excellent at prophecy. Don't mock what you do not understand."

"Anyway," I said, trying to change the subject. "I had

to deal with him, but by the time I got back to the booth, you were gone."

She smiled. "I'm sorry we got off on the wrong foot. I've just never had a roommate. Can we start over?"

"Okay," I said slowly. "Listen, I really need to go talk to Giguhl."

She frowned a bit at the mention of the demon cat. "Okay, I'll get some drinks, and when you come back you can tell me all about this sexy hexy."

I let that go as she disappeared into the kitchen. I took a moment to gather myself before I confronted the pissed-off furball in the other room. No doubt about it, I was going to get the tongue-lashing of a lifetime. I had a few things to say to him, too.

I opened the door to my room expecting mayhem, but what I saw instead was Giguhl lounging on the bed, licking his paws. I shut the door and walked in slowly.

"Okay, I'm going to try to remain calm. And you're going to give me some answers, got it?"

He paused from his licking to give me a disdainful sniff. That was as close to acquiescence as I was going to get.

"What the hell were you thinking out there?"

"That I needed to pee and *someone* forgot to take me for my nightly walk before she left."

"Crap, you're right. But did you have to pee on her plant? Couldn't you have gone into the bathroom and used the tub or something?"

"Look, lady, I saw an opportunity for freedom and I took it. It's not my fault I've been stuck in this freaking floral crypt for two days. Cats need freedom to roam, you know?"

I rolled my eyes. "Does this roaming also include shredding furniture?"

He shrugged. "Sometimes."

"And the pillow humping?"

"I have needs!"

"You can't do that shit here, Giguhl. She'll make us leave."

He sat on his haunches and glared at me. "You can't expect me to just sit around here all the time trapped in this room. It's bad enough I'm trapped in this furry carcass. Talk about insult added to injury."

"Speaking of which, why is that? You could have changed back to demon whenever you wanted, right?"

He looked down and pawed at the bedspread. "Not exactly." He mumbled something I didn't catch.

"Come again?" I said, moving closer.

He sighed. "I said, I can't change back. I tried and it didn't work."

"Why not?"

"I think it's because you told me to stay in cat form unless you told me otherwise."

"I'm not following."

He looked up. "I think that when you survived the test, I kind of became your minion."

"What?"

"Yeah, see normally only the summoner has power over me, but somehow it switched to you—or some of it did. It must be related to your surviving when I staked you." He paused to give me a look to let me know he still thought that was weird. I agreed, but I had bigger issues than trying to overanalyze what most vampires would consider a blessing.

"Anyway," he continued, "I basically have to do what you say."

A laugh escaped my lips. "Now that's funny."

"I'm glad you find it amusing."

"Let's test it. Giguhl, change back to a demon."

A burst of green light and the smell of singed hair filled the room. Waving a hand in front of my face, I squinted through the smoke. When it cleared, Giguhl sat bare-ass naked on the bed, scowling.

"Ack, cover yourself." I grabbed a pillow from the floor and threw it at him. "Now I'm going to have nightmares."

He caught the pillow and placed it over his lap. "It's bad enough that I have to obey your every command—let's not add insults to the mix."

"Sorry. It's just so weird. I've never had a minion before." He huffed and crossed his arms. "Aw, come on. It's only temporary."

He looked up. "Oh? Have you found the mage who summoned me yet?"

An image of Adam's face flashed in my mind, along with his ridiculous deal. "Not yet. But," I said when Giguhl's face fell again, "I have another plan."

"What's that?"

"I'm going to find a reversal spell and send you back myself."

Giguhl snorted. "Right. Good luck with that."

"Hey! I'm half mage, so I have to have some powers, right?"

"Pardon me for not being more excited about playing guinea pig while you test out your latent magical skills."

"Look, I'm doing the best I can here." But was I? One

call to Adam right then and Giguhl could go home. But I had no interest in paying the price for the mancy's help. Assuming he was telling the truth.

"In the meantime," I said, changing the subject. "You're going to have to behave yourself. If Vinca kicks us out, it could jeopardize my mission."

"And that's another thing," Giguhl said. "Seeing as how I'm your minion and all, don't you think it's time you told me about this secret mission?"

"No."

"Come on, Sabina. Who are we going to kill?"

"First of all, what makes you think I'm going to kill anyone? And second, if I was, what are you going to do, pee on them?"

"Please, you're an assassin. It's highly unlikely you're here to take in the sights. And second, I have powers you haven't seen yet."

"What powers?"

"That's for me to know and you to find out."

"You're a real pain in the ass, you know that?"

He didn't respond, just smiled, revealing pointy yellow teeth.

"Look, I need to get back out there. Change back into a cat."

He opened his mouth to protest, but before a sound came out, the room sizzled with electricity and the green cloud returned. When it cleared this time, Giguhl the cat sat on the bed glaring at me. "That hurts, you know."

"Sorry, but I can't imagine Vinca would appreciate a naked demon strutting around her apartment. I promise I'll take you on more walks. And I'll let you out when

Vinca's not here. But you can't go around acting like an animal."

He raised brow. "Forgive me, but you're the one who wants me in cat form. If I act like an animal, you have no one to blame but yourself."

"Fine! Jeez. Would it help if I got you some cat toys or something?"

He sniffed. "Don't insult me."

"I was trying to be nice. But if you want to sit here and sulk, be my guest."

I left before he had a chance to get in the last word. The door was just closing behind me when his voice carried down the hall. "Don't forget the catnip!"

15

I'm surprised to see you back so soon. Is your new living situation satisfactory?" Clovis reached for my hand and placed a soft kiss on my knuckles. My skin tingled where he'd touched me. I pulled the hand back when he seemed to linger over it.

"Yes, Vinca is very nice," I said. "May I?"

He gestured to the chair opposite his. "Please, make yourself comfortable. I'll admit I'm intrigued to learn the reason for your visit."

I settled into the seat as I gathered my thoughts. I didn't want to seem too eager.

"I've given it some thought and I've decided that joining you is the wisest course of action."

His smile was immediate. "That's excellent news. However, I'm curious about your sudden change of heart."

"You can thank Vinca for that," I said. "She's convinced me that I can trust you."

He steepled his fingers and regarded me closely.

"So it has nothing to do with needing shelter from the Dominae?"

I shrugged. "I'll admit that factored into my decision. But I would never take your offer if I didn't believe your cause was worth joining."

He nodded. "I can't say I'm not pleased with your decision. If you're amenable, we can take care of the initiation tonight."

He said it casually, as if he referred to filling out forms. I knew better than to relax. As powerful as Clovis was, he wouldn't take my word. I'd have to prove myself. And from what Vinca told me, I wouldn't enjoy it.

"That would be fine." My tone was businesslike. But inside, my impatience and anxiety took the form of nausea.

"Let me summon Frank and we will begin shortly." He stood to call his assistant, but I stopped him.

"What exactly do these rites entail?" I couldn't help myself. I needed something to go on to prepare myself for what was to come. Surprises weren't something I dealt with well.

"Patience, my dear," he said with a smile. "You'll know soon enough."

Soon enough turned out to be an hour later. As I waited in his office, I fidgeted. I'd tried to sit still for as long as possible, but ended up moving around the room looking for something to occupy my hands. According to his bookcases, Clovis seemed to have a fascination with the Spanish Inquisition, which did nothing to calm my nerves. He also had quite a collection of spell books, many with cracking leather spines. To distract myself from my nerves, I thumbed through a few, looking for a

reversal spell that might help me with the Giguhl situation. The problem was most of the spells were written in
something that looked like Sumerian. I decided to "borrow" a few anyway.

The door opened a few moments after I hid the books
in my bag. Frank, looking solemn, asked me to follow
him. He led me down a labyrinth of corridors. We passed
a guard here and there but no other people or beings
crossed our path. As we approached a set of doors, the
hair on the back of my neck stood on end. This place
smelled different from the common areas I'd seen so far.
It'd been a while since I'd had any, but it was hard to mistake the scent of sex—musky and sweet. Instinctively, I
knew we were about to enter Clovis' private rooms.

Frank paused just outside the doors. Watching the
wooden panels, I saw him produce a blindfold from his
back pocket.

"Turn around," he said quietly. I stared at him for a
moment. What was it with this guy and blindfolds? It's
not like I couldn't find my way back to this room. His
face betrayed no emotion as I considered my options. I
didn't have any. I nodded slightly and turned with my
head held high, not wanting to seem subservient. If I was
going to do this, I was going to do it for real. No cower-
ing or fear about what was to come. Grandmother would
have been proud.

The wall disappeared behind the veil of the black cloth
covering my eyes. Frank tied it on tight, but not painfully
so. I rolled my eyes around, adjusting to the darkness.
Not a sliver of light passed through the cloth.

I felt Frank's hand on my shoulder as the doors in front

of me creaked open. A slight breeze escaped the room. The air was even more saturated with the carnal scent.

Even with the blindfold, I could tell the room was large by the echoes created by our footsteps. Refusing to appear dependent on Frank, I walked forward confidently—no careful shuffling. The clicks of my heels told me the floors were concrete, which might also account for the cooler air in this room. I'd taken several steps before a slight pressure from Frank's hand indicated I should stop.

"Don't move," Frank whispered in my ear. His footsteps echoed as he walked away. When I heard the doors close behind me, I assumed he'd left me standing there alone. I tried to remain calm, yet prepared for anything. Unfamiliar vulnerability hung around my throat like a noose. Remembering my hands weren't bound, I ignored Frank's last instructions and I lifted one toward the edge of the blindfold.

"Do I need to bind your hands, as well?"

My body jerked at the unanticipated sound of Clovis' voice. He was standing uncomfortably close. As I dropped my hand slowly, I cursed myself for not having sensed his presence. The fact he'd caught me off guard put me even more on edge. Doubts started creeping in, but I pushed them aside.

"Sabina." He breathed in. A warm palm cupped my cheek. I jerked from the unanticipated contact. Silently, I cursed my inability to control my own body. I took a deep breath. That's when I realized the scent I'd detected earlier—the sex—was actually coming from him. It was as if his body was throwing off narcotic pheromones.

"Please forgive the blindfold. I'm afraid it's a necessity."

His voice was different—deeper with a husky timber. Jesus, he even sounded like sex.

I nodded to acknowledge his statement, not trusting my voice.

"Are you frightened, Sabina?" Instead of concern, I heard amusement in his tone. I gritted my teeth, trying to regain control.

"No." My voice broke a little bit. I cleared my throat. "I just don't like these games you're playing."

"Just wait. They get even better." He chuckled. "Are you ready to prove your loyalty?"

"Bring it on," I said, raising my chin to show him I wasn't intimidated.

He took my hand and led me forward. We walked a few feet before he halted me. "Please sit." His polite manner held an undertone of menace. He helped me lower into a chair with wooden arms. I'd just settled myself when I felt a cold metal cuff click over my right wrist. He quickly cuffed the other hand before I could react.

I struggled against the bonds, kicking out with my feet, but only hitting air. "You bastard!" I said. I strained against the cold metal, hoping my strength could break them. They didn't even budge. The shackles must have had copper lining, which weakened my strength.

"Are you quite finished?" Clovis asked from behind me.

My breath puffed in and out harshly, making it hard to respond. "Why?" I managed to ask.

"It's for your own protection, really," he said. "If you fight me while I feed from you it will arouse my predatory instincts."

My blood turned to ice, even though I'd already suspected what his test would entail. Again, I wondered how my grandmother could ask me to do this. She understood the gravity of allowing another vamp to take a vein. By letting Clovis do this, I was, in essence, saying he was now my master. The thought caused my stomach to clench.

I took a deep breath to quell the rising panic. The combination of blindfold and restraints was making me feel claustrophobic and my other instinct threatened to take over—survival.

"Take. Off. The. Blindfold." I was gasping for air now, not caring that I was betraying a weakness.

Almost instantly, the cloth disappeared. I blinked against the dim light in the room as my eyes adjusted. I looked around, trying to get my bearings. The chamber was vast, with candle-lit sconces along the walls. My eyes shot to Clovis, who stood in front of me now, just out of kicking distance. He wore a long, black silk robe with a red dragon embroidered over his heart. He stood patiently, seeming content to let me finish my scan of the room.

To his right, about twenty feet away, stood the largest bed I'd ever seen. Carved ebony posts stood at the four corners with a red silk canopy balanced on top. The real kicker, though, was the yards and yards of black satin covering the mattress. The thing looked like something out of a Goth porn film.

My eyes shot back to him. He smiled wide, showing his fangs for the first time since I'd met him. "Shall we begin?"

It was do-or-die time. If I balked or said no, it would destroy any chance of succeeding in my mission. But deep down, the primal part of me yearned to cry uncle and run away with my tail tucked between my legs. Not only did I not want to submit to Clovis, or anyone else for that matter, but I also didn't like the idea of him taking some of my power along with my blood. He'd be taking part of me—the very life force that made me who I was. My grandmother's words came to me then. I didn't have the luxury of being squeamish. I had a job to do, and dammit, I was going to succeed.

I took a deep breath and nodded my acquiescence.

"Ah, Sabina," he said. "Your strength continues to impress me. I can hardly wait to taste you."

He moved forward. My hands curled into claws under the metal restraints. I struggled to sit still as he bent down. His breath caressed my throat. The invasion of personal space caused me to jerk back, but he grasped my jaw with one hand to hold me in place. I blinked rapidly as he ran his lips over my jugular. A memory of the vamp in the parking garage doing the same thing caused bile to rise in my throat. Before I could chase away the memory, Clovis' fangs broke skin. Searing pain shot through my neck, causing me to gasp.

After a moment, the pull of his mouth on the vein was matched by a pulsing in regions further south. A new sensation of pleasure-pain pulsed through me. He wrapped an arm around my shoulders, pulling me closer. My body yearned toward his. He sucked harder as if trying to swallow me whole. And Lilith help me, I wanted him to. I didn't stop to think about why I suddenly wanted to give him my blood, I just did.

The whole ordeal lasted too long and not long enough. He pulled his fangs away, but came back for one final caress with his tongue. He murmured something, but I was too dazed to understand it.

His face came into view, blurry through the tears I hadn't noticed falling. Inexplicably, his eyes glowed red in the dim light and a pair of small horns bulged from his forehead. They disappeared so quickly, I wondered if I was hallucinating. His mouth and chin glistened red when he smiled. "You're mine now, Sabina Kane."

My head felt like it was full of helium and my hands were shaking. At the same time, I was squirming with need. No one had ever told me it would be like that. It wasn't so much that I gave him blood; it was more like he'd fucked my vein. And now, inexplicably, I yearned for him to fuck other parts of me.

His eyes glowed in the dim light as he watched me. "You taste like sex and magic," he said. "I can feel your power running through me." Clovis stretched his arms out wide, expanding his chest. His robe gaped, exposing the hard planes of his pecs, which were sprinkled with droplets of my blood.

I shifted in my seat, hoping to ease the ache in my groin. Clovis seemed to notice my discomfort and smiled.

"How do you feel, Sabina?" he asked. His eyes showed me he knew exactly what was going on. But I'd be damned if I was going to beg.

"F-fine," I lied. "Are we done yet?" I needed to get out of there or I was going to do something else I'd regret.

"We're finished," he said. "However . . ." He let the word hang in the air, as if he expected me to ask more questions. I didn't give him the satisfaction. I was too busy trying to think unsexy thoughts.

"If you need assistance relieving some of the . . . side

effects, I'd be happy to lend a hand." He actually leered
at me. By this point, I was tired of his dramatics. I just
wanted out of there. Regret was starting to pour through
me like acid. I didn't know what he'd done to my mind to
make me so pliable during the feeding, but it was wearing off. Plus, my neck was killing me.

"I really need to get going," I said. "Could you please
take off the cuffs?"

He looked disappointed. "If you insist."

He made quick work of the locks. "You know, Sabina,
we would make an excellent team."

I rubbed my wrists and then shook them, hoping to
regain feeling. "Team?" I was too distracted by my impatience to leave to pay much attention to him.

"Think about it. You're half mage, I'm half demon.
We're both vampires. Together we could be unstoppable.
A power to contend with."

"I'm not looking for power." I stood and gingerly
touched the wounds on my neck. Already they were healing, but the pain remained.

He laughed. "Don't be naive. Everyone wants power,
Sabina."

I looked him in the eyes. "Not me."

He stared at me for a moment. "Perhaps you will
change your mind."

"Don't count on it," I said. "Are we done here?"

He nodded and stepped back. "We need to discuss
your role in the sect."

"Sounds good," I said, backing toward the door. "But
I really need to get home to ice down my neck. Can we
talk about it tomorrow?

He paused for a moment. Shock showed in his eyes.

He wasn't used to being blown off. That was too damned bad, because I wasn't staying in his presence another minute.

"Tomorrow night will be fine," he said finally. "And, Sabina?"

I turned from where I was about to open the door and waited.

"We're not finished," he said. He looked at the bed meaningfully. A threat lurked in his eyes—or was it a promise?

I nodded, not knowing what to say. "Good night, Clovis."

I stumbled down the temple steps and into the night. The cold air was like an antiseptic, cleansing me of the stench of what I'd just done. I took a couple of deep breaths, hoping to clear my head. Self-recriminations swirled in my brain.

How could I have let Clovis take my blood? The thought of my blood flowing through him made me ill. What was worse, even though he'd been the one feeding, I felt as if I'd absorbed some of his darkness into myself. It was though I had a black mark on my soul.

Sure, I wasn't the most pure of beings—I killed for a living, after all. But one thing I'd never done was sell myself out for anyone or anything. And here I'd done just that for the Dominae.

Part of me wanted to march back in there and kill Clovis. The Dominae be damned. But the dutiful part of me, the one that had gotten me into this mess, argued that my mission was to find out his plans first. Killing him now would equal failure.

I hopped on the Ducati and brought it to life. The engine roared under me. I'd never felt so weak. Yet had Clovis been right? Did everyone crave power? I'd told him I had no interest in it, but I felt powerful every time I carried out a mission for the Dominae. Acting as executioner made me feel like an avenging angel dispensing justice in a world full of gray.

I took off down the road, speeding as if I could escape myself. I could only hope that the meeting tomorrow with Clovis would give me the information I needed. Then I would be free to kill him and return to my life.

But as the wind buffeted my body, I felt hollow, as if I'd somehow lost part of my soul back in that room.

16

Vinca said nothing about the marks on my neck when I got home. She had a knowing look in her eye, but it lacked judgment. To distract myself from thinking about what I'd let Clovis do, I grabbed the spell books out of my bag.

"Do you have a computer I can use?"

"Sure," Vinca said. "Do you need the Internet?"

I nodded. When she came back, she had a sleek little notebook computer, which she sat up for me on the coffee table.

"It's ready to go," she said. "Whatcha doing?"

"I just need to do a little research."

She must have sensed my reluctance to discuss it because she wandered off, leaving me to do my thing in private. When she returned, she set a pint glass next to me.

"What's this?" I asked.

"I have a friend who works at a blood bank. I figured it'd be easier for you if you didn't have to run out to feed all the time."

I looked at her for a moment, touched by the gesture. I wasn't used to someone thinking about my welfare, and it was kind of nice.

I wasn't sure of the etiquette of thanking my nymph roommate for hooking me up with a blood supply. "Thanks," I said, simply.

She watched me as I lifted the glass and took a tentative sip. I suppressed a grimace of distaste at the flavor of cold blood mixed with silicone. After all, she'd gone to the trouble, and I was so hungry I downed the rest of the glass in one gulp.

"Someone was hungry," she laughed.

"Starving," I said. "Thanks, Vinca. That really hit the spot."

"Okay, I'll let you get back to it."

I nodded and watched her go down the hall to her bedroom. It looked like having a roommate did have some benefits after all. My neck tingled and my mood instantly lifted as the blood did its magic. No wonder I'd felt so crappy after I left Clovis. Loss of blood and sacrificing my dignity tended to make me a tad touchy. But now I was able to turn my attention from what happened earlier to my new task.

I moved the glass aside and got down to business. As I typed "Sumerian dictionary" into the search engine, I thought about how much the world had changed over the last few decades. If I had found Clovis's books thirty years earlier, I'd be slubbing my way to a library or looking up linguistics experts at a local university for help. But now with a click of the button, I had thousands of pages of information at my disposal. I had to admit that as much as I disliked mortals, some of their inventions sure made a vampire's life easier.

I started clicking through pages. After a few minutes, Vinca came back in and told me she was heading out to do some work in the flowerbeds. I worked in peace for about five minutes, until Giguhl slunk out of my room.

"Is she gone?" he asked.

"Yeah." I clicked on a page with an extensive list of cuneiform symbols with definitions. When the page loaded, I shifted in my seat, excited to be getting somewhere.

A small, warm body rubbed against me, but I ignored it as I compared the symbols in the books to what was on the screen. A throat cleared. I scribbled notes. A head butted my elbow, causing my pen to scratch a black line across the page.

"Hey!" I said. "Do you mind?"

"May I ask what you're doing?"

"No." I scribbled a bit more and then read over the words. The spell seemed straightforward. All I needed was to light a white candle, sprinkle some salt, and chant a Sumerian phrase. Easy peasy.

"Where'd you get the books?" Giguhl asked.

"I borrowed them from Clovis."

"What did Clovis borrow in return?"

I swiveled my head and looked at him. His eyes were on my neck. My hand flew to the sore spot instinctively. "Also none of your business."

He looked at me for another moment, but eventually gave up and went to curl up on the other end of the couch. I hated it when he pouted.

"If it makes you feel any better, I think I've found a spell to send you home."

His little ears perked up, but he didn't look at me. "It's not nice to tease, Sabina."

"I'm not teasing. Actually, I can't believe how simple it is."

Obviously intrigued, Giguhl padded back toward me, eyeing the book on the table. "Is that it?"

"Yeah. You want to give it a try?"

"Are you sure you can handle it? I mean, you've never done magic before, right?"

"It seems pretty straightforward. You game?"

He jumped off the couch and looked back at me. "Sure. What's the worst that could happen?"

Twenty minutes later, we had our answer.

"I can't freaking believe this!"

I cringed. "I'm so sorry."

"I'm bald!" Giguhl continued. "I look like a freak."

"It's not that bad," I said. But it was. Oh my lord was it bad. I'd never seen an uglier cat in my entire life. "Look at the bright side, you won't have to worry about shedding anymore."

A deluge of expletives both in English and demon followed this observation.

Behind me, the front door opened and Vinca walked in. Her gasp was almost lost in the wave of profanity coming from the hairless demon cat.

"What happened?" Vinca whispered to me.

I shrugged, but Giguhl had plenty to say. He paced in front of us. His gray skin wrinkled disconcertingly as he stalked around the room, swishing his naked tail. "What happened? I'll tell you what happened: She's the worst mage ever," he said to Vinca.

I glared at him. "Hey, now, you knew going into this that I've had no training. Just because I have genes from my Hekate side of the family doesn't mean I know Jack shit about spell casting."

"No shit, Sherlock."

"I said I was sorry." I crossed my arms and plopped onto the couch. I knew I shouldn't be angry that he was upset, but I was. He knew the risks. I looked at Vinca. "I tried to send him home using a spell I found in a book. I guess I got the translation wrong."

Vinca grimaced and looked at Giguhl with sympathy. "At least you're not a toad or something." I smiled at her, thankful she was trying to help. She walked over and picked up the spell book, which lay on the table next to the white candle I'd lit for the spell. "Where'd you find this?"

I grimaced, not wanting to admit I'd stolen it from the male she worshipped. "I borrowed it from Clovis."

"How did you translate it?"

Warmth spread across my cheeks as I ducked my head. "The Internet. I found a Sumerian translator engine."

Vinca's mouth fell open and her eyes widened. "This isn't Sumerian."

My stomach dropped. "It's not?"

"It's Hekatian." Behind us, Giguhl groaned and said something I didn't understand.

"It can't be," I said. "The symbols matched those on the Web site."

"It's an easy mistake. The languages developed in the same region around the same time so the symbols are almost identical. But the pronunciations and meanings are quite different."

"That's it," Giguhl said. "All bets are off. You have to let me change back into my demon form."

Guilt and embarrassment warred for supremacy in my gut. I nodded, figuring it was the least I could do for him given my screw-up. "Giguhl, you may change into the demon." To Vinca, I said, "You might want to cover your eyes." She stared back at me, wide-eyed with curiosity.

Giguhl sat back on his bald haunches and closed his eyes, waiting for the transformation. When nothing happened, he opened one hairless lid. "Why isn't it working?"

"I don't know. Try it again."

He stood on all fours and seemed to focus his eyes on a distant point in the room. Every muscle in his body seemed tense as he concentrated. After a few seconds, his legs shook with effort. "It's not working." His voice sounded panicked. He screwed his eyes shut and his little mouth pursed into a grimace. When that didn't work, he blew out a large breath and collapsed.

"What's going on?" Vinca asked.

I had a sneaking suspicion, but I didn't want to say it. Giguhl said—actually he yelled—it for me. "When she screwed up the spell, she took away my ability to shape-shift. I'm stuck in this hairless carcass!"

Vinca patted my arm. "You know, it's amazing you're so bad at this stuff."

I'd had it. Tension and embarrassment combined into anger. "What do you guys want from me? I was raised by vampires, remember? It's not like they were going to send me to mage school or wherever it is the Hekatians learn this stuff."

Giguhl dragged himself off the floor and came toward me. I tuned out his latest rant as I put my head in my hands and tried to figure out what to do next.

". . . that mage you mentioned." I caught the tail end of Vinca's statement and then the room fell silent. I looked up to find the hairless cat—lord, he looked spooky—and the nymph looking at me expectantly.

"Huh?" I said.

Vinca rolled her eyes. "Do you think that mage you mentioned could help you with this?"

I realized she was suggesting I go to Adam for help and began shaking my head. Before I could speak, though, Giguhl jumped in.

"Mage? You never mentioned a mage. Do you think he'd help us?" He looked so hopeful I hated to disappoint him, but that was so not an option.

"No way, that guy's crazy," I said, hoping they'd drop it.

They both started speaking at once, trying to convince me. As I half-listened I thought about Adam's offer to help me learn magic. Of course, I couldn't take him up on it. All I knew about him was that he was insane.

"Sabina, call him," Giguhl was saying. "Please? I don't want to be a hairless cat for the rest of eternity."

My stomach clenched. He walked over and stood on his hind paws. His bald little front paws landed on my knees and he pleaded silently with wide eyes. His batlike ears fell back as he switched to meowing at me.

"Stop it. That sad little kitty thing isn't going to work on me."

"Come on, Sabina," Vinca said. "Look at him. He's shivering, the poor thing."

I looked at her with disbelief. "I thought you hated him."

She shrugged. "That was before you turned him into the ugliest cat on the planet. Besides, I'm a sucker for stuff like this."

Great, I now had a pitiful cat and a bleeding-heart nymph on my case. I considered lying to them. I could just tell them I didn't have a way to contact Adam. The truth was his business card was sitting in the pocket of the pants I'd worn the other night. I decided to take the middle road.

"Look, I've got a lot going on right now. If you'll give me a couple of days, I promise I'll try to get in touch with the mancy. But I'm not—" Their cheers cut off my words. I was going to tell them I couldn't promise any miracles, but it was obvious they wouldn't listen anyway. My only hope was to hold them off with excuses while I tried to find some other way to help Giguhl. The other option—asking Adam for help—was the last thing I wanted to do.

17

The next night, I left Vinca to deal with Giguhl. To make him feel better, she'd run out and bought him a trunkload of stuff from the pet store. He'd protested, but by the time I left, Vinca had bribed him with catnip into trying on a little red sweater. He looked ridiculous, but seemed to be basking in Vinca's attention. I left them around nine to go face Clovis.

When I arrived at the Temple, Clovis leaned in for a kiss, but I shied away. He noticed the move and backed off with a knowing smile.

"I trust you're not suffering any ill effects?"

I'd really hoped to pretend last night hadn't occurred. Obviously, Clovis had other plans. I simply nodded and took a seat, ready to get down to business.

"You said that once I passed my initiation you'd tell me about my role in your organization?"

He hesitated at my abrupt change of subject, but quickly recovered. As he switched into business mode, I surreptitiously wiped my palms on the legs of my jeans.

"How familiar are you with the Dominae's business dealings?"

The question took me off guard. Frowning, I said, "A little. Honestly, if it didn't involve killing someone, I wasn't privy to much."

"So you're not aware of their recent foray into winemaking?"

I nodded, recalling the wine they'd given me. "Actually, I did know about that. The last time I met with them, they let me try their blood-wine. It was excellent."

He leaned forward. "What did they tell you about it?"

I shrugged, figuring it was safe to tell him what little I knew. "Not a lot. Just that they were expanding their business interests. They said they were also marketing real wine to the humans to earn more income. The blood-wine would be marketed to the vamp population. Why?"

"They didn't mention anything about mages?"

I shook my head, wondering where he was going with this.

He pulled a manila folder from one of the drawers. Placing a hand on it, he said, "We've had several reports recently about mancies disappearing—friends of Temple congregants and the like. I had my team check out the cases to see if I could help in any way. What they discovered is shocking."

I sat patiently, trusting he'd connect the two seemingly unrelated subjects together when he was ready.

"Tell me, Sabina, what happens when vampires ingest the blood of mancies?"

My whole body jerked, realizing where he was going with this. "The vamp absorbs some of the mage's powers," I said slowly. "Are you insinuating the Dominae are kidnapping these mancies?"

"I'm not insinuating anything. The Dominae *are* kidnapping the mancies and harvesting their blood."

It couldn't be possible, I thought. Any fool knew if the Hekate Council found out the shit would hit the fan. The centuries-old truce between the races would be broken. The result would be another war.

"But . . ." I began. "Why would the Dominae want to antagonize the mancies that way?"

"It's simple: power. The Dominae have recognized their dwindling control over the vampire population. Do you realize over the last six months alone, I have recruited hundreds of vamps to my cause?"

I knew he spoke the truth. After all, hadn't the Dominae sent me to kill him because he was threatening their power?

"But why antagonize the mancies? They have to know it will lead to war."

He crossed his arms and regarded me levelly. "What better way to rally the support of the vampire community than to create a common enemy?"

Holy shit, he was right. I wasn't buying it completely, but there was a certain twisted logic to his thinking.

"And think about it, Sabina," he said. "If the Dominae can arm their vamp army with blood filled with mancy magic they'll be almost unstoppable."

My stomach sank. In centuries past, when the vampires and mancies fought, the mancies always had the advantage. A vampire had to be close to attack—hand-to-hand or fang-to-vein. But mancies could use their powers from miles away. If vamps had the power of magic combined with their superior fighting skills behind them, they could wipe out mage-kind. This certainly put a new spin on things. But if the Dominae wanted me to kill Clovis to prevent a war, why would they feel the need to have a secret weapon? Unless they were just being proactive. That had to be it. Still, if the Hekate Council found out the Dominae was behind the mancies' disappearances, they'd be forced to declare war first. If I didn't know better, I'd think the Dominae wanted a war. But why?

Wait a second, I thought. Clovis is full of shit. The Dominae wouldn't do something so foolish. And even if they did, why should I care?

"Okay, so if what you're saying is true, why does it matter to me? I am a vampire, after all."

"Correction, you're only half-vampire. Doesn't it bother you that your own kin could be eradicated from this planet?"

"Considering I've never met any of my family on that side? No."

"Then how about this? How long do you think the human race would last if vampires didn't have their truce with mancies keeping them in check? It would be a bloodbath—literally. When the dust settled, there would be no humans left from which to feed. How long until the vamp population turned against itself?"

The hairs on the back of my neck stood on end as the implications hit me.

"Again, I have to ask why? Why would the Dominae want to bring on their own version of the Apocalypse?"

"My source—"

I held up a hand to stop him. "Just who is the source?"

"I'm afraid I can't divulge his identity. But I can tell you he's getting his information from a member of the Undercouncil."

So Grandmother was right about the source of the leak. Now I just needed a name. "Which member of the Undercouncil?"

He ignored me. "As I said, my source has been sending me troubling reports about Lavinia Kane's increasing fanaticism. As the Alpha, your grandmother holds power over the others. And it's common knowledge her own daughter—your mother—broke the sacred laws and mated with a mancy, which led to her death. In short, Lavinia wants to make the Hekate Council pay."

It couldn't be that simple. Could it? Surely my grandmother didn't want to risk an all-out war over a personal grudge. I stopped and regrouped my thoughts. For a minute there, I'd almost forgotten about my mission. Clovis was my enemy, even if he didn't know it. But more important, he considered the Dominae his enemy. He'd tell me anything to get me to help him destroy their power. Besides, my grandmother might be angry about what happened with my parents, but surely she wouldn't risk a full-out war. Would she?

"If you're right, and frankly I'd need proof, what role could you possibly see me playing in this?"

"I want you to destroy the vineyards."

"Me? How the hell am I supposed to do that? It's not like I could just stroll in there."

"Your skills as an assassin make you an expert at reconnaissance and moving about undetected, correct?"

"Sure, but—"

He wasn't finished. "You come up with a plan to take

over the vineyard, and I'll make sure you have the man-power to carry it out."

I'd reserve judgment on the simplicity of that assignment until I could gather some more information. I had bigger questions gnawing at me.

"What's in it for you?" I said.

He lifted his hands as if trying to convey modesty. "We all have a stake in the survival of our kind, Sabina. I'm simply trying to do what I can to right a wrong."

"Bullshit." The word escaped my lips like a gunshot.

He stared at me in shock for a moment, as if amazed someone would dare question his sincerity. He leaned forward with his arms on the desk.

His voice was lower yet harder when he said, "Fine. I'm hoping to expose the Dominae's plan and secure my place as the new leader. With them out of power, I'll be able to convince the Hekate Council to refrain from seeking retribution."

I leaned back to consider his words. Part of me admired his honesty. The other part understood he'd just given me the information I'd come to gather for the Dominae. But I knew I needed more to bring to them before I fulfilled the final stage of my assignment. They'd want details.

"And what is in it for me if I agree to help you?"

He chuckled. "Who said you had a choice? After all, Sabina, wouldn't the Dominae be interested to find out that you're no better than David Duchamp?"

My stomach did a somersault followed by a nosedive.

"If memory serves, you were David's executioner."

I swallowed hard as I remembered the betrayal on David's face when I pulled the trigger.

Clovis wasn't done. "Did you know that David and I only met once? I approached him to see if he'd be willing to work for me. Do you know what he said, Sabina?"

I shook my head because if I opened my mouth, I might throw up.

Clovis leaned his elbows on the table. "He told me to go to hell."

"You're lying." I choked out the words. "He was working for you. That's why they had me kill him."

Clovis frowned and shook his head. "They *lied*."

My eyes closed, trying to block out the words. Hadn't David told me not to trust anyone? I'd assumed he meant Clovis, but could he have included the Dominae in that warning? My head started to throb as the mission that had seemed so straightforward suddenly felt more like a web of deceit and I didn't know who was the spider.

"Just imagine, if they'd murder David just because I spoke to him," Clovis said, "what would they do if they found out how far you made it in the process? That you allowed me to feed from you?"

I stared at him so hard I felt like my eyeballs might ignite. He had no idea how empty his threat was. After all, my grandmother not only approved of him feeding from me, she'd made it clear it was expected. I clenched my jaw, fighting to keep some perspective despite the painful implications. Clovis might be telling the truth. Maybe my grandmother did only see me as a pawn in whatever plan she had brewing. I suppose part of me knew that already, but didn't want to face facts. And it hurt, a visceral pain in my midsection. But I'd do best to remember who was my real enemy here—Clovis. Using David's death to threaten me sealed his fate. "That won't be an issue."

He leaned back with a grin, misunderstanding my comment. "I knew you were a smart girl."

I clenched my fists under the table, so he wouldn't see. If I could just hold back my anger for a few more minutes, I could escape his office and go put my fist through something.

"Why not just call in the Hekate Council now? Why use me? Why trust me when you know the Alpha is my grandmother?"

"Why trust you? An interesting question, Sabina. Let's just say I have my own reasons." His smile was downright reptilian. And for the first time I wondered if I was being played. Was it possible he knew I was still working for the Dominae? But why allow me this far into his circle of trust?

"As for your other question, I can't risk the Hekate Council finding out because they're likely to just declare war first and ask questions later. No, your lineage will help ensure my victory."

"My lineage?"

"You're of noble bloodlines on both sides of your family. Having you behind me will lend weight to my negotiations with the mancies."

"I highly doubt that. They disowned me from the minute I was born."

His eyes narrowed. "Who told you that?"

I really didn't want to get into a discussion about my checkered family history. "Look, it doesn't matter. If you think it will help, then fine."

He looked like he wanted to say more on the subject, but let it drop. "What will you need to get started?"

I thought for a moment. "I need to see this place myself and read through any information you have before I answer that question."

"No problem," he said. "I'll have Frank drive you."

I shook my head. "I need to go alone, without distractions. I'll also need wheels." I couldn't take the motorcycle; it was too flashy for undercover work.

He smiled. "Done. You have forty-eight hours. We need to move quickly before the Hekate Council gets wind of this."

"No problem."

Assuming we were finished, I stood to leave.

"I'll have Frank arrange for transportation immediately."

I nodded and turned to go.

"Oh, Sabina?" he said. I stopped on my way to the door to look at him. His eyes held the same red glow I'd witnessed the night before. "I don't need to remind you of the consequences of fucking me over, do I?"

Goosebumps spread over my limbs. "No."

He rose and came toward me. I gulped, fighting my instinct to turn and run. He ran a finger down my cheek.

"Good, because I'd hate it if you forced me to harm that smooth skin of yours."

I swallowed, hoping my voice wouldn't crack. "You can trust me."

He smiled and leaned in. His nearness made my limbs turn leaden, as if surrendering.

"How about a kiss to seal the trust between us?"

I nodded even though I felt ill at the thought. Remembering how easily he'd taken control of me the night before had me on edge.

He smiled and pressed his mouth against my lips. My

body pressed against his of its own volition. He leaned down and scraped my neck with his fangs. A sigh escaped me as his tongue replaced the sharp points.

"I can't wait to taste your blood again." He whispered this against the moist skin, sending a shiver through me.

Abruptly, he pulled away. "I'll see you in two days."

Dismissed.

I blinked, trying to regain my mental equilibrium. He watched me with a knowing half-smile. Self-revulsion washed over me. How could I be so weak? It was as if his touch hypnotized all the sense from my head. I shook my head a little, trying to clear it.

"Okay, see you then," I squeaked. I turned quickly and escaped the office before I could make more of an ass out of myself.

18

I pulled off the highway near St. Helena, about an hour north of San Francisco. Giguhl had his nose pressed against the window of the minivan, checking out the scenery. He wore a black sweater and four matching microfiber booties that Vinca insisted he needed to keep his paws warm.

Traffic was heavy, even though most of the vineyards had closed for the night. Since it was grape harvest time, tourists flocked to the small towns of Napa Valley to take in some local flavor. It didn't take long for me to see the sign for Immortal Vineyards. The picture of a vampire in full cape and fangs holding a glass of wine was a dead giveaway.

The vineyard was set back from the main drag, down a winding dirt road. I pulled off into the attached parking lot, which was already full of cars. According to the information Frank gave me, the vineyard center played up its vampire theme by opening only at night. Visitors seemed to enjoy the kitsch without ever suspecting vamps really ran the place.

"Okay, Mr. Giggles, here's the deal. We'll split up. I'll go in the visitors' center, you head out onto the grounds. We'll meet back here in an hour."

He pulled his nose from the window, leaving a little smudge on the glass. "First, it's bad enough I have to wear this stupid sweater," he said. "But I'll be damned if I'll let you destroy my dignity further by calling me that insulting nickname."

"The sweater looks good on you. Brings out the yellow in your eyes." I said. We both knew that I wasn't about to stop using the name.

"Flattery will get you everywhere. But I'm serious about the nickname, Sabina. It's animal cruelty."

"Tough titty, Mr. Kitty."

"You're a real bitch, you know that?"

I nodded. "So I've been told. Now, if you're done whining, can we do this?"

"What am I looking for again?"

"Secret rooms, anything with security-cameras, guards, you name it."

"Got it. Look for a room with a sign with a big arrow that says, 'Kidnapped Mancies Here,'" he said. "Come on, Sabina. Do you really think they'd keep them here, in this public place?"

"That's what Clovis said." I shrugged. "Besides, they're already hiding in plain sight with this whole vampire theme they've got going."

"All right," he said, sounding unconvinced. "For the record, though, I really hope Clovis is full of shit."

"That makes two of us. See you in an hour." I opened

the car door and stepped out into the damp night air. He jumped out the door and landed soundlessly on the gravel lot. As I watched, he shot off through the dark and disappeared behind the main building.

Clovis's claims about David not really being a traitor rushed back to me. As sick as it sounds, I really hoped he was lying and that David was the betrayer the Dominae painted him. Otherwise, I'd have to take a long hard look at my grandmother's motivations for sending me on this mission. The very idea she might have lied to me made me ill. I steeled my spine and reminded myself that Clovis was no fool. He was trying to fill my head with doubts to further his own plans. I'd do best to remember that going forward.

I headed up the path to the replica castle housing the visitors' center. The thing looked like something straight out of Transylvania—all crenellations and gargoyles. To the right of the path lay a clearing designed to look like a graveyard. Some wiseacre had made up fake headstones for some of the most famous vampires in history— Erzebet Bathory, Vlad Tepes, Gilles de Rais. I ignored them and continued to the wide oak doors leading inside.

Sconces shed an eerie glow on the fake spider webs and aged stone walls. Just like every bad movie about my race ever made, the room played up every false vampire stereotype.

Along one wall stood a bar, which resembled a black lacquered coffin with a closed lid. Behind it, a woman dressed in a high-collared black cape and a pair of fake fangs poured samples of the vineyard's wines. Kitty-corner to the bar was a wall filled with vampire souvenirs— bumper stickers, stakes, crucifixes, strands of garlic.

Little did most mortals know that the last two items actually had no effect on real vampires. Sure, we weren't thrilled about crucifixes, but that was more of a principle thing than a real fear. As for the garlic, I loved it roasted and spread on crusty French bread. However, the vamp community had long encouraged these particular myths. If mortals knew our real weaknesses, it could spell disaster.

A perky blonde approached me as I looked at a bumper sticker that read, "Vampires do it all night."

"Welcome to Immortal Vineyards," she said. "Can I help you with something?"

I put the bumper sticker back, embarrassed to be seen with it. "Do you offer tours?"

"Yes, in fact we have one starting in five minutes. It meets by the bust of Bela Lugosi," she said without a trace of irony. "In the meantime, why don't you head over to the blood bar and sample some of our wines? Be sure to taste our Sanguinarian Shiraz. It's to die for." She smiled at her bad pun and winked at me. I barely managed not to flash my fangs and hiss at her.

She left to accost some other unsuspecting person, leaving me free to wander to the bar. A few other people leaned against the coffin, sipping from small glasses of wine. It didn't take long for the fake-fanged brunette to approach me.

"Good evening, I'm Drusilla," she said. "Might I tempt you with some bloody good wine?"

At that point, I seriously considered leaving. All the kitsch and puns were about as charming as a poke in the eye. However, I needed to figure out if Clovis had been telling me the truth. So, I forced a smile at the idiot and nodded.

"I've heard good things about the Shiraz," I said.

She nodded. "Yes, ma'am. Our Sanguinarian Shiraz is our newest vintage," she said as she took a bottle from behind the bar and poured a sample into a small glass. "It's an earthy wine with notes of chocolate, raspberry, and leather."

I raised an eyebrow at that last thing. "Leather?"

She laughed. "It works, believe me."

I held her eye as I took a tentative sip. The only thing I tasted was wine. It didn't suck, but what did I know from wine? I made appreciative noises, and she refilled the sample before moving on to another visitor.

Luckily, the tour group started gathering right then. I slammed the rest of the sample and walked over just in time to bring up the rear. The group consisted of a white-haired couple, a pair of newlyweds—obvious from the gratuitous tonsil-hockey—and two ladies with Texas twangs and big hair. A guy dressed in a tuxedo and cape with movie star hair and ridiculous neon white fangs welcomed us.

"Good evening, my name is Ivan. Who's ready to explore the inner workings of the only vampire-owned vineyard in the world?" As he spoke through the plastic fangs a line of drool formed at the corner of his mouth. Amateur.

The others cheered. I stood back and wondered what they'd do if they knew a real vampire stood right behind them.

Ivan led us through a short hallway into what appeared to be a museum. Interactive displays sat alongside movie paraphernalia from some of Hollywood's more famous vampire flicks. A sign on one wall read, "Vampires and Wine—A Retrospective."

About ten minutes into it, I was ready to impale myself with a corkscrew. Ivan's ridiculous blather about vampire lore and the intricacies of winemaking were enough to make me long for the sweet release of death.

I looked at my watch—only thirty minutes until I had to meet Giguhl. Time to get serious about my reconnaissance.

I raised my hand, interrupting Ivan's soliloquy about tannins. "Yes?" he said, sounding annoyed by the interruption.

"Can you point me to the little girls' room?" I asked. The entire group turned to look at me, except for the newlyweds, who were playing grab-ass by a diorama depicting the life of a grape.

"It's down that hallway," he said, pointing to a door at the opposite end of the museum from where we entered. Ivan had already turned back to the group, dismissing me and my bladder without a second glance.

The door led to a hallway lined with offices. After a quick scan for any signs of surveillance, I started peeking in doorways. I didn't really expect these offices to offer much in the way of clues, which is good since I didn't find any. At the end of the hall was the bathroom, and next to that were double doors with small windows. I glanced through them to see they led to a warehouse. *Bingo.*

I made quick work of the lock on the doors and slipped through them. Again, no cameras or guards were around. I figured once I saw them I'd be close.

I scooted by large pallets of empty wine bottles and large oak barrels. In the distance, I could hear the sounds of workers talking and machinery churning. I went the other direction, toward another set of doors. This time, as I neared them, I saw the cameras. Just before I got in range, I ducked behind a crate to devise a plan.

"What are you doing here?" a deep voice demanded. My heart burst into a rapid staccato as I swung around, ready to defend myself. Only instead of a guard or employee, Giguhl sat a few feet away laughing at me.

"Dammit, you scared the crap out of me."

He laughed, a spooky noise coming from an even spookier-looking cat. "You should have seen your face."

"Shut up," I said. "How'd you get in here?"

"The other end of this warehouse has an open delivery dock. No one was around, so I slipped in."

"Did you find anything?"

He shook his head. "Nada. Although the security on that door tells me that's the place."

"Any ideas on how to get in there without being noticed?"

"Well, see that guy coming our way?" he whispered.

I peeked over the lid of the crate. A vamp male pushing a cart was headed straight toward the door. The cart carried a defibrillator and several bags of blood. *Not exactly standard winemaking tools,* I thought.

"I'll take him out, steal his uniform and pass card." I started to move when a paw nudged my ankle.

"No, dummy, I'll just run over and slip onto the cart. Once I'm in, I'll take a look around."

"And just how are you going to get back out?" I asked.

"With my catlike reflexes, of course." He shot off before I could stop him. One second he was a fleshy gray blur and the next his ratlike tail disappeared between two boxes on the lower shelf of the cart.

The male, totally unaware of his stowaway, slid his keycard through the reader and the doors air-locked open. Just like that, Giguhl was inside.

I waited a few seconds for an alarm to sound, worried the cameras had picked up the cat before he got on the cart. When nothing happened, I sat on the floor. Soon, though, my nerves—combined with ass-numbing concrete—had me fidgeting. What-ifs plagued me as time seemed to limp forward.

The sound of footsteps made me jerk upright. This time when I looked around the crate, I saw someone else approaching with a cart. A young vamp with strawberry blonde hair pushed a large laundry bin in front of her.

I didn't have time to think because she was closing in fast. I snuck around the backside of the crate and ran behind some discarded oak barrels to emerge behind her—and out of view from the cameras.

"Excuse me?" I said. Her head swiveled in my direction. Her eyes narrowed as she stopped in her tracks.

"This is a restricted area, ma'am," she clipped.

I started forward. "I was just looking for the bathroom."

She sized me up, but I was way ahead of her. I rushed her before she could utter another syllable. I'd left my gun in the car, so I used the only weapon available—my fist. A quick right hook had her staggering back. I caught her and spun her around, covering her mouth with my hand.

"Listen, I don't want to kill you but I will if you make me," I said. "Now are you gonna be a good girl?"

She nodded quickly, but I felt her muscles tense for a scream. "On second thought," I said. With my free hand, I cracked her neck. Not a mortal wound for a vamp, but given her youth one that would have her out cold for a while. She'd need a good infusion of blood to repair the damage, too.

I threw her unconscious body into the bin after grabbing her pass card, which had been clipped to her blouse. Praying the security didn't involve anything fancy like fingerprint scans, I slowly pushed the cart toward the doors.

A quick swipe of the card reader resulted in a buzzer and a red blinking light. My blood pressure spiked. I looked down at the card and realized I'd run it through upside down. Cursing myself for my nerves, I calmly turned the thing over and reran it. This time, the airlock hissed and the doors yawned open.

The well-lit area inside the doors looked more like a hospital than a winery. Institutional white linoleum spanned the short corridor. I moved forward, pushing the cart ahead of me. It had a squeaky wheel that sounded like a siren to my ears. Elevator doors stood at the end of the area. I pushed the button and waited.

A few moments later, the doors opened and I rode down what seemed like several floors, despite the fact there was only one button on the panel. The doors opened and I hesitated, shocked by the scene before me.

It looked like something out of an intensive care unit. Vampires dressed in scrubs moved among rows of hospital beds. The muted beeps of monitors were back-drop to the hushed voices of the attendants.

In the beds, bodies were hooked up to respirators. Feeding tubes ran out of their noses and IVs dripped something clear into their veins. But most alarming of all, were the IVs attached to their other arms. Dark red blood poured out of their veins in a steady flow, filling up blood bags. The room smelled of antiseptic with an undertone of blood and slow death.

"You there," someone called out to me. The voice sounded very far away and echo-y, like someone called through a metal pipe. "Hello? You must be new."

My muscles felt wooden as I slowly moved in the di-rection of the voice. A petite female vamp dressed in black scrubs stared at me. She had a stethoscope hanging around her neck and a chart in her hand. Her eyes were intelligent and her expression patient, yet annoyed.

"Put those linens in the storeroom," she said. "Be sure to take the soiled ones when you leave."

She pointed a finger, its nail crusted with dried blood, in the direction of the room. I nodded slowly and began pushing the cart. As I moved, my eyes were drawn to the bodies like magnets. Clovis hadn't been lying. The Do-minae were keeping these mancies in a vegetative state so they could steal their blood. My mind rebelled despite the proof right before my eyes. Their pale bodies lay inert as their life force dripped slowly from their veins.

I moved faster now, the initial shock wearing off in favor of abject panic. I tasted bile at the back of my throat. My skin felt too tight and all I wanted was to get away from the constant beep of the machines.

The storeroom was lined with shelves of medical supplies. I unloaded the sheets covering the woman. A quick check told me her pulse was going strong. I felt bad about covering her with dirty sheets, but I had no other choice. I dumped them on her, making sure to leave a breathing space.

I couldn't leave until I located Giguhl. Just as I turned to go, I saw him huddled under one of the beds near the storeroom. His eyes met mine. I'd never seen fear in his eyes before that moment. I wondered if mine had the same glinty look. I nodded and pushed the laundry cart forward. My feet felt leaden as I moved. The attendants scurried from one bed to the other, too busy to notice me or the cart with the squeaky wheel.

As I went past, Giguhl scampered from under the bed and leapt into the cart. At that moment, an alarm sounded from one of the beds on the far side of the room. Afraid we'd been found out, I stopped, my muscles tensed for action.

"Shit, he's going tachy," one of the male vamps yelled. The female I'd talked to earlier rushed over with the defibrillator. Relief and revulsion washed through me. I'd seen enough. In fact, I'd seen too much. I practically ran to the elevators. It seemed like an eternity before I pushed the cart through the airlock and we were free.

By the stack of crates, the cat leapt out as I unloaded the stinking linens from atop the woman. Someone would find her soon. By then, Giguhl and I would be long gone.

"Follow me." Giguhl ran in the direction of the cargo bays. We passed by a few workers, who did double takes as we ran past. I supposed that the image of a hairless cat in a sweater being followed by a stressed-looking chick in stiletto boots could have been funny. I was too anxious to get the hell out of there to see any humor in it.

We jumped off the ramp. I scooped up the cat and used my preternatural speed to race through the night. The cool cleansed some of the lingering stench of death, but not nearly enough. I felt coated in it, soiled by it. My mind spun in tight circles, trying to find some way to justify the Dominae's motives for the atrocity I just witnessed. No easy answer presented itself. The more I tried to find an explanation I could live with, the more I feared Clovis had been telling the truth.

Giguhl didn't say a word as I threw open the minivan door and dumped him inside. I peeled out of the parking lot and turned back onto the highway. Neither of us spoke for a long time. Then finally, Giguhl said, "Why?"

I stared straight ahead, clenching my jaw. "That's what we're going to find out."

My brain felt like it was about to short-circuit from trying to compute all the variables into some sort of logical explanation. I needed more answers before I figured out how to sort through everything.

"Where are we going?" Giguhl asked.

"It's time to have a conversation with the mage."

19

The card Adam gave me listed only a cell phone number. About twenty minutes outside the city, I called it. He picked up after the second ring.

"Lazarus."

"It's Sabina," I said. "We need to talk."

He didn't hesitate. "Meet me at the Fog City Hotel."

A while later, I pulled the minivan into the porte-cochere of the hotel. The valet guy opened my door. He jumped back in surprise when the hairless cat jumped out ahead of me.

"Sorry, he needs a potty break," I said.

The guy took the keys without a word and handed me a ticket. I chased Giguhl over to a small patch of monkey grass.

"I can't take you anywhere," I said under my breath.

"Bite me."

"Keep up the backtalk and I just might."

The hotel wasn't what one would term five-star. But it wasn't shabby either. Adam's room was on the second floor. I bypassed the lobby by slipping down the first hall-way I saw. From there I took the stairs two at a time up to the next floor. The last thing I needed was some nosy hotel employee telling me the cat wasn't welcome.

Adam's room was the second on the right from the stairs. I knocked and waited.

"What's our plan?" Giguhl asked, squirming in my arms.

"Just keep quiet," I said. When Adam didn't open the door after two more knocks, I pressed my ear to the wood. I didn't hear any movement.

"Are you going to ask him about how to send me home?" Giguhl whispered.

"Not yet," I said. His body went slack from disap-pointment. I sighed. "Listen, if you just play along and be a good kitty, I promise I'll talk to him about it soon."

"Okay." He sounded crestfallen, but resolved.

Pushing my guilt to the side, I knocked again. Why would Adam leave when he knew I was on my way?

Left with no other choice—at least to my mind—I de-cided to let myself in. Giguhl muttered a protest, but I shushed him and transferred his scrawny frame to my left arm. I turned the doorknob hard and forced my right shoulder into it. The door cracked open. I looked to my left and right to be sure no one noticed my B&E before slipping into the room.

I pushed the door against the slightly splintered door-frame. From the outside, it wouldn't be noticeable. Turn-ing back toward the room, I stopped short.

Standing in front of me, wearing nothing but a white towel, was a scowling, wet mage. Giguhl squirmed from my arms and streaked further into the room.

"What the hell do you think you're doing?" Adam demanded. With one hand, he held the towel, and with the other, he dragged me further into the room by my arm. "And what the hell was that thing?"

"Whoops, sorry," I said. "You didn't answer so I thought you'd stepped out. And that," I motioned in the direction Giguhl fled, "was my cat." I wasn't ready to introduce him to the demon he'd sent.

"First, that was not a cat. It looked like a bald weasel or something." He looked at the door. "Second, did it occur to you to call my cell phone?"

Distracted by his damp, sculpted chest and the happy trail of golden hair, which disappeared beneath the towel, I didn't answer. Just above the edge of the white terry cloth, I saw a small tattoo, which resembled a three-pronged maze in the shape of a circle. The symbol wasn't familiar, but the placement just above his happy place was . . . intriguing. In fact, up close and personal, I couldn't help but realize for the first time that Adam was a total hottie.

He crossed his arms, bringing my attention back above his waist. Seeing his scowl again, I realized I needed to focus.

"When you didn't answer my knocks, I figured you might be hurt," I said. "I didn't have time to think."

"As much as it warms the cockles of my heart to think you were rushing to my rescue, I'm not buying it."

I wasn't about to tell him that part of me had been hoping he'd stepped out for a few minutes. Then I would have had some time to rifle through his things. "I'll pay for the damage."

He blew out a breath, making the towel sag a little. I

held my own breath hoping to get a glimpse of the Promised Land. He cleared his throat, bringing my gaze north. His right eyebrow arched. "See anything you like?"

My cheeks warmed, but I wasn't about to give him the satisfaction of admitting to my embarrassment. "I was just noticing your tattoo," I said.

He didn't look like he believed me, but let it pass. "It's Hekate's wheel. And it's not a tattoo."

I must have looked confused because he went on. "All mages have this birthmark somewhere on their body," he said. "Where's yours, Sabina?

I looked away. Mine was different from Adam's. An eight-pointed star, just like the symbol on the Lilith amulet at the Red Moon, sat on my right shoulder blade. Remembering what my grandmother had said about keeping it hidden, I decided to change the subject. "Are you gonna put some clothes on or what?"

Out of the corner of my eye, I saw him smirk. He decided to let me get away with my evasion over the birthmark issue. "I'll be right back."

I moved further into the room. Giguhl was sitting on a table, looking at a piece of paper.

"Hey, stop that," I whispered.

"You've gotta see this," he said.

I picked it up and felt my eyes grow too big for their sockets. "Holy shit."

"Rooting through my things, Sabina? Isn't that a little clichéd?" Adam was back and he sounded amused.

I swung around, the damning evidence in my hand. "Why do you have this?" I thrust the printed layout of Immortal Vineyards at him.

"Why don't you tell me?" he said, ignoring the print

out and sitting on the bed. "You went there tonight, didn't you?"

My mouth fell open. I opened it and closed it several times as I sputtered. "You followed me?"

He shook his head. "Not technically, no."

"How did you know then? Technically."

He shrugged, seeming unconcerned by my growing agitation. "We all have our little secrets, Sabina. I'll tell you mine if you tell me yours."

"Cut the shit," I said, growing impatient. "Why are you still following me?"

"Like I told you, our family sent me to find you and make sure you're safe. So, you gonna tell me why you went?"

I sat in the chair next to the table where Giguhl was now napping. "Oh, you know, just had a sudden hankering for some wine."

"Right. And it just so happens the vineyard you visited is owned by the Dominae? Last I heard you weren't exactly on their good side."

"Weird, huh?" I said with a shrug.

"I'd say so." He was playing along. "Sample anything good?"

"They have an amusing Shiraz you'd probably like. Although, it was a bit tannic for my taste."

"Interesting." He leaned forward, so his knees brushed mine. "Now are you going to cut the shit and tell me why you were really there?"

"No," I said, pulling away. "That's privileged information. If I told you, I'd have to kill you."

"That would be a pity," he said. "After all, if you kill me you'll never get the answers you came to me for."

I stopped, wondering if mind reading was one of his powers. He laughed then, "Mind reading isn't one of my powers. I just figured this wasn't a social call."

I shifted in my seat, cursing myself for being so easy to read.

"Now that the witty banter portion of the evening is over, why don't you tell me why you're here?"

His posture was relaxed and his manner open, but I noticed a slight tension around his eyes. I felt a little tense myself as I tried to think of a way to question him about the missing mancies without his guessing the reason.

"Okay, so I've been thinking about what you said. Why would the Hekate Council send you now? I mean, I'm fifty-three years old. They've had plenty of time to track me down."

He leaned forward with his elbows on his knees. "Your existence was kept secret from us until recently."

"Kept secret? By whom?"

"The elders of the Council knew, of course. However, it wasn't until recent events that they felt the need to find you. They only entrusted the information to me and one other."

A dozen questions popped into my head. I started at the top. "What recent events?"

He stood and started pacing as if the activity would help him gather his thoughts. "How much do you know about the *Praescarium Lilitu?*"

"That's odd," I said. "You're the second being who's mentioned it to me recently."

"Who else mentioned it?"

Not wanting to explain why I'd gone to the occult

shop, I shrugged. "Doesn't matter. I always thought the prophecies were a myth."

"Yes and no. No one's ever seen them. They're guarded by a secret sect."

"The Caste of Nod?"

His eyes narrowed. "What do you know about them?"

"Nothing really. Like I said, I thought it was all a myth."

"The Caste is über-secret and from what I hear they'll do anything to keep it that way. As for the book, it's rumored to be a collection of prophecies."

"And?" I wasn't impressed by his dramatics. So far, it sounded like Nostradamus-type shit.

"And," he said, "Some of the prophecies have been coming true."

"Wait, I thought you said no one's ever seen them. How would anyone know if they're coming true?

"Oral traditions exist among the spiritual leaders of the races, passed down from generation to generation. So some of the prophecies are known by each race's leaders—more or less."

I frowned remembering Grandmother's dismissal when I'd mentioned the book to her. If Adam was telling the truth, surely she would have access to some of this information. Given recent revelations about the Dominae, I wouldn't be surprised if Grandmother kept this secret, too.

"What kind of prophecies are we talking here?"

"Big stuff, like wars and the second coming of Lilith."

"I see." Obviously, Adam was a few drops short

of a pint. I played along anyway. "And what has been happening?"

"Over the last couple of months, several mages have vanished."

My stomach felt like it had been dropped off a ten-story building. "Vanished?"

"Gone. Poof. No one has heard from them and no bodies have been found," he said. "There's a vague prophecy the Council believes relates to their disappearance."

My mind was too busy absorbing this information to respond. If the Hekate Council knew about the missing mancies, then there was no way I could let Adam find out about what was happening at the vineyard. He'd organize an army to storm the place. And the war would begin.

Adam was watching me, his manner wary, as if he expected me to launch out of my chair and disappear into the night.

"I know it sounds far-fetched, but that's all I know."

"I believe you, actually," I said. If nothing else, his explanation proved he was indeed sent by the council. But their reason for sending him still confused me. "So what are you supposed to do?"

He came and sat across from me in the other chair. He looked at me over Giguhl's sleeping form. "I'm supposed to find them, and I think you can help me do that."

I blinked and looked away quickly.

"Sabina? What aren't you telling me?"

Oh, shit. A flash of memory from earlier in the night came to me. A black-haired woman strapped down to a bed with tubes and wires sucking out her life force like bloodthirsty snakes. When I saw her, and the others, lying there, helpless, I'd felt the first stirring of . . . well,

I guess one might call it conscience. But I couldn't very well tell Adam all this. I would be causing a war just by saying the words.

"I know where they are," I said.

His body jerked in shock, causing the table to rock. The movement startled Giguhl awake.

"Where are they? Tell me," Adam demanded.

"I can't," I said.

He grabbed my hand and squeezed it, as if trying to force the truth from me. "Sabina, please." The weight of my knowledge bore down on my shoulders, making them ache.

"Adam, I can't tell you."

"Whatever you're involved with, I want in." His eyes burned with intensity. I wondered briefly if someone he knew was being held in that cold room that smelled like death. Someone he loved?

"You can't be involved. It's . . . complicated."

"Fuck complicated," he said.

As much as I agreed with his assessment, I couldn't tell him what was happening. Too many thoughts were tumbling through my head. I needed to get away and sort through everything.

"Look, I—" My phone rang. Adam looked at me, waiting for me to continue. I held up a finger and picked up the phone. The Dominae were the only ones with this number. I hit the button to take the call.

"This is Sabina," I said.

"We need to talk." It was my grandmother, and her words sent a chill through me. After listening for a couple more minutes, I hung up.

Adam looked like he was ready to shoot off the bed, he was so tense.

"Listen, something's come up. I need to go."

He stood, looking pissed. "What? Now?"

"I'm sorry. It's important."

"We're not done talking about this, Sabina."

"Yes, Adam, we are. You can't be involved."

I picked up Giguhl, who yowled at the rude awakening. I tucked the cat under my arm and headed for the door. Adam grabbed my free arm. "You know I'm going to find out everything you know."

I stared him down, not letting his fierce scowl threaten me. "You can try, but the day I work with a mancy is the day I give up drinking blood."

20

$\mathcal{A}$ limo picked me up at the designated spot near Fisherman's Wharf. A few minutes later, it drove over the Golden Gate Bridge. A fog had rolled in at some point, and the lights bathed the bridge in an unearthly vermillion haze. The limo continued northbound on the 101, toward Marin. I wondered if they were taking me to the vineyard until the limo left the highway near Muir Beach.

The car eventually turned off a winding road into a gravel drive hidden behind a stand of trees. The driveway turned into a cul-de-sac, at the end of which was a modest wooden cabin. When I say modest, I mean that by Marin County standards, where a million-dollar wooden cabin was a steal.

I opened the door and walked toward the house. No exterior lights decorated the place, but my catlike vision allowed me to find the path leading to the door. I couldn't see any guards, but I felt their presence, watching me from shrubs and trees surrounding the cabin.

I didn't bother knocking on the door, just let myself in. The male standing in the small entryway didn't seem surprised by my entrance. He merely held out a hand to indicate I should follow him. The cloak-and-dagger shit, combined with my nerves, made my neck muscles cramp. I closed my hands into fists, trying to release some of the built-up adrenaline, but it didn't help.

A servant led me into a surprisingly large main room. Floor-to-ceiling windows lined one wall. During the day, the views of the bay must have been amazing. But right now, they only showcased inky night with a few muted dots of light across the water.

The servant told me to wait there and left. The room held a large sectional sofa done in cognac leather. An oriental rug spanned the floor under the glass coffee table. A bar sat in the corner with several barstools. Despite its size, the room was welcoming and cozy. I could picture a group of friends gathering for drinks and conversation. But I knew better than to expect an impromptu cocktail party in my honor.

I was pacing in front of the stone fireplace when I felt Lavinia's energy. It struck me like a hot wind, making the hair on my arms prickle. One second I felt her and the next she appeared before me. I blinked, trying to figure out if she had moved too quickly for my eyes to detect her or just appeared out of thin air.

"Sabina." It was said quietly, but the power behind the voice was like an echo.

I lowered my head, not meeting her eyes as a sign of respect. "Domina."

"Please sit, child. We have much to discuss." She moved toward the sofa. I waited until she arranged her black skirts before sitting at the other end of the sofa. I perched on the edge, not comfortable enough to relax into the inviting cushions.

A servant appeared and set goblets on the table before us. After all I'd seen at the vineyard, I had as much interest in the contents of the crystal as I would in kissing a snake. When the servant left, I spoke. "I was surprised to receive your summons. I didn't realize you were coming to San Francisco."

Lavinia leaned forward and picked up her own drink. She took a sip and then ran a fingertip along the rim of the goblet.

"I was in the area checking on our vineyard."

My head jerked up. "Problems?"

"No, nothing like that. I just wanted to see how things are progressing with a pet project." She took another sip. "The time has come for you to kill Clovis."

Shocked by the abrupt change in subject, I looked up quickly. "You told me to find the mole first. Clovis confirmed it's a member of the Undercouncil, but I haven't gotten a name yet."

"Don't bother. We've already found him. No thanks to your efforts."

"What? When?"

"We've had operative in L.A. keeping tabs on all the members of the Undercouncil. It seems one of the members was having an affair with one of Clovis' spies."

My blood went cold. I knew what she was about to say.

"Distasteful, really, for a vampire as old as Nicolo Vera to allow himself to be manipulated by such trash. You knew Ewan McGregor, yes?"

Her use of the past tense made me go cold. I closed

my eyes and swallowed the bile rising in my throat. The stupid son of a bitch. How could Ewan be so careless? I opened my eyes again and cleared my throat.

"Yeah, I knew him."

"Interesting. Did you have any friends who weren't traitors, Sabina?"

"That's not fair. I had no idea what David and Ewan were up to. And if you'll recall it was me who made David pay for his treachery."

She opened her mouth to speak, but I swiped a hand through to the air to stop her. "Speaking of which, did you know David refused to work with Clovis when they met?"

She tossed back her head and laughed. "And who told you that, Sabina?" I didn't answer. We both knew who told me.

She leaned forward and sniffed the air in front of me. "He has fed from you."

My mouth went dry. For a moment, I'd forgotten whom I was dealing with. "Yes, Domina."

"Tell me something, Sabina. Who raised you?" Her tone was casual, but I knew better than to relax.

"You did."

"And who taught you the skills you needed to survive?"

"You," I whispered.

"Who did you swear fealty to when you were sixteen?"

I straightened a bit. "The Dominae."

"Correct on all accounts. So, please explain why you are challenging me based on the lies of our enemy? Has he seduced you so thoroughly that you have become blind to the truth before your eyes? He will do anything to achieve his goal of overthrowing our power. Are you going to allow yourself to be used as a pawn by some half-demon scum?"

I swallowed and shook my head. I'd lost my focus and allowed myself to doubt the Dominae because Clovis used his charm on me. It was time to come clean. "He knows about the vineyard. He plans on saving the mancies and then using the situation to wrest control of the race from you." Part of me felt relieved, but the other wondered if I was making a huge mistake.

She thumped the goblet on the table and rose. Crimson liquid splashed over the side and slid down the cup like a bleeding wound. She paced in front of the table. "Kill him."

I stammered, trying to think of a way to hold her off. "Domina, surely—"

She slashed a pale hand through the hair. "Tomorrow."

My stomach coiled. "I understand your urgency. However, I can't just walk in there with guns blazing. His guards will kill me before the first shot hits home."

She crossed her arms and skewered me with a look. "Losing your life for your race is an honor."

In the ensuing silence, all of my thoughts took on crystal focus. *Honor.* The word haunted me my entire life. She'd drilled the concept into me from such a young age, it was practically my first word. Later, honor sealed my lips when she'd told me I couldn't become an acolyte at the temple. Honor made me ignore my better judgment when she'd told me to kill David. And now, she expected me to accept a death sentence—all in the name of honor.

"I understand," I said. She nodded, assuming I accepted the possibility of death. She didn't get that I understood something else entirely.

I'd always believed my grandmother cared about me. She wasn't warm or affectionate, and she drove me hard, but I figured that was just her way. If nothing else, our blood ties should be proof of some sort of connection. But her careless disregard for the possibility of my death showed me the truth. She saw me as a pawn—a means to an end. Well, this pawn wasn't going to lie down and die.

"What of the mages at the vineyard?" I asked.

"Excuse me?" Lavinia's eyes flashed with fire.

"What happens when the Hekate Council finds out what you're doing?"

"You dare?" Her voice rose. "Do not forget your place, child."

"Clovis isn't the only one who knows. If word gets out—"

She waved my concern away with her hand. "War is inevitable. It's only a matter of when. Your job is to kill Clovis before he can use the situation to stage a coup. If he manages to get into power, the Hekate Council will wipe out our entire race."

Clovis. Someone else who saw me as a pawn. While my grandmother's attitude left me feeling empty, Clovis had caused the death of two of my friends. He needed to be taken out of the equation.

"But why harvest the mage blood? It seems like an unnecessary risk."

"When the war comes, the blood will give us a fighting chance against the Hekate Council. We will finally be able to fight fire with fire."

My pride demanded I protest, but something else—something weak and needy—begged me to ignore my misgivings. I wasn't proud of my need for her approval. Like a junkie, I rationalized my need, hoping one more hit would result in the high I craved.

"But you'll only use it if it comes to war, right? You aren't planning on forcing a war?"

Lavinia laughed. "Don't be ridiculous. Why would I intentionally try to start a war?"

I nodded and chewed on my lip as I thought it over. A memory of the mages at the vineyard threatened to test my conscience. But I shoved it away. They were mages. I was a vampire. Clovis was the enemy. My grandmother was family. Put that way, my choice was clear.

When this was all over, I'd have to do some serious thinking about my life choices. All this political maneuvering gave me heartburn. Maybe I just needed a vacation. Or maybe I'd strike out on my own for good, and leave the intrigue to my grandmother. The thought made my stomach cramp.

Now wasn't the time for existential crisis. I pushed thoughts of the future aside and focused on the here and now. I'd forget what I saw at the vineyard and do my duty. "I understand, Domina."

Her fangs flashed, making her look like a cobra ready to strike. "Excellent."

I didn't sleep well the next day. Despite the blackout curtains Vinca had installed in my room, I was aware of the progression of the sun. Each minute brought me one step closer to completing my mission.

I finally gave up on sleep about two in the afternoon. The cat slept on a pile of discarded clothes in the corner. Even in sleep, he seemed to feel the tension rolling off me in waves. His little paws jerked and his ears flicked occasionally, as if he was dreaming.

I used the time before sunset to come up with a plan. If I could get Clovis alone, I could do the deed and then get out of there before his body was discovered. I just had to figure out a way to get close enough without him suspecting my motives.

At around four o'clock, I got dressed and woke up the cat to tell him good-bye. He wanted to come with me, to help with the plan. I'd broken down the night before and admitted everything. I figured he'd seen enough to deserve the truth. But something told me to keep him out of this. If something happened to me, I couldn't risk Giguhl getting caught.

At five, I arrived at the temple. The place seemed deserted except for mortal guards, since most of the disciples would just be waking up for the night. One of the guards called Clovis on the phone, alerting him to my presence. At his direction, I followed him to the office.

Clovis was already there, sitting, as usual, behind his desk, looking clean-cut in an expensive suit. I wondered if he ever slept, or if his mixed genetic code allowed him to be awake in the daylight like me.

"You're back." He waved to the guards, dismissing them. "Did you have a nice trip?" His voice dripped with sarcasm. I didn't have the patience to deal with wordplay.

"I saw them," I said. "You were right." I glanced to my right, where a window overlooked the courtyard. The place was deserted at this hour. Most vampires didn't rouse until about seven, and the other acolytes were all in class.

"Of course I was right," Clovis said. He rose and came around the desk. He perched in front of me, his leg touching mine.

Seeing my opportunity, I leaned forward. "I shouldn't have doubted you. The Dominae need to be stopped."

Clovis reached for my hand and pulled me up. I went willingly, allowing him to bring me between his thighs. "Have you given any more thought to my offer?" His voice was husky, seductive. I gritted my teeth, trying to resist the pull he had on me when we were close.

"Which offer is that?" I moved in closer, licking my lips.

His eyes flared at the blatant invitation. With one hand, he stroked my cheek. I closed my eyes and moved into the caress. With my right hand, I slowly reached under my leather jacket, feeling for my gun in my rear waistband.

"To share my bed," he whispered.

I opened my eyes to meet his. His eyes were glowing again. I hesitated with my hand on the gun as a wave of arousal hit me. That's when I realized he must be using some demon mojo on me, causing me to feel this synthetic arousal. The knowledge freed me somewhat from the haze threatening to distract me from my task.

Smiling, I leaned in further, placing my lips at his ear.

Gripping the gun now, I said, "All I'm going to share with you is—"

A knock on the door interrupted. My heart skipped a beat and I jerked back a fraction, hiding the gun at my side. Frank stuck his head in. "Boss," he said. "Oh, hey, Sabina." He dismissed me and focused on Clovis. "We've got a problem."

"What is it?" Clovis said in a clipped voice.

When Clovis stood, I fell back behind him in shock. My hand went damp as it gripped the butt of my gun. I stood behind Clovis, my heart still hammering against my ribs. It would be so easy to take my gun and place it against the back of his head. Before he or Frank would know what was happening, I could pull the trigger. Bang. Clovis is dead.

Only, if I did that, Frank would put a bullet between my eyes before I got to the window and freedom. I struggled, trying to figure out what to do. Clearly, if it were up to my grandmother, I'd forfeit my life to get the job done.

". . . mancy was found trying to break into the compound."

Frank's words ended my internal struggle. Surely, Adam wasn't that stupid.

"We've detained him in a holding room."

"Has he talked?"

"Not yet, sir, but we're working on it." Frank's gaze drifted toward me. "However, he did ask to see Sabina."

I closed my eyes and prayed for patience. The gun slid easily into my rear waistband.

"Sabina, do you know anything about this?" Clovis

asked. I opened my eyes to find both Clovis and Frank eyeing me with suspicion.

"Maybe," I said. "Is he a tall guy with sandy hair?"

Frank nodded.

"Then, yeah, I think I know him. Stop beating him, please."

Frank looked to Clovis for instruction. "Bring him in here." Frank nodded and spoke into a walkie-talkie, telling the guard on the other end to bring in the prisoner.

Clovis looked at me again. "Want to tell me what this is all about?"

I heaved a big sigh. "It's a long story."

"Humor me."

I gave Clovis the CliffsNotes version of my experience thus far with Adam, leaving out his claims about my mancy family sending him. I hoped Clovis wouldn't notice my hands shaking as I talked. Adrenaline still gushed through me. Inside, I was berating myself for failing the Dominae. The truth was, even though the interruption wasn't my fault, I still could have taken one for the team and accomplished my mission. But I'd been scared. I didn't want to die.

Just as I wrapped up my story, another guard entered the room, pushing Adam ahead of him. The mage's right eye was swelling shut and his arms were bound behind him with handcuffs. The cuffs must have been lined with brass, which flattens and grounds magical energy.

Adam wouldn't meet my eyes as I stared him down. He was too busy having a one-eyed stare-off with Clovis.

"And who might you be?" Clovis's tone was casual.

"Adam Lazarus," he said. He stood straight with his shoulders back and his abraded face stubborn.

"Would you mind explaining to me why you were breaking into my sanctuary? Was the front door too obvious a choice?"

"This was the only way I knew to get in to see you," Adam said. "And her." His head jerked in my direction, but he still didn't look at me. If he had, he probably would have rethought his little plan. I was pretty sure my eyes would have fried him on the spot.

"Well, you've got your audience," Clovis said. He leaned back in his chair. "Speak your piece."

Adam seemed confused by the ease at which he was given the stage, but he recovered quickly. "I was sent by the Hekate Council to investigate the disappearance of several mages. I have reason to believe you have information regarding this matter." He paused for Clovis's reaction, but received none except a slight nod.

"Sabina admitted she knew where the mages were being held, but wouldn't give me any more information." His eyes cut to me then, unapologetic. "So I followed her here, since she's obviously working for you."

"And?" Clovis asked, sounding bored. I was so tense, my nails dug into the armrests of the chair. Part of me wanted to punch Adam for his stunt, and the other was scared for him.

"And I want in," Adam said.

"What use do I have for another mage when I have Sabina sitting right here?" Clovis said, nodding to me. I started to protest but his look shut me up.

"With all due respect to Sabina, she is untrained in magic. While I'm convinced she has latent skills, she is unable to use them."

Clovis rubbed his bottom lip, as if weighing this information. "And how do I know I can trust you?"

"A simple phone call to the Hekate Council will verify my identity."

"Therein lies the rub," Clovis said. "I'm afraid the Hekate Council must remain in the dark about certain aspects of this situation."

Adam's jaw tensed. "If you don't let me in on this, I will tell them that you are withholding information that affects the well-being of their followers."

"However do you think you'll pull that off? After all, what's to stop me from killing you right now?"

"I called my contacts at Council headquarters in New York before I came here. If they do not hear from me in half an hour, they will send a force to retaliate for my murder."

"You're bluffing," Frank said.

Clovis waved a hand at his assistant. "I see," he said. "I have to admit I admire your bravado. However, I cannot let you in on this unless I have assurances you will not reveal information to the Council."

"If it will save lives, I promise I will not reveal anything you tell me to the Council—until after the situation has been resolved."

Clovis looked at me. "What do you say? Should I spare his life and trust him? Or should I have Frank take him out back?"

Adam looked at me, his eyes daring me to condemn him. I was still pissed that his stunt screwed up my plan. However, while I didn't agree with his tactics, his obvious eagerness to help his people was touching. I couldn't really think of anyone I'd risk my life to save. Perhaps I wanted to understand how he was capable of such loyalty. Perhaps I felt bad for him. Or perhaps I knew I could trust him the moment I realized he was telling the truth about himself in the hotel. Regardless, after making Adam hold his breath and suffer while I made up my mind, I turned to Clovis.

"I trust him."

21

$\mathcal{V}$inca's eyes widened when she saw Adam follow me through the door. "Well, hello there." She came forward with a little extra swing in her hips. "I'm Vinca."

Adam looked amused by her blatant interest. "Adam."

"So you're the sexy hexy I've been hearing all about," she said. Adam looked to me for confirmation. I hated that she made it sound like I'd been giggling about him during a slumber party. I frowned at both of them and went to my room.

Vinca's flirtatious voice followed me down the hall. I found Giguhl napping on my bed.

"Wake up," I said. "We've got to talk."

He opened one eye and regarded me with a look I can only describe as disdain. "You're disturbing my beauty sleep," he said over a yawn.

"You'd have to be Rip van Winkle for that shit to work, my friend."

He ignored my jibe and took his time stretching. "Is Clovis dead?"

"There's been a change of plans." I quickly filled him in on everything.

"How do we know he won't go to the Hekate Council?" He was fully awake now. If he'd been in demon form, he'd probably have stroked his chin. Instead, he rhythmically swished his hairless tail like a metronome.

"We don't."

Giguhl's ears perked up just as I heard footsteps in the hallway. I turned in time to see Adam raise his hand to knock on the doorjamb.

"Were you just talking to your cat?" he asked, looking at Giguhl.

"Yeah, so? Lots of people talk to their pets." I walked toward him to push him out of the room before Giguhl could spill the beans about his true identity. I wasn't ready to go there.

Giguhl stood and stretched. "So you're the one who summoned me?"

Adam's eyes grew large as he looked to me for explanation. I threw my hand in the air. "We can talk about that later. We have some things to discuss, you and I."

"Looks like that's my cue to leave," Giguhl said, hopping off the bed. As he passed Adam he said, "Good luck, dude. You're going to need it."

Adam watched Giguhl's bare rear end sashay out the door and down the hall. "I summoned a demon. How did you change him into a cat?"

"Don't change the subject," I said. "You want to tell me what you were thinking with that stunt?"

He hooked his thumbs in the front pocket of his jeans. "Don't act so shocked, Sabina. You forced my hand."

"Don't pin this on me. You seriously screwed things up by barging in there like that."

"How did I do that? Clovis seems fine with me helping."

"Not that." I gritted my teeth together.

"What then?"

I couldn't very well tell him he'd botched my assassination of the male I was supposed to be working for. "You just fucked things up for me, okay? There's more going on here than meets the eye."

"Look, I apologize if my actions complicated your life," he said. "However, that's not really my problem, is it? You have your goals and I have mine."

"And screw anyone who gets in your way, right?"

"Spare me the self-righteous indignation. I highly doubt your motives are selfless."

He had me there. "I'm only going to say this once. Are you listening?" He nodded curtly and crossed his arms. "If you screw me over like that again, I'll go vampire on your ass. And trust me, your little magic spells won't be able to begin to repair the damage I'll do."

He stepped toward me. The stubborn tilt of his chin told me my words hadn't had quite the effect I'd been going for. "I tell you what. Any time you want to go, as you so eloquently put it, 'vampire on my ass—'" he did those little finger quote things, "you just bring it right on. Because, frankly, it'd be freaking hilarious."

"You think I can't take you?" I got in his face, showing a little fang for effect.

"Don't make me laugh." Confidence radiated from

every plane of his face. Like gunslingers in the Wild West, we squared off, each daring the other to break eye contact. He might have a bag of spells up his sleeve, but I had him beat in the speed department. I hooked my leg behind his knee, knocking his legs out from under him. His ass hit the ground before he knew what was happening. He blinked once, twice. "Ow!"

"Who's laughing now, magic boy?" A laugh bubbled up in my throat as he rose slowly, rubbing his ass. The sound barely escaped my lips before he waved a hand through the air. A weird tingling sensation started in my feet and snaked its way up my legs. I looked down and gasped. My feet hovered six inches off the ground. "Hey!" I tried to move my arms, but they lay useless at my sides. "Put me down."

Adam smiled and did another gesture in the air. My world tilted on its axis. The tips of my hair brushed the rug as Adam's inverted face came into view.

"This isn't funny!" I said.

"On the contrary, it's quite amusing from this perspective. Did you know your face turns a lovely shade of pink when you're pissed?"

"I've veered right past pissed and straight into apocalyptic." Blood rushed to my head, making me dizzy. "Put me down!"

"Not so fast. Since I have you at my mercy, I think it's time we get a few things straight."

"Screw you."

"Might be interesting given the position, but no thanks," he said. "Now, I've been thinking about this, and it's time you agreed to begin your magical training."

"Right. Like I want to spend even more time with you than I'll already be forced to endure."

"Seriously, Sabina. It's long past time you learned," he said. When I refused to answer, he sighed. "I'm not letting you down until you agree."

I shook my head, refusing to dignify his threat with a response.

"You're turning purple."

Blood pounded behind my eyeballs. I gritted my teeth against a wave of nausea. Inside, I was yelling at myself for being so stubborn. Maybe if I agreed to the training, he'd help me send Giguhl home and forget about making me meet my mancy family. So why was I being so pigheaded?

I knew the truth. It was just hard to admit it to myself. I was embarrassed. It was bad enough Adam had bested me at my own game. It was even worse I needed his help. Admitting that really chapped my ass.

"Sabina?"

I rolled my eyes up to look at him. "Fine! One session."

"Five."

"One and you help me send Giguhl home."

"You don't have much experience with negotiation do you?"

My head hurt and I was starting to see little stars superimposed on his face. "That's my final offer."

"You're no fun," he said. "Okay, we'll start with one."

Just as quickly as it began, I found myself standing upright again. Vertigo rushed through my head and I swayed right into Adam. He reached to steady me, but I pushed away and sat on the edge of the bed. The room spun for a moment as my equilibrium returned. The lightheadedness passed quickly, replaced by embarrassment. I took that and twisted it into anger, an emotion I felt more comfortable with.

"You asshole!" I said, standing again.

Adam's shit-eating grin did nothing to bank the fire in my belly. "You deserved it after that cheap shot. My ass is still sore."

"Good!"

"Seriously, Sabina? You might want to look into some anger management classes. You're awfully touchy."

"Touchy!" I took a menacing step toward him. He didn't move, just looked at me with a challenge in his eyes. I paused, realizing he'd been trying to get a rise out of me all along. Not wanting to give him any further satisfaction, I clenched my fists and forced myself to calm down. I counted to ten. He was still grinning. I took two cleansing breaths. He cocked an eyebrow. That did it.

"Fine! You win. Are you happy?"

"Yep."

I stalked out of the room, embarrassed by my lack of control. I'd given my opponent the upper hand the minute I lost my temper. It was a rookie mistake, and I knew better.

Vinca and Giguhl were curled on the couch watching *Oprah* when I stormed out. Their eyes widened, seeing me in full fang. "Did you kill him?" Giguhl asked.

Vinca nudged the cat and pointed behind me. Adam strolled into the room, looking like he didn't have a care in the world. He smiled at my roommates before winking at me. I clenched my fists, knowing he was trying to goad me into embarrassing myself in front of my friends.

"Wait a second," Vinca said. "What's going on here?"

"Nothing," I said. "Adam's leaving." Two sets of eyes moved from me to Adam, as if watching a tennis match.

Adam looked at his wrist. "Actually, I don't have to be anywhere for a while. Anyone want to order pizza?"

"I do!"

"I do."

"No!" I said, staring down the two betrayers on the couch.

"That's three against one, Sabina. Sucks to be you." The cat grinned at me, which looked just as odd as it sounds. Just for that, I silently vowed to hide all his catnip.

"Fine," I said. "I'm going out."

Adam raised an eyebrow, which was as good as calling me a coward. "Before you go, what time do you want me here tomorrow?"

I eyed him with suspicion. "For what?"

"To begin your magic lessons, of course."

"Magic lessons?" Giguhl perked up. The hope on his face made me bite back the retort I'd been about to toss. I narrowed my eyes at Adam. He'd just set me up. Again.

"Be here at dusk. You'll have thirty minutes before we need to go to the temple for our first strategy meeting." I expected him to argue at the short time I'd given him. Instead, he smiled.

"Okay," he said with a shrug. He then dismissed me, turning to my friends. "How about pepperoni?"

As they debated the merits of anchovies, I turned to the door. Part of me hoped one of them would try to convince me to stay. How had Adam worked his way into the group so quickly? And how did I end up feeling like an outsider just as fast?

I grabbed my coat from the chair and opened the door. With a final glance over my shoulder, I saw the three of them laughing. Vinca stared at Adam with obvious sexual interest, while Giguhl looked like he had a serious case of hero worship.

I stalked out into the night, slamming the door behind me. Their laughter carried through the wood, following me through the courtyard.

Screw them, I thought. This was why I didn't believe in friendship. You couldn't trust anyone to be loyal for the long haul. An image of David's face flashed in my head.

Nope, you couldn't trust anyone. I was proof of that.

I returned two hours later, my cheeks warm despite the cool night air. The recent infusion of fresh blood, courtesy of a mugger who'd been stalking women in a local park, did wonders for my mood. I always did get a little bitchy when my reserves ran low. At least, that's what I told myself as I thought about the scene I'd made earlier in front of Adam.

While I was out, I had some time to think about how to handle the fact I'd botched Clovis's assassination. I knew Lavinia was waiting for my call. There'd be hell to pay when I didn't check in. My only hope at this point was to try again the next night. After my training session with Adam, we'd head over to the temple to plan the attack. After the meeting, I'd ask Clovis to meet in private about some detail of the plan. That's when I'd do it. Sure, it meant taking an extra day, but I hoped the Dominae would overlook that in light of my success. Until then, I just had to avoid my cell phone.

Vinca and Giguhl looked like they hadn't moved from the couch since I'd left. A pizza box sat on the table in front of them, the lid open to reveal a few discarded crusts and one greasy piece of pizza. Looked like Giguhl won the great anchovy debate after all.

"Hey guys," I said. My eyes scanned the place for signs of Adam. Only the faint scent of sandalwood remained.

Giguhl, who lay with his distended, fleshy belly in the air, didn't move his eyes from the screen but managed to raise a paw in greeting. Vinca jerked at the sound of my voice. "Hey, Sabina. I didn't hear you come in."

"What are you watching?" I craned my neck to see the TV, but Vinca clicked it off with the remote. Giguhl protested but she ignored him.

"Just some ridiculous mortal movie," she said. Her pink cheeks made me suspicious.

"Which one?"

"I don't remember the title," she said, suddenly very interested in a piece of lint on her pants.

"Oh, shut up," Giguhl said. "It was *The Lord of the Rings*." He stood slowly and stretched, his alarmingly large belly wobbling as he did so.

Vinca's eyes shot to mine. I grinned at her. "Don't be embarrassed. That elf was hot."

A giggle escaped her. "Damn straight."

"My favorite is that Sauron," Giguhl said. "That dude knows from evil."

Vinca shot him a glance and shook her head. "So, where did you head off to in such a hurry?"

"Just grabbed some dinner," I said. "Needed some fresh air."

She lifted an eyebrow. "Hmm, I wonder why? Wouldn't have to do with a certain sexy hexy, would it?"

"If you mean the annoying asshole who was here earlier, yes."

Vinca and Giguhl traded a glance and then looked at me. "Please," Giguhl said. "You're so hot for that mancy you're about to spontaneously combust."

I ignored them both and went to the kitchen to grab a drink. Vinca followed me. "Do you want to talk about it?"

I popped the top to a soda and shook my head. "Nope. Nothing to talk about."

"So you aren't mad I was flirting with him?"

I hopped up on the counter and took a long swallow. The bubbles burned a path down my throat. "You were flirting with him? Hmm, didn't notice."

"Really? I must be losing my touch. After you left, I was throwing some of my best moves out there. He didn't even seem to notice, so I finally gave up."

"Maybe he's gay," I said. Who was I kidding? The male fairly reeked of heterosexuality—the kind that made a female's naughty bits tingle.

Vinca snorted. "Right. That's why he was sporting wood when you came out of the bedroom."

I choked on my drink, sputtering. "What?"

"Oh come on, Sabina. When you two walked out of there you looked guilty and he looked about ready to explode. It's so obvious you're into him."

"Please. I am not." And I meant it. I wasn't exactly one to giggle and fawn over a guy just because he had a nice face and an amazing ass. Besides, Adam was a mage. I didn't even want to think about the Freudian ramifications of being interested in a mage. After all, it had worked out so well for my mother. Not to mention, I could barely fit into the same room as Adam's ego. That guy had a serious attitude problem.

Vinca leaned into the counter, eyeing me. "Whatever you say. But I predict you two will do the deed before the next full moon."

I rolled my eyes. Thus far, Vinca's prophecy skills left a lot to be desired. Of course, this time it worked in my favor since there was no way I was going to do the nasty with that pompous, arrogant mage.

"Good thing you're not a gambler. I hate taking money from innocents," I said.

"We'll see," she said. We were quiet for a moment, the only sound in the apartment was Giguhl's snores echoing from the living room. When she finally spoke again, Vinca was more serious. "I want to help with the rescue mission."

I'd been mid-sip again, but managed to swallow before I answered. "No way."

"Come on, Sabina. You know you could use me in case anyone got hurt."

"It's too dangerous," I said.

"Adam said he didn't think it'd be a problem."

My teeth automatically clenched. "Adam isn't in charge."

"Stop it," she said, her voice taking on a steely tone I'd never heard from her. "Have you considered how to disarm the security without setting off the alarms?"

I cut her off, knowing where she was going with that. Members of the faery races were well known for being able to alter electromagnetic currents, which would come in handy with the security cameras and alarms around the vineyard complex. Still, I couldn't risk it. Especially since I didn't plan on being involved with the rescue. If I wasn't there, I couldn't protect her.

"Adam can handle it."

She crossed her arms and scowled. "It's not fair. I'm not some delicate flower, Sabina. I have skills you can use."

I jumped off the counter and approached her, feeling bad but not that bad. "Look, I appreciate the offer. Really. But it's just too dangerous. If something happened to you, I'd feel horrible."

"I'm not your responsibility. I can take care of myself."

"I'm sure you can. But I won't have you risking yourself on my watch."

"I could go to Clovis, you know."

"Good luck." I already knew his answer. Clovis wanted the team small and lethal. Nymphs weren't exactly known for their bloodthirsty battle skills.

Her hand landed on my arm, her eyes imploring me to listen. "Please, Sabina. I want to help. Anything."

I sighed as I felt some of my resolve crack. I knew what it felt like to be underestimated. "You can help with the logistics—gathering supplies and whatnot." She let out a whoop of triumph, but I stopped her. "However, you'll stay behind during the attack."

"That's okay," she said. "I'm just happy to help any way I can."

Her smile was contagious. I felt my face crack into a grin.

"You know, when you first got here I had my doubts," she said.

"Oh yeah?" I leaned back against the sink, surprised by her candor.

She nodded. "I'm ashamed to admit this now, but Clovis asked me to spy on you." She looked up at me through her lashes, as if worried I was going to get angry. I wasn't angry—or surprised. I'd figured as much.

"And well, I'm relieved at how this has all turned out. I know it was rocky at first, but I'm glad we're friends."

My chest contracted. Friends? When had that happened? I'd never had a female friend before. Most of the other assassins in school were males, and the profession lent itself to being a loner more than a social butterfly. And now, inexplicably, I had a nymph for a friend. I wondered if she'd still think that after I killed Clovis. I knew better. The trust shining in her eyes would die and I'd go from friend to traitor.

Again.

22

If there are two things that don't mix, it's pizza and cats. Giguhl groaned half the night with heartburn and emitted the most noxious gas I've ever had the misfortune to encounter. At one point, it got so bad I opened the bathroom door and turned on the fan. The cat darted past me, heading straight for the toilet. I left the door cracked to give him privacy and fell back into bed amid the sounds of dry heaves and yowling.

When I managed to fall asleep with a pillow over my head, nightmares plagued me. In one, David was alive and hunting me through a thick forest. I woke with a start, his words echoing in my ears, "Betrayer!" My breath came in labored gasps and cold sweat coated my skin.

When I managed to fall asleep again, I dreamed of my father. I hung upside down on some sort of torture device, my hands and feet bound. He told me to use my magic to rescue myself. Yet as hard as I tried, I couldn't break free. My father shook his head and said, "You're such a disappointment."

Finally, my own yells woke me. I was sitting up when my eyes opened. Giguhl sat at my feet, watching me warily. "Are you okay? You were shouting."

I ran a hand through my rat's-nest hair and tried to get my bearings. I closed my eyes and willed my heart to decelerate by taking slow breaths. In my solar plexus, I felt the sun hovering at the horizon.

"What did I say?" I asked finally.

Giguhl's ear twitched. "Something like 'it's not my fault.' "

I cringed, remembering the reason I'd been yelling. Though I'd never met my father, I knew without a doubt he'd been the mage in my dream.

Knowing I'd never get back to sleep, I tossed off the covers and stood. Adam would probably arrive at the butt crack of dusk just to annoy me anyway.

"How are you feeling?" I asked Giguhl.

"About five pounds lighter," he said.

"Poor, Mr. Giggles," I said. "That'll teach you to stay away from people food."

"I'd rather be gassy all night than forced to endure that horrible slop that passes as cat food."

"Suit yourself. Only next time you're sleeping in the living room. You gave a whole new meaning to 'nocturnal emissions.' "

He sniffed and jumped from the bed, dismissing me. At the door, he paused, waiting for me to open it for him. I sighed and did his bidding. He left without looking at me.

"You're welcome," I called. His only response was a tail twitch as he rounded the corner into the living room.

I felt a grin tease the corner of my lips at his behavior. Shaking my head, I pivoted toward the bathroom. If luck was on my side, I'd have time for both a shower and a gallon of coffee before Adam made an appearance.

By now, I should have learned that luck, if she was a lady, was a mean-spirited bitch with a grudge against me. I'd barely stepped out of the shower when I heard the doorbell. Dripping like a wet dog, I grabbed a towel from the rack and did the world's fastest dry-off. Five minutes later, my hair was in a makeshift but damp bun. After tossing on jeans, a white tank, and my black cowboy boots, I inspected myself in front of the mirror.

"Makeup," I said to my pale reflection. A couple of coats of mascara, a little cream blush, and some lip-gloss worked wonders. I told myself the enhancement was merely a concession to my sleep-deprived complexion. However, part of me didn't feel right appearing before Adam clean-faced. I needed some war paint before I faced my first lesson in magic.

Someone knocked on the bedroom door. Knowing I couldn't put it off any longer, I went to answer. Before I opened it, I rubbed my damp palms on my denim-clad thighs.

Adam lounged against the doorframe. "Morning," he said with his trademark grin.

"Hey." The word came out like a croak.

His gaze traveled south, pausing briefly over my chest. I crossed my arms, suddenly wishing I'd thought to put on a bra. I cleared my throat.

"You ready to get started?" His eyes met mine again.

"I guess so," I said. "Do I need anything?"

He shook his head and stepped back to make way

for me. "I thought we'd start in the courtyard. It's a nice night."

"Sounds good." I felt like I needed to clear my throat again. And I was having trouble meeting his eyes. Weird. Guess I was more nervous about this magic stuff than I thought. Of course, given the distrust Lavinia instilled in me about all things mage, maybe it wasn't such a surprise.

Giguhl and Vinca had made themselves scarce. I wondered if this was their lousy attempt at matchmaking or if they were just scared to be around once I started casting spells. After a quick detour to the kitchen for coffee, Adam followed me outside. A bistro table and two wrought iron chairs sat next to the pool. Adam motioned to it and I took a seat, adjusting the chair so it faced the street.

"Worried someone's going to sneak up on you?" Adam said. Then, he did the same thing. I ignored this and busied myself looking everywhere but at him.

Despite the temperature, the pool lights glowed. The chlorine's sharp scent mixed with the smoky aroma of fallen leaves. I took a deep breath, trying to relax.

"This isn't the Spanish Inquisition, you know."

I looked at Adam. He smiled at me across the table. The lights from the pool accentuated the pleasing symmetry of his face. Realizing I was staring, I shifted in my seat. "I'm fine. Just didn't sleep well."

He nodded and reached into his backpack. "I thought tonight we'd just cover some basics. How much do you know about mages in general?"

I shrugged. "Not much. You're not immortal, but you

live extremely long lives. I guess the magic helps with
that."

He nodded. "It helps. The oldest mage I know of lived
to be a thousand years old."

I felt my eyes widen. "He must be pretty strong to live
so long."

"She," he corrected. "Ameritat was the leader of the
Hekate Council." His voice held a note of regret. Almost
as if to distract himself, he pulled a book out of his bag
and set it on the table. "What else?"

I looked up, racking my brain for something. "Honestly? Most of what I've been told isn't so positive."

He chuckled. "No, I guess it wouldn't be. Let's skip
the vampire propaganda and go straight to the basics of
magic, okay?"

"Fine with me."

"The first thing they teach all mage youth is that magic
must always be used with caution. Because it messes with
the balance of nature, you have to be weigh potential repercussions before casting any spell."

"What kind of repercussions are we talking about?"

He leaned his elbows on the table. "Depends on the
magnitude of the spell. Are you familiar with the butterfly effect?"

I nodded. "Something about a butterfly flapping its
wings in Africa can cause a hurricane on the other side
of the world."

"Very good," he said. "Magic basically works on that
principle. The larger the spell, the more serious the consequences. I've seen big spells cause earthquakes, torna-
dos, even tsunamis."

"What about the smaller ones?"

"Those are harder to track. Might be something as big as a rain shower or as small as an acorn falling from a tree. Could happen five yards away or fifty miles. Plus, you never know when it will happen—in five minutes or fifty years."

"That sucks," I said. "But if you don't know what will happen, why worry at all?"

"The point isn't knowing what will happen, it's being aware that everything we do affects the whole. All of us—mages, vampires, humans, and the rest—affect the balance of life."

"If you start singing 'Kum Ba Yah' I'm out of here."

That got me a frown. "Sabina, this is serious. You can't just go around hexing people or casting spells willy-nilly."

"I was kidding, jeez."

He cleared his throat and pulled a book out of his backpack. "This is a textbook used in mage schools. It's pretty elementary, but it gives a good overview of the basics." He pushed the book across the table. I picked it up and flipped through it. He wasn't kidding. It read like the Dick and Jane version of *The Book of Shadows*. "There'll be a test tomorrow."

I brought my head up, ready to tell him where he could stick his test. But stopped myself when I saw his smirk.

"Gotcha."

"Nice one," I said. "Can we get to the good stuff already?"

"Not yet. You need to learn about the basics before we move into introductory spell casting. That book will help."

Just then, my cell phone rang. Grimacing, I picked

it up to check the number. Lavinia. Cursing under my breath, I hit the end button and then powered the phone off. If things went as planned, I'd be able to call her back later with news of my success.

"You could have taken that," Adam said, nodding toward the phone.

"I didn't recognize the number." He didn't look convinced but let it drop. "Okay," I said. "What else, Teach?"

"That's it for tonight."

My mouth dropped open. I'd gotten myself all worked up and all he did was give me some stupid book? "That's it?"

"I don't want to rush this. You've got a lot to learn and tossing you into intermediate casting might overwhelm you."

"Wait a second," I said. "You're making it sound like I'm in this for the long haul."

"Aren't you?"

"Hell no. We agreed on one lesson. I thought you'd teach me a few spells and that'd be it."

He sighed and tilted his head to look at me. "Don't you get it? I'm here to help you claim your birthright."

"What are you talking about?"

"Sabina, you've lived your life so far as if you were a pureblooded vampire. But you're not. Half of your blood is mage. And until you accept that you'll never be whole."

I sat back in my chair and stared at him, dumbfounded by his audacity. "I think we're done here." The scrape of the chair legs against concrete made me cringe as I stood.

"Sabina," Adam said. I ignored him and continued to

the apartment. Behind me I heard him curse followed by his chair being pushed away from the table. "Wait!"

"See you at the temple!" I yelled. The door slammed behind me.

Two hours later, I was ready to stab myself in the eyeball with the pen I was tapping on the notepad in front of me.

"If we go in through the west entrance, we can disable the cameras," Frank said.

"But why would we do that when I can simply disable them with a spell?" Adam argued.

Vinca and I looked at each other as the two men continued to debate the various methods of entry. The meeting had already gone on too long, most of it consisting of Adam and Frank arguing over every last detail of the plan.

"Frank, how many vamps can we count on to help us?" I interrupted.

Frank's glare shifted from Adam to me. "I've got five of Clovis' personal guard."

"Shit," I said. "We need a lot more than that. They've got security all over that place."

"I can probably get some faeries involved," Vinca offered.

Frank snorted. "What are they going to do, blow pollen on them?"

Vinca stuck her tongue out at him. "Don't underestimate fae folk, vampire. We've been known to kick some bloodsucker ass. Would you like a demonstration?"

Frank started to lean forward, his eyes hot. I put a hand on his arm. "Stop it," I ordered. "Vinca, I appreciate your offer, but I need you to focus on gathering the weapons and supplies right now." Vinca leaned back in her chair with a frown.

"I can put a call out to some of the covens in the area," Adam said.

I shook my head. "Absolutely not. We can't chance the Hekate Council stepping in."

"But—"

I held up a hand, cutting him off. "No. We'll have to make do," I said. "Now, let's start by going over what we know about the facility."

An hour, and a lot of shouting, later, we'd come up with a rudimentary plan. It wasn't fleshed out, but it was a start. Frank stood and stretched.

"I need to go brief my men." He stalked out without another word.

Adam watched him go. "That guy's got an attitude problem."

"No doubt," Vinca said.

I sighed and stood, gathering papers. "Look, this isn't ideal for any of us. We just have to manage with the resources we have. If either of you has a problem with the plan, you are free to walk away now."

I looked at each of them, hoping they'd bow out. The plan we'd come up with was a suicide mission. Neither spoke.

I stood and began gathering the papers on the table. "Adam, I'll need your list of supplies by tomorrow evening. That should give Vinca enough time to get it all together by week's end."

Adam nodded, eyeing me. I ignored him. Vinca rose

to leave. "Thanks for including me, Sabina. I'll see you at home."

I nodded curtly and went back to my shuffling. After she left, Adam continued to lounge in his chair.

"Don't you have some place to be?" I asked.

"I thought we were going to continue your training," he said.

I stopped and stared at him. The gall of this guy. "The deal's off."

"No, it's not."

"Yes," I said firmly. "It is. It's obvious we have different goals here."

He leaned back in his chair and tossed the pen he'd been holding onto a set of blueprints. "You're scared."

With deliberate slowness, I placed the palms of my hands on the table and leaned toward him. "What did you say?"

"Come on, Sabina. It's obvious. My comment earlier about realizing your potential stung your pride. But more than that, it scared you," he said. "And you want to know why?"

I shook my head and pursed my lips. "No, but I'm sure that's not going to stop you."

He leaned his elbows on the table. "You've spent your whole life living in this little bubble where the rules were clear. The Dominae brainwashed you against all of mage-kind, and embracing that side of yourself terrifies you."

"You know what terrifies me, Adam?" I said. "That you think I'm so gullible that I'll buy that psychobabble bullshit. You don't know me. And you certainly have no right to sit there and pontificate about what I'm thinking or how I feel. I meant what I said, no more training. It's not because I'm scared or because deep down, I'm a lost little girl. It's because I'm not interested."

He watched for a moment, his expression unreadable. Finally, he stood and came around the table. "You're not interested? That's fine. But if you don't agree to continue with the training, I'll walk out of here and tell the Hekate Council everything."

My eyes narrowed and my fists clenched. "You're a real bastard, you know that?"

He smiled and picked up a stack of papers from the table to hand to me. "I've been called worse."

I closed my eyes, wondering how things had gotten so complicated. If Adam went to the Hekate Council now, war would follow, no doubt about it. If I could hold him off, there was a chance I could convince the Dominae to change their minds. Granted, the chance was small, but I had to try.

When I opened my eyes, Adam's smile had faded into a frown. He seemed to be holding his breath. "Fine. The training continues. But no more life coaching, okay?"

He nodded. "Deal."

I knew conceding was a sign of weakness. However, if things went according to plan, I'd off Clovis that night and be gone before Adam could schedule another lesson.

Thinking about the devil made him appear at the conference room door, as if I'd summoned him. "Sabina?"

I turned quickly. "Yes?"

He eyed Adam and me, his gaze taking in our closeness. "Did I interrupt something?"

I backed away a step. "No, we were just discussing the plans." I glanced at Adam, willing him to confirm my statement. Instead, he merely looked at Clovis with a small smile hovering on his lips. I wondered why he'd want Clovis to think something else was going on.

"Sabina, may I speak to you in private?" Clovis said. It was stated as a question, but his tone made it clear I didn't have a choice. That was fine with me because I had plans for Clovis.

"Sure," I said. "Excuse me." I said this last to Adam, who nodded.

"Tomorrow evening then?" He was obviously referring to our next training session, but his tone implied otherwise.

Distracted, I nodded and gathered my things. I walked to the door where Clovis waited. When I looked up, he was staring at Adam. A quick glance backward confirmed Adam was returning his stare. Freaking males, I thought, they couldn't be more obvious about their territorial dispute if they'd both peed on me.

"You ready?" I asked Clovis. He reluctantly ended the stare-off to smile at me.

"Always, my dear." He placed a hand on my hip to guide me through the door. Before he closed it, I caught a quick glimpse of Adam scowling at us.

"Frank said the plans are coming together nicely," Clovis said, leading me down the hall. His words interrupted my confusion over Adam's sudden possessive behavior.

I nodded. "Yeah, I'm a little worried about the lack of manpower, but I think it'll work out."

"Surprise will be on our side," he said. "Besides, the mage should be able to back up the team should any magical intervention be necessary."

I didn't like the way he'd said "the mage." He spat the word out, like it had been a bad taste in his mouth. I didn't comment because I was finally paying attention to the direction he was leading me.

"Isn't your office in the other direction?"

He moved the hand from my lower back to wrap his arm around my shoulder. I was suddenly glad I'd shoved my gun into my boot instead of its normal place at the small of my back. "I thought we'd meet in my chambers."

He didn't wait for a response, just guided me confidently toward his rooms. I didn't protest because the privacy of the chambers suited my plans just fine. When we got to the doors, I noticed no guards were on duty. So, Clovis wanted extra privacy for our "meeting"? That was fine with me. It'd be easier to escape once the deed was done.

He led me into the rooms and shut the doors behind us. Once again, my senses were assaulted by the overpowering scent of sex. I found it odd I never noticed the smell on Clovis outside this room.

"Can I offer you a drink?"

I shook my head, not trusting him or his libations. "I'm fine, thanks."

He shrugged and went to the bar, pouring himself a tumbler of something amber-colored. He swirled the drink around for a moment, watching me across the room. I stood still under his scrutiny, despite my sudden urge to fidget.

"You've been holding out on me, Sabina."

I tamped down the brief spurt of panic his words created. "How so?" Deliberately, I sauntered toward him.

"You know damned well what," he said. He took a gulp from the glass and slammed it on the bar. "I've made it clear I want you in my bed."

Relief flooded me for a moment. I'd been worried he knew something about my working for the Dominae or the plan to kill him.

"And I told you I needed more time."

He came forward, his hands gripping my shoulders roughly. "I don't like games."

"Good, because I'm not playing them," I said. I wanted to push his hands away but decided it would only anger him further. "I've just got a lot on my mind. When I come to your bed, I want it to be with a clear head."

"You said when you come to my bed, not if," he said, moving in closer. I felt light-headed, which seemed to be normal now whenever he was this near.

"I never said I wasn't interested." I toyed with his tie and lifted the corner of my mouth in a flirtatious smile.

He bent down and placed a kiss on my neck, just over my jugular. "If you won't let me have your body—yet, perhaps you'll allow me to taste your blood again." He ran a tongue over the spot, causing a stream of concentrated electricity to run from my neck to my groin.

My brain went all foggy as desire pooled in regions south. I knew it was wrong to allow him to feed from me. If I had my way, he'd be dead in the next five minutes. But he had some effect on my body that I couldn't deny. Part of me considered allowing him one last taste before I damned him to Irkalla.

He scraped his fangs over my vein. The resulting pleasure-pain sent a shiver down my arms. The logical portions of my brain screamed at me to remember how dirty I'd felt the last time. But I didn't care. Inside, I felt an overwhelming urge to do something wrong, something I'd regret, something to relieve all the pressures built up in my life lately. I went lax against him, my body giving him permission even though my head denied it.

My mind shifted restlessly through itself, bringing up quicksilver images. The gun in my boot. Mages strapped to gurneys at the vineyard. My grandmother's disappointed face. David's body smoldering next to a grave.

Clovis's breath caressed my skin, hot and moist. It mingled with my own rapid breaths. "You want this," he whispered. "You want to give me your blood."

My head felt both overfull and deliciously light at once. My breath came in shallow pants as my heart skipped a beat and then kicked into overdrive. Clovis' musky pheromones assaulted my nose as a coppery taste overtook my tongue. The onslaught of physical and mental stimuli compounded until I felt overwhelmed. Clovis' fangs pressed against my skin, pushing against my vein. The sharp canines were about to break through when my heart went from pounding to galloping. I felt the skin give way and his fangs begin to sink into the soft tissue. I couldn't catch my breath. Before I knew what was happening, I shoved at him, clawing and kicking against him until he fell back. Collapsing onto the floor, I curled up into a ball.

My heart rammed against my chest like a piston. I hyperventilated against the pain, sure I would die when the bomb in my chest exploded.

"Sabina?" In some part of my mind, I was aware of Clovis' hand landing gently on my shoulder. I ignored it in favor of freaking out. In my head, I shouted to myself to calm down. I'd never felt so out of control of my own body.

"Breathe," Clovis commanded.

I forced myself to take in deep, slow lungfuls of air. My pulse kicked up for a second before skipping a beat. The new rhythm felt slower, yet still too fast. Another slow breath and my heart ratcheted down another notch.

Somewhere nearby glasses clinked together. Clovis shoved a cool glass into my shaky hand. "Drink."

My skin felt too tight and my jaw ached from clenching as I looked up at his concerned face. "Drink it," he repeated. Through a fog, I squinted at the glass. Recognizing the red fluid, I brought it to my lips. The first sip exploded on my tongue, making my mouth water and my fangs throb. The rest went down in one swig. It spread down my throat and through my limbs like a balm. I closed my eyes and licked my lips, trying to get every drop. I knew Clovis was watching me, but I was still too panicked to worry about appearing weak in front of him.

When I opened my eyes again, my breathing had returned to normal and my heart had slowed its rhythm. My head felt full of helium and my hands were shaking, but I felt more in control. Clovis stood before me, his eyes sympathetic but calculating.

"Better?"

I nodded, wiping the back of my hand over my lips. "Yeah."

He sat on a chair I missed when I collapsed. He didn't say anything, just watched me. Conscious of his gaze, I cleared my throat and set the glass on the floor. My palms were sweaty even though I felt cold.

"You want to tell me what that was all about?" he said finally.

"I haven't fed in a while," I lied. I didn't know what the hell had just happened.

"Sabina, hunger's effects are rarely that severe unless you're close to starvation."

I shrugged. "I don't know what it was. Stress maybe."

He nodded and patted my knee, a strangely paternal gesture from a man who'd just tried to seduce me. "Maybe you should put your feet up." He reached down to lift my boots onto his lap. Remembering the gun in my boot, I jerked away. His eyes shot to mine, surprised by my skittishness.

"I just need to go home." I tried to stand. My knees wobbled, causing me to reach out and grab his shoulder for support.

"Are you sure you're okay?" Real concern weighed down his voice.

"I just need to get some rest," I said. "I'll be good as new tomorrow."

He stood slowly, watching me as I tried to steady myself. "You could lie down here."

My eyes shot to the bed made for sin. "Thanks but I'd be more comfortable in my own bed."

He looked so disappointed I almost laughed. Almost. The fact I'd just screwed up another assassination sucked all the humor out of the situation for me. I briefly considered just pulling my gun out right then and taking care of it once and for all. However, I knew I wouldn't get far, as weak as I felt. Clovis was too strong to come at without all my facilities in order.

I ran a shaky hand through my hair. My hairline was damp with sweat. "I'm sorry about, well, you know."

He shrugged, a slightly befuddled expression marring

the dark beauty of his face. "No harm done. I'll see you out."

I shook my head, causing hair to fall in my face. "That's all right."

Before he could argue I walked as fast as I could to the door. I needed to get far away from Clovis and his narcotic pheromones to clear my head.

By the time I reached the front doors, I felt a little better. The combination of blood and fresh air did a lot to restore my strength. Frank slouched by the front door, almost as if he'd been waiting for someone.

"Wore you out, huh?" He actually smirked at me.

I stopped and looked at him. "Excuse me?"

He came forward, slinking. "Clovis always has that effect on the ladies." He winked at me. Winked!

"Whatever," I said, reaching for the door handle. Frank's hand landed on mine. I rounded on him. "Back off."

"Ah, come on," he said, toying with a few strands of my hair. "Didn't Clovis tell you? He doesn't mind sharing."

I bared my fangs at him. "Back off."

He didn't heed the warning. Instead, he moved forward and grabbed me by the arm. "You'll find being nice to me will help you with the boss. What do you say, Sabina?"

I grabbed his free arm and twisted it around behind his back. "I say if you ever touch me again, you'll pull back a bloody stump."

With most males, this threat would have been enough. But Frank obviously had training to back up his cockiness. With his feet, he shoved backward, slamming me into a wall so hard I released his wrist. He grabbed my arm and spun me around into a choke hold.

"If you wanted foreplay, you just had to ask," he whispered in my ear.

A comforting surge of adrenaline propelled me as I grabbed his arm and hugged it to me for leverage. With my free hand, I reached back and grabbed the back of his shirt. By adjusting my weight, I managed to flip him over my shoulder easily. His body hit the ground like a sack of potatoes drenched in too much cologne. He lay still for a moment, shocked by the impact. I placed the heel of my boot against his neck.

"You need to learn some manners," I said. "And while you're at it, try a breath mint."

The playful confidence had fled from his eyes, leaving only malice. I'd seen that expression before on men I'd bested. The wounds to their pride hurt far worse than any injury I could inflict.

"You'll regret this," he said, fangs flashing.

"Maybe, but I'd regret fucking you a lot more."

With a final twist of my heel into his trachea that left him gasping, I turned and marched out of the temple. As the door slammed behind me, I knew I'd made a new enemy. But damned if I didn't feel better.

23

The next evening, I woke up feeling even better. I'd slept the sleep of the dead, blessedly undisturbed by dreams. I could hear the TV in the other room and the sounds of Giguhl and Vinca talking.

I lay in bed for a few moments, trying to compel myself to get up. Adam would arrive soon for another lesson and I hadn't had a chance to look over the book he'd given me. Not that I wanted to, but I certainly didn't want another lecture from him.

My little episode with Clovis confused me. Instinctively, I knew analyzing it too much wouldn't help matters. However, if I couldn't get a handle on my stress, it could cause more complications. After all, that little anxiety attack had ruined my chance at killing Clovis and that certainly didn't do anything to calm me.

In assassin training, the first lesson is always to remain calm. Metaphorically losing your head usually results in literally losing your head. It worried me that I'd become so affected by everything going on, I couldn't do my job. I needed to find a way to release some of my stress before I got myself killed. The only question was how. It's not like I was exactly the yoga type. No, the best way I'd found to fight stress was to administer a good ass kicking. But even though my skirmish with Frank helped a little, it hadn't offered the kind of release I needed.

Then, of course, there was the possibility I'd hit some sort of slump. I'd heard of other assassins losing their edge and having to leave the field. Looking at it objectively, I'd have to say screwing up two assassination attempts in as many days might qualify as losing my edge. But I wasn't ready to hand in my guns—yet. After all, if I wasn't an assassin who the hell was I?

With a sigh, I picked my cell phone off the bedside table. Five missed calls. Lavinia had to be furious by now. I needed to figure out my next step, but first I needed to shower.

When I came out of the steamy bathroom, I found Adam lounging on the bed. "What the hell?" I yelped, pulling the towel tighter around my breasts.

"Evening, sunshine," he said.

"Get out." I pointed with my free hand at the door.

"Who woke up on the wrong side of the bed?"

I marched over to the dresser and grabbed some clothes. Ignoring him, I walked straight back to the bathroom and closed the door.

"You're no fun." Adam's muffled voice came through the door. I stuck my tongue out at the panel.

A few moments later, I emerged again, this time clothed in jeans and a long-sleeved black T-shirt. Adam was right where I'd left him, looking amused.

"I didn't know you were so modest."

I dragged the comb through my hair. "Yeah, well, there's a lot you don't know about me."

"I'm starting to get that impression. For instance, I had no idea you and Clovis were an item."

I swung around so fast my wet hair lashed my cheek. "What?"

"You and Clovis."

"We're not an item." I tugged at a few tangles to cover my embarrassment. I so did not want to discuss my love life with Adam.

"If you're not already, you will be soon. I saw how he looked at you last night."

"Look, whatever you think you saw, you're wrong. Nothing is going on between Clovis and me." Except that he's fed from me and I have to kill him, I silently amended.

"Okay, fine, you don't want to admit it. That's cool. I'm just saying even if you're not interested, he is."

"Drop it."

He shrugged and leaned back into the pillows. "You're touchy tonight."

"You know what? You're right." I said, abandoning my hair. "I think maybe we should reschedule the lesson."

Adam sat up. "Hey, I was just kidding."

I sighed. "I know. Look, it's not you. I'm just kind of stressed out right now. I don't think I'm up for it."

Adam opened his mouth to respond when Giguhl walked in.

"What up, peeps?"

I looked at my hairless cat for a moment. " 'What up, peeps'? You've been watching MTV again, haven't you?"

"Word." Giguhl bounded onto the bed. "So what's up?"

"Sabina just told me she doesn't want to work on her magic."

Giguhl's eyes swiveled to me just as I started making slashing motions to my neck at Adam. Caught, I stopped and smiled weakly.

"Sabina, you promised you'd take this seriously." His wrinkly, hairless face was stamped with disapproval.

"Can we talk about this later?"

"No, we cannot. You promised you'd get Adam to help you send me back."

Adam held up his hands. "I already told her I'd help. But my question is: How did you end up as a cat?"

Giguhl shook his head sadly. "The magical misfit over here screwed up a spell."

I stepped in. "Hey, I tried, didn't I? It's not my fault the spell book was wrong."

Giguhl shot me an annoyed look. "Whatever helps you sleep at night, Red."

"Wait a second," Adam slowly dragged his gaze away from Giguhl and focused on me. "You did this? What were you thinking doing magic without any training?"

My cheeks flushed under Adam's stare.

"Have you considered the possibility that Giguhl is your familiar? Most mages have them."

"I'm not really a mage, and he's not my familiar," I said quickly. "He's kind of like a sidekick or something."

Giguhl huffed. "Sidekick my scaly ass. I'm clearly the brains in this operation."

I sent him a look to let him know he wasn't helping.

"Don't look at me like that," he said. "I'm still pissed about having to wear those sweaters."

Adam's eyes widened. "Sweaters?"

I waved him off. "Long story."

Adam rubbed his temple, as if doing so would massage some sense into the situation. "I'm so confused right now."

"Join the club."

Adam opened his mouth to respond, but Giguhl interrupted. "Let's get back to that thing you said about zapping me," he said to Adam. "You're the one who summoned me, so you should be able to send me back to Irkalla, right?"

Adam let out a disgusted sigh and turned to Giguhl. "What tier are you?"

Giguhl sat up straighter. "I'm a fifth-level mischief demon."

"What area of Irkalla do you come from?"

"Gizal, in the southern region near the Pit of Despair."

"Wait," I said. "Can you really send him back?"

Adam nodded, not looking happy. "Yeah. But I wouldn't recommend it. He's still here for a reason."

Giguhl and I ignored Adam and exchanged a look. "Do you want to go back right now?" I asked.

He shrugged. "I guess. I mean, if it's okay with you."

He looked so hopeful that my stomach dropped. I didn't want my friend to leave. But I knew it was unfair to deny him this chance.

"Will he be able to come back?" I asked Adam.

Adam nodded. "Yes, but you'll definitely have to have more training."

I looked back at Giguhl, who was practically squirm-ing with excitement on the bed. I smiled at his enthusi-asm even as my heart felt bruised in my chest. I'd gotten so used to having him around. Even though Adam said I could learn how to summon him again, it wouldn't be fair to do so anytime soon. Taking a deep breath, I said, "If it's what you really want, then it's okay with me."

Giguhl jumped off the bed and wound around my legs. I couldn't hold back my smile at his affection. As he purred "thank you, thank you, thank you," I fought the tightness in my chest.

He pulled away and turned to Adam. "Well, mage, what are you waiting for? Send me home."

Adam looked at me for confirmation and I nodded, despite the churning in my stomach. He picked up his backpack from the floor. From it, he took out a large vial filled with white crystals.

"Sabina, pay attention because your real lessons begin now," Adam said. "Giguhl, stand over there." He pointed to an open space on the floor near the door. When Giguhl was in place, Adam circled him, pouring the white grains around him.

"This is salt. It helps focus the energy of the spell. Blood is best, but salt will do in a pinch." He was all busi-ness now. Next, he took a book from the bag. "Since the demon is from a lower level, you have to tailor the spell to return him to the right place. With more powerful de-mons, it's not as important because their energy is drawn to Irkalla like a magnet."

As he flipped through the book, Giguhl watched me. "Sabina, before I go, I need to tell you something." I tore my glance from Adam to look at my friend. "No matter what happens, remember to trust yourself. Loyalty has its place, but your first responsibility is to yourself."

"Don't go getting all Oprah on me now, demon," I said. The comeback was lost under the tremor in my voice.

"I'm serious," he said. Adam made a show of being engrossed in his book. "Trust your instincts."

The sarcasm drained from me, like a melting piece of armor. "I'm going to miss you," I said, finally putting words to the feelings churning inside me.

"I'm gonna miss you too, kid. Just listen to the mancy here, and he'll teach you how to bring me back if you need me."

"If you two are done with the heartfelt good-byes, I'm ready to do this," Adam said.

Adam began to chant in an ancient tongue I assumed was Hekatian. Within seconds, Giguhl's body became transparent, with a shimmery green aura. "Good-bye," he said just before his outline blinked away entirely.

The whole thing was over in just a few seconds, but it seemed like a lifetime had passed. Adam looked at me and closed the book. "You okay?"

I nodded and rubbed at my eyes, which had mysteriously begun to sting. "You know, I've been trying to get rid of him, but now that he's gone, I wish he wasn't."

Adam placed a hand on my shoulder, an intimacy I didn't shrug off. "The sooner you commit to your training, the sooner you'll know how to bring him back."

Vinca stuck her head in the doorway. "What the heck's going on in here? Why was Adam chanting? Why is there salt all over the floor? And where is Giguhl?" Her rapid-fire delivery made my head spin. Adam stepped in, no doubt understanding I needed a few moments. As he explained what was going on, I walked over to the circle. The collar Giguhl had worn lay in the center. I picked it up and watched the light dance off the metal spikes. I didn't know why I felt so sad. Most of the time, the opinionated demon annoyed the crap out me.

"Sabina? Are you okay?" Vinca asked. I looked up. Vinca and Adam were both looking at me with hangdog expressions. I took the collar, wrapped it around my wrist and tightened it to form a bracelet.

"I'm fine." I stood and straightened the pillows on the bed. Needing a distraction, I said, "Adam, let's talk shop."

Adam smiled a real smile, not his normal smirk. Without a word, he went to grab his backpack from where he'd left it on the floor.

"I guess I'll leave you guys to it then," Vinca said. I nodded, but wasn't really paying attention. Now that I had a reason to learn magic, I was determined not to screw up again.

Adam pulled a small book from his backpack and handed it to me. The faded red leather cover had no markings and when I opened it, the pages were blank. "What's this?"

"It's a journal. That's your starter grimoire. I want you to take notes on all the spells I teach you. Eventually you'll want to buy a more substantial book that you can fill with your own charms and potion recipes."

"Do you have one of these, too?" I asked. He nodded. "Can I see it?"

"Mine is back in New York under lock and key. Most of us are very protective of our personal grimoires." He pointed to the book. "Since you're just starting out, be sure and keep it with you at all times. That way you can jot down questions for me or ideas you have."

I was strangely touched by Adam's gift. I knew it was just a stupid journal, but it felt more important than that.

"Thanks," I said.

He tilted his head and his lips quirked into a smile. "No problem." Our eyes held for a few moments. I broke the contact and cleared my throat. Adam stood straighter and shuffled his feet. "Anyway, tonight we're going to learn about creating and breaking circles."

I grabbed a pen from the bedside table and opened the book. Before he could begin, however, my cell phone rang. My heart picked up speed, knowing who was calling. I paused, trying to decide what to do. If I took the call, I'd no doubt be ordered to report to her immediately. Obviously, that option held little appeal.

Adam frowned when I let it ring. "Who is it?" he asked.

I clicked the "end" button. "No one."

24

*H*er goon found me the next night. I was heading to my favorite feeding ground when the black car pulled up next to the curb. A male vamp with wide shoulders and a no-nonsense attitude stepped out of the car. He wore a black suit with the Dominae's emblem, a gold fleur-de-lis, embroidered on the pocket. I didn't argue when he told me my presence had been "requested." It was time to face the music with my grandmother.

She waited for me in the house where we'd met a few days earlier. As I walked slowly into the room, her eyes took in everything. Self-conscious, I straightened my spine and tried to project confidence I didn't feel. Her anger was more pungent that the smell of ashes coming from the fireplace behind her. I knelt down and waited for acknowledgement.

"How dare you ignore your orders." Not exactly the warm greeting I'd hoped for.

I slowly stood and tried to look abashed. "Grandmother, I'm sorry I haven't returned your calls. There have been complications.".

She slashed a hand through the air. "I don't want to hear excuses, girl. Clovis is alive. You failed. End of story."

I shook my head, trying to figure out how to spin my miserable failures. "Actually, I think I've found a better way to approach his death."

She raised her eyebrows, but still appeared skeptical. "This had better be good. The other Dominae are ready to put a price on your head."

My heart kicked up a notch, but I soldiered on. "What if we waited until the vineyard attack? That way we'd not only kill Clovis but also his best men. His organization would be crippled without anyone to assume the reins."

She went still, her face expressionless. My instincts urged me to continue, to justify, but I held them back. Silence conveyed confidence.

"Why should I trust you now when you have repeatedly failed?"

That stung, but I gritted my teeth and ignored the slight collapse in my confidence. "Think about it. The attack will be chaotic. I should have plenty of opportunity to kill Clovis and his guards." I swallowed, hating what I was about to say, but knowing it would assuage her. "If you still have doubts about my abilities, you could even set a small contingent of your guards in ambush, ensuring the deed is done properly."

She tapped her chin with her forefinger, considering my plan. "It could work," she said finally. "However, when all of this is done, don't think there won't be repercussions for your failures."

I bowed my head. "Yes, Domina. I understand."

"I'll talk to Tanith and Persephone. In the meantime, you must fill me in on the plans. I assume you have not failed in that area as well?"

Resentment churned like acid in my belly. I knew I'd screwed up, but did she have to rub it in? I'd warned them from the beginning that I wasn't a spy. My job usually entailed following someone and putting a bullet in them. All this cloak-and-dagger bullshit wasn't my strength.

"Well?" Grandmother's impatience with me was clear. I tamped down my pride and nodded.

"I know the plan."

"Excellent. You may tell it to me now."

As I went over the plans with her, I reminded myself to be grateful for this second chance. A small voice in the back of my head worried about how Adam and the other mages might fare during the ambush. I put a muzzle on it. My first loyalty was to my own kind. I was raised a Lilim. Despite my recent experiences learning more about my mage heritage, I didn't want to live a dual life as both vampire and mage. The Dominae wouldn't stand for it. My grandmother would freak if she ever found out I'd been taking lessons in magic, let alone that I was consorting with mages and nymphs.

I tried to convince myself that hanging with Adam and Vinca was just part of my assignment. That it didn't mean anything. But the truth was, along with Giguhl, they had become my friends. Well, maybe *friend* was too strong a word. I didn't hate them like I did most beings.

But they'd hate me when they found out I'd been playing both sides of this. I could only hope I'd be long gone before they realized my role in the ambush. And if not, well, there wasn't much I could do about it. Duty came before . . . not hating them.

This time, when Adam showed up for training I was dressed, caffeinated, and ready to go. Vinca let him in, and when he saw me sitting casually on the couch his eyebrows shot to his hairline.

"You're up early."

"That's because someone I know has a nasty habit of showing up at least a half-hour early for training sessions."

"Fair enough," he said. I couldn't put my finger on it but he seemed almost nervous. His normal easy smile seemed forced. "I assume you're ready to get started?" I nodded and set my mug on the coffee table.

"I thought we'd take a field trip for tonight's lesson." I noticed tension in his shoulders, almost as if he expected me to balk.

"Oh? Where?" I kept my tone casual, but something wasn't right.

"It's a surprise."

Curious, I shrugged. "Whatever you say, Teach."

He relaxed a fraction then and turned to Vinca. As they bantered, I shrugged off my earlier suspicions. Perhaps I was letting my meeting with Lavinia get to me. Guilt and doubt plagued me at odd intervals. Like earlier, when Vinca already had a fresh pot of coffee made especially for me when I woke up. For some reason, I knew she'd be the most hurt by my betrayal. Even though she wouldn't be at the vineyard during the attack, she'd be devastated when she found out I was responsible for

Clovis's death. Further, I didn't want to think about how losing Clovis would affect her. She worshipped him and truly believed in his teachings, even if he didn't.

"Sabina?" Vinca said, interrupting my maudlin thoughts.

"Hmm?"

She rolled her eyes. "I said, don't you think Adam looks nice tonight?"

That was a major understatement. Tonight he'd skipped his usual urban commando look and opted for faded jeans and a tight black sweater. The black brought out the golden highlights in his hair and made the green in his eyes deeper, like moss. Not to mention the way the shirt clung in all the right places to his impressive biceps and taut chest. No doubt about it, the mage was a hottie.

I shook myself. "I guess so," I said with a shrug.

"Oh, stop," he said. "You're going to make me blush."

Vinca giggled and slapped his bicep playfully. "Don't listen to her," she said, sending me a mock frown. "You're a total stud."

He smiled at her. "Don't try to charm me, nymph. I know all about how you girls operate."

Vinca batted her eyelashes at him. "*Moi?* I wouldn't dare think of seducing you. I prefer my males like rocks—dumb and hard."

Adam laughed out loud and even I cracked a smile. Vinca sashayed away, her hips swaying. I shook my head at Adam. "She's a piece of work, isn't she?"

He chuckled. "I pity the poor male she really sets her sights on. He won't stand a chance."

I grabbed my purse. "You ready to go?"

He blinked at my abrupt change in subject, but walked

to the door. I didn't like the green spike of jealousy I'd had when Vinca had been flirting with Adam. I didn't have any right to it, but there it was. It didn't seem to matter that their flirtation had been a joke.

Adam opened the door for me and indicated I should precede him. I swung my hair over my shoulder and didn't meet his gaze as I passed. However, I couldn't help taking a deep breath of the pleasing scent of spicy soap mixed with sandalwood. Someone should bottle that stuff.

"I thought we'd take my car," Adam said as he followed me down the walkway to the street. The beep of a car alarm disengaging caught my attention. A black SUV sat across the street.

"Nice wheels," I said.

"It gets me around," he said. I frowned at his understatement. The thing was huge with blinged-out rims. When he opened the door for me, I noticed soft Corinthian leather and burled wood on the dash.

His mood had shifted again as he pulled away from the curb. I tried to breech the silence. "So, you're from New York?"

He nodded as he turned onto the freeway, heading north. "Manhattan."

"Where is the Hekate Council headquartered?"

"North of the city."

At that point, I figured out he wasn't in a sharing mood. I settled back into my seat with a sigh, watching the city speed past.

When we crossed over the Golden Gate, I started to get restless. "Where are we going?"

He jumped, almost as if he had forgotten my presence.

He glanced at me out of the corner of his eye and shifted in his seat. "Muir Woods."

"The national park?" I asked. "Isn't it closed this time of night?"

He shot me a look. "For mortals."

I nodded, thoughtful. "What? Are you going to teach me about plant life or something? We should have brought Vinca."

"No, not plant life."

I frowned, wondering at his mysteriousness tonight. "Adam, just tell me, already."

"We're going to meet a faery by the name of Briallen Pimpernell. Sound familiar?"

His question seemed a tad too casual. "No," I said. "Should it?"

He pulled off the 101 where a sign directed us to Muir Woods. "Yeah," he said finally. "It should."

"Why do I have a feeling this isn't just some random field trip?"

He stopped at a red light and turned to me. "Because it's not. Briallen was there when you were born."

My stomach lurched. "What?" I whispered.

"I lied to you when I said we were training tonight." Adam pushed the accelerator. I barely felt the movement because of the shock of his admission. "We're going to meet with Briallen because it's time for you to learn the truth."

I was almost too scared to ask, but I did anyway. "What truth?"

"I'll leave it to Briallen to tell you."

25

The faery greeted us on a stone bridge that spanned a bubbling creek. Night sounds served as an organic soundtrack to our hushed introductions.

Despite my wariness after Adam's cryptic remarks in the car, I found myself liking Briallen Pimpernell right away. She stood barely five feet tall with a body shaped like a pear. The wrinkles around her eyes and mouth served as evidence of a lifetime of laughter. She took my cold hand in her soft, warm palms and smiled.

"My, how you have grown, young lady. Last time I saw you, your small face was purple with rage as you screamed for your mother's breast."

I felt myself flushing, embarrassed for some reason I couldn't fathom. Perhaps it was the fact this woman gave the impression of knowing everything about me. The knowledge was in her alert eyes, which darted like a small bird's, catching every nuance.

"I'm afraid I don't remember you," I said.

"Ah, well, we shall remedy that soon enough. Please,

come out of this soggy night. My cottage is nearby if you can stand to walk for a bit longer?"

Adam nodded for both of us. "Thank you. I appreciate your taking the time to meet with us."

She nodded and waddled off across the bridge. Adam looked at me, as if checking to make sure I wasn't going to bolt in the opposite direction. Funny. If you'd asked me back in the car, I'd have guessed the same thing myself. But now, after meeting the faery, I felt intrigued to know whatever she could tell me about my birth.

Without a word, I marched after her, despite my aching feet. Not for the first time since our hike into the woods started an hour earlier, I wished Adam had thought to tell me to change my shoes before we left the apartment. While he wore broken-in Doc Martens, I had opted for high-heeled boots. Not the best footwear for picking one's way through undergrowth or bounding over fallen logs. More than once, my heels had sunk into the damp stew of moist earth and leaves. Mindful of this, I took to mincing on my toes. I must have looked ridiculous, but Adam never said a word. Proof he also felt tension over the meeting with Briallen.

A few minutes later, lights appeared ahead. The soft glow came through small windows at the front of a cottage nestled between a copse of trees and another creek. A cheerful plume of smoke rose from the chimney.

Adam had caught up with me and plodded along, silent. "I didn't think anyone could live in a national park." I commented under my breath.

"They can't. Faery magic prevents the mortals from detecting her presence."

I made a silent O with my mouth. Again, I wondered

how I could have lived so long and not known more about the other races. Of course, the answer was my grandmother. She'd kept me fairly sheltered at the temple in my youth, teaching me about vampire history and customs. That education included instilling a healthy distrust of anything nonvampire.

Briallen shooed us inside the warmth of the cottage. The scents of herbs and fire mingled to create a homey atmosphere. This impression was buttressed by cozy-looking chairs and aged wooden tables throughout the small space. Adam and I both had to duck down to fit under the thatched ceiling.

The faery bustled around, pushing mugs of spiced wine into our hands and urging us to take seats. I carefully perched on the edge of a rickety wooden chair with a flat cushion covered in calico. Adam followed my example in the chair next to mine. Briallen set out a plate of cheese and bread before finally sitting in a tattered armchair across from us.

"Forgive my excitement," she said. "It's not often I have such esteemed guests in my humble abode."

Adam waved off the compliment. "We are the ones who are honored." I darted a glance at him, wondering where he'd learned such diplomacy.

Briallen chuckled away his flattery. "Now, you said you wished to discuss the circumstances of sweet Sabina's birth?"

I blushed, utterly charmed by the woman's innate goodness. She fairly glowed with maternal warmth. Beside me, Adam grasped his mug in both hands and leaned forward, resting his elbows on his knees.

"I was hoping you could tell us about Sabina's parents."

Briallen's head tilted to the side, like a curious bird. "I'm afraid I never met the father." She sent me a sympathetic glance. "He passed before Phoebe came to me."

"Why did she come to you?" I said. I ignored Adam's look and focused on the faery.

"Surely you've been told the story?" She looked from me to Adam, who shook his head.

"Actually," I cut in, "I know a little. But not about the birth. Mainly just the circumstances leading to it."

Briallen clucked her tongue. "Well, then, we shall start from there." She took a deep breath, as if relaxing into her tale. "Back then, births happened at home. My breed—we call ourselves the Spae—specialized in these matters and were often sought out by members of all the species to assist. I suppose you could say we were midwives of a sort. I had developed somewhat of a reputation in these parts and my services were in high demand." She flushed, as if embarrassed to brag on herself. I nodded eagerly, encouraging her to continue.

"That summer, I was contacted by emissaries from both the Dominae and the Hekate Council. They said they had a delicate matter and needed my assistance. They said a forbidden match between a mage and a vampire had occurred. The young vampire female was with child and they needed me to oversee the birth. This news shocked me because usually anyone found breaking these laws was put to death immediately. However, when they offered me a king's ransom to do the task, I naturally assumed those involved were most likely of noble classes, which might explain why they were allowed to live.

"I agreed readily to the terms, despite their odd-ness. You see, normally I performed my services at the client's home, arriving once the female was already in labor. However, in this case, they wanted me to shelter the girl here starting immediately. She was only about four months along, so you can imagine my surprise that they wanted her to stay with me for the remaining eight months of her year-long pregnancy."

"Wait. My mother lived here?" I looked around the room, as if some trace of her lingered.

Briallen smiled, seeming unperturbed by my inter-ruption. "Patience, child."

I nodded and sat back in my chair, trying to put a lid on the questions bubbling at the tip of my tongue. Adam placed a warm hand on my arm. The sight of his golden skin resting on my own pale forearm reassured me.

"Where was I?" Briallen said. "Oh, yes, so even though the terms were quite unusual, I agreed. Of course, the money made a difference, but more than that I was curious. As far as I knew, I would be witness to the first mixed-blood birth in many centuries. The thought of being part of this historic event exhilarated me even as it frightened me."

"Why were you frightened?" Adam asked.

She shrugged a rounded shoulder. "In addition to the obvious political implications, I was terrified the child might die. Or what if the melding of the two species resulted in deformities? In those days, before the dark races began to rely on modern medicine, many of my colleagues lost their lives due to a belief the midwife had somehow hexed the child."

I leaned forward, completely engrossed. She had a

knack for storytelling, and I wondered idly if it was a distinctly faery trait or a personal one.

"Phoebe arrived a week later, accompanied by Lavinia, your grandmother," she said, nodding at me, "as well as a maid, whom your mother would use for feedings. Your grandmother left quickly, as if she could barely stand the sight of her daughter. Phoebe seemed heartbroken, but whether this was from your grandmother's quick departure or the sad circumstances that brought her to my door, I cannot say."

"What did she look like?" Adam asked, voicing the question in my own head.

Briallen smiled wistfully. "She was a vampire princess in every sense. Her hair was the color of fresh-picked strawberries, and it fell in soft curls around her face. Her skin was pale as milkweed down, with a sprinkling of freckles over her nose. She had fawn eyes, bright with intelligence. The only imperfection I could detect that first day was the swollen circles under her eyes, indicating many recently shed tears. However, on that first day she had steel in her spine, as if daring me to judge her. I did not.

"She spoke as little as possible for the first few weeks. She'd sleep all day, in the little room just through that door." She pointed to a roughly carved door to the right of the fire. "At night, she would take long walks through the forest, refusing any offers of company. Every so often, she allowed me to examine her. I tried to talk to her about innocent subjects, like the weather or her favorite flowers, but she remained closed. Until one day.

"The maid and I were chatting in front of the fire about herbal remedies, when the door crashed open and Phoebe

rushed in. She talked so fast, we could not understand
her. I tried to calm her, worried she might make herself
sick. That's when she told me she'd felt the babe's first
kick. For the first time since she'd come, I was blessed
with a smile. It was as if that little flutter had opened
something inside her. From then on, she made more effort to discuss the pregnancy. She knew very little about
the process and confided a great deal of worry about
what was to come. We had long talks about her symp-
toms and concerns. She even started inviting me with her
on her walks. We'd talk about the life growing inside her
within the comforting womb of the forest, which seemed
to relax her somewhat.

"One night, we walked in companionable silence
under the towering redwoods, so tall you could barely
see the underside of the first branches in the dark. By
this time, I quite enjoyed our nightly excursions. Phoebe
had a keen intellect and could talk about a variety of subjects with great authority—literature, history, the Great
Mother—but never the one subject I sensed she longed
to talk about most. Until that night under the redwoods.
'I suppose you've been wondering about the father,' she
said. I confessed to a certain curiosity, but told her she
need not discuss him if the subject was too painful.

"Your mother sat on a lichen-covered log, her hair
glistening in the moonlight. If I had not known better, I
would have guessed her to be a wood sprite, she looked
so at home in the setting. I waited patiently, knowing she
would open up to me when she was ready. She started
slowly, choosing her words carefully. 'His name was
Tristan,' she said. 'He is dead.'

"I couldn't help my gasp at her admission. She didn't

seem to hear it, lost as she was in her own memories. Sadness embraced her like an aura. Over the next hour, she told me how they had fought their forbidden attraction and how ultimately they were helpless against it. She said she knew it was wrong, yet she loved him. It was obvious to me, she spoke not of adolescent love, that fleeting emotion fueled by hormones. No, Phoebe's love for her mage was real, the kind that stands the test of time and even death."

I felt Adam's eyes on me. Turning to look at him, I was suddenly aware of a curious wetness on my cheeks. "You okay?" he asked.

"Oh dear," the faery said before I could answer. "I'm sorry if I've upset you, child."

I swiped my hands over my cheeks. "I'm fine. Please go on."

"You're sure?" Adam said. At some point, his hand had moved from my arm to grasp my hand. Now his grip tightened reassuringly. I nodded for Briallen to continue.

"Do you know the story of his death?" Briallen asked gently.

"Yes, he was found dead not long after my mother found out she was pregnant. The murderer was never caught."

Briallen sat up straighter. "Who told you this?"

"My grandmother. Why?"

"My child, I'm sorry but your mother told quite a different tale. According to Phoebe, your father disappeared and was assumed dead. No one ever found his body."

I frowned, wondering if the old woman's memory wasn't as reliable as I'd thought. "But that can't be right.

Why would they assume he was dead if they never found his body."

Adam cleared his throat and shifted. I glanced at him, but he didn't meet my eyes.

"Phoebe told me they discovered blood in his rooms," Briallen said.

"Perhaps my grandmother was trying to spare her feelings?" I guessed.

The faery frowned, seeming unconvinced, yet said, "Perhaps. I'm afraid that's one mystery we cannot solve this evening. Regardless of how your father disappeared, it was obvious Phoebe was heartbroken. And who could blame her? The entire ordeal smacked of a Greek tragedy. However, I was glad for one thing. Phoebe obviously needed to talk about what had happened and what would happen. She had no one else to turn to, so I was happy to be her confidante. During my monthly reports to the Dominae and Hekate Council, I left out these revelations and reported simply on her glowing health and growing girth.

"In fact, at some point, I realized her stomach was expanding at an abnormal rate. In those days, we didn't have fancy machines to see inside the belly, but I knew without a doubt the reason."

Adam's hand tightened on mine. I sent him an annoyed look for the distraction, but something in his gaze stopped me. I started to question the concerned anticipation in his expression, but Briallen, lost in her story, continued.

"Phoebe was about seven months along when I told her the good news. Twins!"

I jumped out of my seat before I knew what I was doing. "What?" My veins felt filled with liquid caffeine.

Briallen pulled back, confusion and shock on her own face. "I—you mean, you did not know? How is that possible?"

I rounded on Adam. "What do you take me for? Who is this woman?"

He held up a placating hand. "Sabina," he said, his voice mellow, like one would use to soothe a wild animal.

"Don't 'Sabina' me! What are you playing at? How much did you pay her to tell these lies?"

Briallen rose and approached me slowly with her hands held out in a pleading gesture. "I am so sorry. I thought you knew."

Adam stood slowly, ignoring the old woman in favor of watching me warily. I couldn't blame him, I certainly felt capable of extreme violence at that moment. "She's telling the truth," he said simply.

My body hurtled toward Adam like a bullet, my speed giving me the advantage. I managed to slam him into the wall before he reacted. I wasn't thinking. The need to inflict pain outweighed logic.

"Sabina, stop!" Briallen's plea was lost in a volley of grunts as Adam and I grappled. A table fell over, sending a basket of herbs crashing to the floor. I punched and kicked and hissed my anger at the mage. Soon, I realized he wasn't fighting back, just warding off blows.

"Fight me, dammit!" I slapped him across the face, the resulting crack sounded unnaturally loud in the small space.

"No." Adam got a hand free and waved it, muttering

something under his breath. I lunged again, but this time, a weird tingling sensation spread through my limbs. I was paralyzed from the neck down. I was too shocked by the sudden loss of movement to speak.

"Now," Adam panted, "You're going to listen." He bent down and righted the table before speaking again.

"Sabina, I know—" He paused. "I know you must hate me right now. But I swear upon my life Briallen's telling the truth."

I shook my head and closed my eyes, trying to block him out. I wanted to run—to flee from him and the truth he was forcing on me. But I couldn't move.

"Her name is Maisie."

I opened my eyes and looked at him for the first time. He looked as bad as I felt. Dark circles of worry weighed down his eyes, and his cheeks were covered in tiny scratches. I noted these things only obliquely. What I focused on was the utter sincerity and regret in his eyes.

"How do you know this?" My voice sounded foreign to me, vulnerable.

He looked down at his hands. "She sent me to find you."

"Why?"

He looked up, meeting my eyes. "She wants to meet you."

"No, why didn't I know about her?"

Briallen's voice cut in. "After your poor mother died only a few minutes after you were born, Lavinia and Ameritat decided the only way to keep the peace was for you to be separated. It was agreed that you should never know about each other to prevent further upheaval within the races."

"Then how did she," I couldn't bring myself to say my sister's name, "find out about me?"

"Maisie was unaware of your existence for a time. However, at some point she started having vivid dreams that were coming true. Your father's mother, Ameritat, realized then Maisie had the second sight. A few years ago, she had a dream about you. Ameritat had no choice but to tell Maisie about your existence with the blessings of the Hekate Council. Only she made Maisie promise never to seek you out while Ameritat was alive."

"So what changed?"

"Ameritat died last year. Now that she's gone, Maisie has risen to her grandmother's position on the council."

Holy crap, I thought. Not only did I have a sister, but also she was the leader of the freaking mancies.

"How can I believe you?" I asked.

He thought for a moment. "There's one thing. Briallen, were there any distinguishing characteristics on the girls when they were born?"

Briallen looked at him strangely for a moment, then her eyes widened. Adam nodded encouragingly, as if already knowing what she was going to say. "Why, yes, now that you mention it. Both had identical birthmarks on their shoulder blades. Eight-pointed stars."

My mouth fell open and my knees went weak. I looked at Adam. Now I knew why he asked Briallen to tell me. Adam would have had a chance to see my birthmark, but Briallen wouldn't have.

"Please," I said. "You could have told her that."

He sighed and shook his head, obviously thinking me too stubborn for my own good. "Anything else?" he asked Briallen.

"They were both born behind the veil."

"Huh?" I asked, turning to her.

She smiled. "It means you were both born with cauls—a thin membrane left over from the amniotic sac."

"Gross." I had no idea why she felt the need to share that little tidbit.

"Actually, they're a sign of good luck," Briallen said. "Usually the child will have psychic powers."

"Usually?" Adam asked.

"Some believe cauls mean the child has been marked by a demon," Briallen said. "But I'm sure that's not the case with you or your sister."

Since my psychic powers left a lot to be desired, I really hoped the faery was just sharing an old wives' tale. Adam didn't say anything, but his face had taken on a thoughtful expression as he looked at me.

"Where do you come into play in all this?" My voice shook as I spoke to him. I felt like my life had suddenly become an episode of *Twilight Zone*.

He shifted on his feet and cut his eyes in Briallen's direction. "The Council trusts me to handle certain delicate matters."

I could tell that was all I was going to get from him. Given my own profession and its resulting need for discretion, I could even respect it. However, I couldn't respect his lies.

"So why not just tell me all this from the beginning?"

His eyes widened with incredulity. "Right. Like you wouldn't have just beat me up and walked away."

He had a point, but I still wasn't happy. "What about the mages? And the training? Were those just cover-ups to get close to me?"

He shook his head quickly. "The missing mages were part of my assignment. I couldn't believe it when I found out you were involved. It was too strange to be coincidence, but I still can't figure out how it could have been anything else. As for the magical training, that was also part of my mission. Maisie felt you might feel more comfortable meeting with her if you understood more about the mage culture."

I thought about this for a moment, trying to sort through the static in my brain. "Let me see if I have everything then." I ticked items off on my fingers. "I have a twin sister who's been raised as a mage. My grandmother has been lying to me my entire life. You are some super secret agent for the Hekate Council sent to find me and educate me about mages. Also, you just so happen to be looking for the same mages I've been ordered by Clovis to free. Does that about cover it?"

His lips quirked. "Sounds about right."

"Actually, it sounds like some screwed-up soap opera from hell, if you ask me." Despite my earlier freak-out, I was finally starting to think clearly again. Sure, I had a lot to sort through. It's not every day a girl finds out she has secret twin sister, or that the person she trusted most in the world betrayed her by keeping that sister a secret. But I was in control of the pain these revelations caused, channeling them into an emotion I was more comfortable with.

His lips twitched. "Good to see the sarcasm returning. Does this mean you aren't going to beat me up any more?"

"Don't count on it, mancy. I'm feeling a little unpredictable right now."

His expression got serious again. "Sabina, I know this probably won't mean much, but I'm sorry."

"Sorry?"

"I know this has to be really hard for you."

"Life is hard, Adam."

"Stop it," he said. "You have a right to be hurt by all this. Or at least angry."

"Oh, I'm angry. I'm so angry I could self-combust."

"Shit, you are going to hit me, aren't you?"

"Don't be stupid," I said. "I'm going to get even."

26

After apologizing to Briallen for my outburst, we left with a promise to visit again soon. She seemed disappointed we were leaving before she could tell the rest of her story. But I'd heard enough. Besides, I knew how it went: My mother died—end of story.

I didn't need to hear how it happened or why. Maybe I should have mourned her loss, but how could I miss someone I never even knew? Especially when I was left to pay for her mistakes. I wondered if my sister had been punished for my father's mistakes, too.

The walk back to the car was uneventful, each of us lost in our own thoughts. Okay, that's not totally true. I was numb and tried to do as little thinking as possible. But those damned thoughts came anyway. By the time we drove away from the park, I knew it was time to come clean with Adam.

"Adam?" I watched the trees pass instead of looking at him.

"Yeah?"

"I need to tell you something." I shifted to look at him. Quickly, before I could stop myself, I started talking. "I never defected from the Dominae. I've been playing Clovis this whole time in order to gather information." He opened his mouth to speak, but I held up a hand.

"It gets worse. My original mission was to assassinate Clovis, but the plan changed." I paused, not wanting to admit to my treachery, to dig the hole deeper.

"Changed how?" He'd gone very still.

"The night of the vineyard attack, a small force of Dominae guards will ambush."

As the seconds ticked by with no response from Adam, I held my breath. The car slowed and he finally pulled to a stop on the shoulder of the highway. He turned toward me, with his arm draped across the top of the steering wheel. "And?"

"And what?" I said, taken aback. "Aren't you angry?"

Adam rubbed a hand down his face. "As far as I'm concerned, it changes nothing. My goal all along was to save the mages being held captive. This battle of wills between Clovis and the Dominae doesn't affect my plans."

"Weren't you listening?" I said, not understanding his lack of concern. "They're going to ambush the rescue operation. You won't be walking out of there with your friends. In fact, you'll be lucky if you walk out of it at all."

"Let me ask you a question," he said, his expression serious. "Why did you tell me all this?"

I tilted my head, trying to understand his angle behind the question. "I guess I just felt like I should warn you."

"Is that all?"

I started to answer, but he held up a hand. "Because

honestly? I think you told me because you're trying to avoid talking about what just happened. I think everything you've learned tonight and over the past couple of weeks has proven the Dominae have done nothing but lie to you from the beginning. And you don't want to face that. To accept that this means your loyalties need to shift."

I crossed my arms and leaned back into the door. "So what? You want me to betray the only family I've ever known for Clovis? Give me a break."

"Not for Clovis, Sabina. For yourself. Don't you think you owe it to yourself to face the fact the Dominae have never accepted you fully because of something your parents did? Don't you owe it to yourself to explore this other half of yourself that you've denied? To learn about the other family who has sought you out? You have the power to do something good here. Help me save them."

The muscles in my neck tightened involuntarily. Adam was another in a line of beings who saw me as a means to their own ends. When I'm merely mad, I yell. When I'm full-on angry, my voice turns to ice. So when I responded, icicles hung from my words. "I find it interesting that you tell me to do something for myself, but what you really mean is you want me to do something for you."

He tipped his chin, acknowledging my verbal parry. "Touché. I do need your help. But that doesn't undercut the principle. This is all going to end badly. Either way, mage-kind and vampire-kind are going to war in the not-so-distant future. You're going to have to choose a side. Are you going to fight for the side that lied to you your whole life? Or are you going to give the Hekate Council, and your sister, a chance?"

"Wait a second." I leaned forward, not believing my ears. "We were talking about the mission. Now you want me to choose sides in a war that hasn't even started yet? And you ask me to trust a sister I've never met? That's not fair, Adam."

"Life isn't fair, Sabina. The sooner you come to terms with the fact your grandmother betrayed you, the sooner we can figure out where to go from here."

I dug my fingernails into the leather seat. "What do you mean 'we'? You're not the one who was betrayed."

"You're right. They betrayed *you*. They lied to you. They used you. They pretended to love you and have your best interests at heart. But the truth is, they never did." His voice was quiet, and the pity I detected there caused something to shift inside me. It was like a light switch flipped on, and its illumination made it impossible to deny the truth any longer.

My chest felt swollen, like a scream was building. I knew if I let it escape, I'd never stop. I skimmed the surface of my feelings, afraid to dive too deep and drown. My whole life was based on lies. *Honor, loyalty, family*—these words were currency used by my grandmother to manipulate me. My eyes stung with the realization that my loyalty had been misplaced. That my own flesh and blood used me. Silly Sabina, hoping one day, if she just tried hard enough, she'd be thrown a few meager scraps of approval. I was a fool. A patsy. A goddamned idiot.

Adam waited patiently, pretending not to notice the hot tears sliding down my cheeks. Pretending not to see me try to hide the rapidly forming cracks in my façade. Watching me pretend I could handle watching my life disintegrate before my eyes. I took one more shaky breath and swiped at the tears. I gathered my pain to me and collapsed it into a tight ball of bitterness.

"They'll pay." Adam reached out to me, but I waved his hand off. "I want to make them—her—suffer for lying to me. For making me feel like a freak my whole life." My voice cracked. I cleared my throat and speared Adam with a look. "But that doesn't mean I'm suddenly switching allegiances to a race I don't even know. That's trading the devil I know for the one I don't. From now on, the only loyalty I have is to myself."

"Fair enough," he said. "All I'm asking is that you give me a chance to teach you about the mage side of yourself. To introduce you to your own flesh and blood—your sister."

I started shaking my head before all the words had left his mouth. I so was not ready to meet my sister. Hell, I still wasn't sure if I believed she existed. Adam saw this and took my hand. This time I let him.

"I know it's a lot. You don't have to meet her tomorrow or anything. Let's just get through the next few days. Come up with a plan to get revenge on the Dominae and save the mages. Can you at least agree to that much?"

I thought about it for a few moments. My head felt swollen with conflicting emotions. It was a similar feeling to the one I had with Clovis just before that anxiety attack hit. I knew if I didn't do something, I was going to lose it again, and that I definitely didn't want to do in front of Adam. I'd made enough of an ass of myself in front of him already. Taking a deep breath, I tried to clear my head of all the static. I told myself to take everything one step at a time. If I tried to process it all at once, I might implode.

My breath escaped with a big sigh. "All right. I'll help you figure out a way to save the mages."

Adam's smile lit up the darkened car. He leaned forward and grabbed me in a tight hug, and for a moment, I let myself enjoy the feel of his solid body against mine. I suppose part of it might have been the attraction I'd been denying for the last couple of weeks, but underneath that was an instinct that I could trust this male with my life. It wasn't often I'd met someone I could trust to have my back in battle, both the physical or emotional kinds. But as I bathed in his scent and absorbed his warmth, I let out a breath. Surrender. I couldn't control what was going to come. But I could control this moment.

Adam pulled back, his hands still on my shoulders, and smiled at me reassuringly. "It's all going to be okay," he said. "Together, we'll figure out what comes next."

I swallowed, overcome by a rush of tenderness. Perhaps I just felt like I needed to lose myself. Or maybe the emotional nature of the night left me vulnerable. All I know is I launched myself at Adam.

Our lips met in an ungraceful mash of teeth and lips. It didn't matter. We figured out the rhythm soon enough. His hands grasped my face as he angled me for better position. I responded by nipping his lower lip with my right fang, giving me just a quick taste of his blood. He groaned, his tongue delving into my mouth. It was as if we tried to consume each other. We were a tangle of lips and teeth and tongues and hands. Our harsh breathing served as an erotic soundtrack for our frenzied explorations.

As is usually the case with ill-advised groping, the harsh ring of a cell phone interrupted our make-out session. "Ignore it," Adam said as he cupped my breast roughly. I gasped as he licked my neck, just above my vein. The phone rang again, sounding more insistent this time. He moved back to my mouth. I ignored the sound of the irritating device as I lost myself in the mage I had no right to be kissing. The ringing stopped soon enough and we continued to explore each other with frustrated caresses.

Until the phone rang again. Adam cursed and pulled away. "I'll just turn it off," he said, grabbing the offending phone from the dashboard. He glanced down at the readout and grimaced. "Shit, it's Clovis. Should I take it?"

I had been sprawled on the seat, panting with lust. My shirt had somehow become bunched under my arms and my black lace bra stood in stark contrast against my white skin. However, that name acted like a douse of cold water on my fevered skin. I sat up quickly and pulled my shirt down to cover myself. Adam watched with obvious disappointment.

"I guess that means playtime is over?"

I nodded and looked away, not ashamed really, just disgusted at my lack of self-control. I was a little long in the fang to be necking in a car on the side of the highway.

Adam blew out a breath and hit the button to call Clovis back. I glanced at him from the corner of my eye and watched him adjust himself with a pained expression. He muttered something under his breath that I didn't quite catch.

"It's Lazarus," Adam said in a clipped tone. "Couldn't

reach the phone. Yeah, well, you've got me now, so start talking."

I felt a small smile form at the corner of my mouth. Obviously, he wasn't talking to Clovis. The only person I'd heard him talk like that to was Frank.

"Now?" he said. "Impossible." He listened for a moment, his frown growing deeper. "I'll be there in an hour. Tough. That's the soonest I can be there." With that, he punched the "end" button and tossed the phone back onto the dash.

"What was that all about?"

He sighed and ran a hand through his hair, which did nothing to repair the damage caused earlier by my own hands. The rumpled locks did nothing to dim his sex appeal. "Frank needs to see me. Said it was urgent and he couldn't discuss it over the phone."

"Just you?" I asked.

"Yeah, he said there's some problems getting some of the supplies I needed."

"That's odd. I wonder why it couldn't wait." This was the first I'd heard of any supply problems. Since Vinca was in charge of that area, I wondered why she hadn't mentioned anything.

"Who knows?" He started the car. "I'll drop you off at the apartment first."

I didn't really want to talk about it, but I held my breath waiting for him to broach the subject of the kiss—kisses, whatever. When he merely put the car in gear and pulled back onto the highway, I relaxed a little.

I watched him surreptitiously as he drove. His posture was relaxed with one wrist draped over the wheel, giving the impression of a man enjoying a nice drive. But the

muscle working in his jaw told a different story. I decided
to keep my mouth shut, knowing we each had bigger issues to worry about.

Soon we were back in the city. Crossing the bridge, I
realized it had been a while since I'd eaten. With all the
stress recently, I hadn't been getting regular meals and it
was wreaking havoc on me.

"Pull over," I said as we neared the park I usually
hunted in.

"Why?" He pulled over anyway.

"I need to feed. You can just drop me off now and I'll
walk home from here."

"Are you sure? I don't mind waiting. Frank isn't going
anywhere."

"No, it's fine. The apartment's only a few blocks
away." I opened the door and hopped out before he could
protest further.

"Sabina?" His voice had an odd tone to it, causing me
to look up. He opened his mouth to speak, but stopped
himself. Our gazes held for a moment too long. Unspoken words passed between us. I knew the gist, though.
The kiss had been nice, but it wouldn't happen again.
"Be careful."

I nodded and smiled. "Don't worry about me, mancy."
With that, I closed the door and walked away. Behind
me, I heard the SUV pull away slowly from the curb, followed by a gun to the engine that sent it speeding into the
night. I didn't look back.

An hour later, my skin felt warm from feeding. I guess
I'd been hungrier than I'd thought because it had taken

four men to satisfy my bloodlust. I dropped the latest blood donor, a would-be rapist who stank of cigarettes. His body landed with a thud at my feet.

I walked toward the exit and pulled my cell phone from my back pocket. When Adam and I had arrived at the woods earlier in the night, I'd turned it off. A press of the button and it lit up, announcing that I had three messages. Bypassing the voicemail button, I scrolled through missed calls. One from Clovis and two from Vinca. I called Clovis first.

"Sabina, where have you been?" Clovis's voice was harsh, almost accusatory.

"Sorry, I forgot to turn it on. What's wrong?"

"Adam is missing."

The ice shot down my spine. "What? That's impossible."

"He was supposed to come by to go over a few details with Frank, but he never showed."

"Yeah, I know, I was with him earlier when he talked to Frank. In fact, he dropped me off on his way to the meeting."

"He hasn't been seen since."

"Maybe he just needed to take care of a few things. Have you called Vinca to see if she's seen him?" Even as I spoke, I remembered the two missed calls from the nymph. Something was up.

"She hasn't seen him either," Clovis said. "I have a bad feeling about this. My spies told me earlier tonight that key members of the Dominae are in town."

My eyes closed as I muttered a curse not fit for respectable company. "I'll be there in five."

Clovis rose when I entered his office. I threw my purse in the chair and got down to business.

"Tell me everything you know," I said.

Frank stepped forward. He didn't look at me as he spoke. Obviously, someone was still angry about getting beaten by a girl. "I called Adam just after midnight, asking him to come by to go over the supplies he'd requested for the raid. He said he'd be here around midnight, but never showed."

"Has anyone gone to look for him?"

Clovis nodded. "We've had people scour the area and check out Adam's hotel room."

"And?" I demanded.

Frank and Clovis exchanged a look, which made my stomach drop. Clovis reached behind his desk and held up Adam's backpack. "We found this near the temple. His car was parked a couple of blocks away."

He handed me the pack. My hand shook so bad I almost dropped it.

"Our guess is he was walking here when someone picked him up."

What he didn't say was the discarded backpack was a sign that Adam hadn't gone willingly. I'd never seen him let the bag out of his sight. I opened it and looked inside. Along with his wallet and cell phone were some baggies of herbs along with several vials filled with various liquids and powders. I opened a bag and sniffed. The scent of rosemary tickled my nose. Just last night Adam had taught me about the herb's antiseptic properties. He made me laugh with a story about how he'd had to bathe in rosemary after he'd accidentally hexed himself as a child.

Clovis cleared his throat, bringing my attention back to the present. "As I mentioned, one of my informants told me your grandmother has been spotted in the city. I think it's a fair guess she has him."

I opened my mouth and snapped it shut. I couldn't tell Clovis I already knew the Dominae were in town because I'd been meeting with them.

"He also told me that activity around the vineyard has picked up. He believed they've been preparing for new arrivals in the lab."

"But why would they take Adam? Do you think they know about the plan?" I asked, playing dumb. Inside I was about to self-combust, but outside I was trying to remain calm.

"It's possible they're suspicious," Clovis said. "However, I think it's more likely they wanted Adam's powerful blood at their disposal."

I stood and gathered Adam's bag along with my resolve. "We go in tomorrow."

Frank's eyes widened. "But we're not ready."

I looked at Clovis for a reaction. He nodded, giving his support of the new plan. To Frank, I said, "We've got surprise on our side. Not to mention they have one of our own, so we've also got pretty serious motivation to kick some ass."

Frank didn't look happy, but nodded. "I'll brief the others."

I turned to Clovis. "We'll need a secure vehicle and someone who can drive in daylight."

Vinca sat on the couch when I got back the apartment. Her arms wrapped around her as she stood. "Sabina, thank Lilith. Did you get my messages?"

I realized I'd totally forgotten to listen to her messages in my hurry to find out what Clovis knew. "No, but Clovis filled me in. We think the Dominae snagged Adam and took him to the vineyard."

Her eyes grew large and sparkled with tears. "What are we going to do?"

"We're moving up the attack. We go in tomorrow." I filled her in on the rest of the plan. "Do you think you can get some of your fae friends together to help? Without Adam's magic, we'll need all the help we can get." I had hoped to keep Vinca away from the fighting, but I knew now that was impossible. Even if I didn't need her help, the fierce look on her face told me I'd have a fight on my hands if I wanted to keep her away now. Obviously, she cared about saving Adam as much as I did.

She nodded and chewed her lip. "I'll make sure they're ready." She left the room to make the calls. I collapsed on the couch and then stood again. Nervous energy built up in me like a pressure cooker. My fingers itched to fight, but I'd have to wait until tomorrow. With nothing else to do, I grabbed my cell phone and hit the button to listen to voicemail.

"Sabina, you need to come to the temple. Adam is missing." Clovis' voice was urgent. The automated voice told me the message was sent at a few minutes past twelve. The system beeped and then I heard Vinca's frantic voice.

"Sabina, are you with Adam? Call me." That message was left at 12:30. The system beeped and Vinca spoke again. "Sabina, something's wrong. Adam's missing. He was supposed to meet Frank, but he never showed. Call me back as soon as you get this." The time was 12:50.

I pulled the phone away from my ear and frowned at it. Something about the timing of those messages didn't add up. I went to Vinca's bedroom and knocked. She was hanging up the phone when I entered.

"Okay, we're all set for tomorrow," she said. I could hear the stress in her voice, but my questions prevented me from trying to comfort her.

"What time did Clovis call you looking for Adam?" I asked.

She frowned and thought for a moment. "It was right at midnight. Why?"

"I just got a chance to check my voicemails from earlier. Clovis called me to tell me Adam was missing at a few minutes past twelve."

"Okay?" she said, not understanding.

"Adam dropped me off at just before midnight. Why would Clovis call me so soon after when he was only a few minutes late?" My head ached as I tried to work out the timing of everything.

"Surely, you don't think Clovis had something to do with this." A frown marred her delicate face. "Do you?"

I shook my head. "It doesn't add up. Why would Clovis want to get rid of Adam? He doesn't have a motive."

She picked up her coat and put it on. "I'm sure it's just a misunderstanding."

Chewing on my bottom lip, I considered the situation from every angle. "Yeah, you're probably right. It's just weird."

She came over and put her hands on my shoulders. "Look, it's been a long night. We're all worried and stressed. Why don't you try to get some rest?"

I nodded absently, my mind still turning things over. "Where are you going?"

"I need to go meet with the other faeries. We've got a few tricks up our sleeves for tomorrow. Those assholes won't know what hit them."

I tried to smile, but my lips weren't cooperating. "Okay. Be careful."

"Will do. And listen, don't worry about Adam. He can take care of himself. Besides, I had a vision earlier. You and Adam standing in a redwood forest. Drums were beating in the background."

"Are redwoods a good sign?"

"Of course. I grew up in the redwood forest near Crescent City. That can't be a coincidence."

I nodded, but wasn't so sure. Vinca's gift of prophecy hadn't exactly been impressive thus far.

"Besides, even without the vision, I'm confident we'll win," she continued. "We're the good guys."

I wished I could feel as confident, but dread pooled in my belly. I wasn't sure if I knew the difference between the good guys and the bad anymore.

Vinca flitted out the door with a promise to be back before sunrise, which at that point was only a couple of hours away. To distract myself, I went to the kitchen and grabbed a beer. My bones ached with exhaustion, but I knew sleep wasn't on the agenda. I had a battle plan to review.

I took the beer into my room and changed into some comfy sweats. When I dropped my boots by the dresser, a flash of red caught my eye. The grimoire Adam had given me earlier sat next to my cell phone. I picked up the red leather journal and flipped through the pages. For the first time, I noticed Adam had filled several pages in the back with black ink, written in bold, masculine script. As I read the beginner spells he'd written for me, my eyes began to sting. He'd included instructions for summoning a demon.

I sat on the bed and thought about how much I missed Giguhl. The demon had his drawbacks, but he'd always helped lighten my mood. But he'd only been gone for two days. Two days that taught me how much I needed my friends.

But now Adam needed me. Those Hekate hooked up to blood-sucking machinery needed me. It felt good to be needed. However, underneath the warm and fuzzies was the leaden weight of regret.

Tomorrow, I would declare war on everything I once swore to protect.

28

I could feel the sun sinking below the horizon as the van sped toward Napa. Frank sat stiffly next to me on the bench. His arm accidentally brushed mine as we went over a bump. He shifted to the right but said nothing. In fact, the only sound inside the van was the rushing air and occasional thump of the tires.

Vinca sat on the opposite bench. Her eyes met mine through the darkness. She smiled a friendly half-smile, but looked away as if the effort cost her.

One of the male faeries she'd recruited for the mission sat with her. The other two sat up front, one driving and one riding shotgun. I wondered what species they were because they each stood more than five feet tall. They couldn't be nymphs because Vinca had informed me that nymphs were always female. They mated with human or mage males. Perhaps these males were the result of those matches. I made a mental note to ask her later.

Darius, the one I figured for the leader given the other's obvious deference, had wavy brown hair pulled back into a ponytail. He looked more pirate than faery with his gold hoop earring and stubble. He spoke little, but he seemed watchful, as if gathering information all the time.

The other two were almost identical in appearance. Each had shoulder-length blond hair and a face almost too beautiful to be male. Even their names were similar—Garrick and Warrick. I assumed they were brothers.

Part of me wanted to deliver a rousing speech to embolden the troops before we headed into battle. The other part of me wanted to throw up. The upcoming fight didn't worry me. I looked forward to kicking some ass. Instead, I couldn't shake the knowledge that after tonight my world would never be the same. I could never return into the Dominae's embrace or live among the Lilim. I'd be an outcast with a price on my head.

It occurred to me that all the suspicion I'd grown up with had proven true. Maybe the mage blood in my veins predisposed me to being a betrayer. Or maybe, as Adam claimed, there was a purpose to all this. As much as I wanted to laugh off the whole prophecy thing, I couldn't reject the idea outright. My immunity to apples might be related. My mage blood could be the reason, but given everything else Adam said, I doubted that was the whole story. Plus, my grandmother had always been very weird about my birthmark. Now, I had to believe it was due to more than just an aversion to a visible reminder of my mixed blood. Apparently my sister had the same mark. Too bad I couldn't ask her about the apple thing, too.

Thinking about my grandmother lying to me all these years made my jaw clench. Her attitude toward me finally made sense. She obviously saw me as an

unfortunate reminder of her daughter's sins. A pawn to
use in her bid to make the mages pay for my mother's
death. Even with the truth staring me right in the face,
I still couldn't understand how someone could be so
cold and calculating. Had she never had a heart? Or did
my mother's death kill it? I shoved that thought aside. I
needed to focus on the mission. Later, I could try to put
the pieces together and figure out what was next.

The van slowed as it left the highway. It was almost
time. My thoughts should have depressed me. Instead,
they made me angry. And I fully intended to punish anyone who got in my way.

Twilight had arrived by the time the van pulled into
the field on the dirt road curling along the backside of
the vineyard. We filed out the back doors, blinking in the
low light.

Four faeries and five vampires lined up in front of me.
Vinca and Frank stood at my sides.

Frank took over, since he was the logistics man. "Remember the plan, faeries go in first. Once they've disabled
the security, vamps attack. Remember, we don't want any
mages harmed. The vineyard center will be closed since
they only open to the public on weekends. We won't have
to worry about any mortals interfering."

"Wait," I said. "The plan was to rescue the mages and
get the hell out of there."

Frank shook his head. "Clovis decided we needed
to stay and make sure the supply of mage blood is
destroyed."

I grabbed his arm and pulled him away from the
group. "What the hell?" I whispered. "Why wasn't I told
of this?"

"Last-minute decision," he said. When I started to tell him what I thought of his last-minute decision, he held up a hand. "I don't want to hear it. Clovis calls the shots. You don't like it, you can leave."

I could tell he was hoping I'd walk away. Instead, I ground my teeth and clenched my fists.

"We're burning twilight, you guys," Vinca called.

I looked from her to Frank. With no other choice, I nodded and stalked back to the group. "Let's move out."

We crossed the road and scaled the fence surrounding the vineyard. Before us, a hill covered in rows upon rows of vines waited. We split up, faeries heading left and vamps heading right with me in the center. Our feet made little sound as we ran across the rocky terrain. Before long, the rear buildings of the winery rose into view. I paused before exiting the cover of the vines, trying to spot guards or workers patrolling the area. To my left, a male faery snuck up behind a guard and snapped his neck with a violent twist. From my right, I heard a gurgle as a vamp took out another guard.

The small faery group headed out of the fields and made their way to the back loading dock. They moved like apparitions though the dusk. Vinca led the team as they disappeared inside the building. I held my breath, waiting for an alarm or the sounds of fighting, but soon Vinca stuck her head out the door and gave the all-clear signal.

Frank's team and I left the field and merged just before the bay doors. Frank motioned the team to split up again once we entered—vamps following Frank, the others taking my lead. The warehouse seemed deserted, except for piles of ashes Vinca's team had left behind as calling cards. I crept forward, toward the secure area, while Frank and his group of vamps took a more circuitous route. I was fine with that because I didn't trust Frank to handle the extraction of the mages. Faeries would have a gentler hand when it came to disengaging the mages from their machines. Their healing knowledge would also help if we had any problem resuscitating anyone.

We got to the doors leading into the containment area. Vinca pointed to the camera above the doors and made a slashing motion across her throat. The security was disabled. I pointed to the doors and she shook her head. None of our people had gone inside.

I pushed through the doors and crab-walked down the hallway. My gun remained in my waistband. I couldn't risk a shot going wild. I flexed my fists, cracking a few knuckles in the process. I waved a hand for the others to stay behind me.

The elevators in front of me dinged, opening to reveal two vampires wearing lab coats in the front of the car. A few more bunched behind them. Acting on instinct, I ran at the first two as they came out, too engrossed in conversation to notice me. In a fluid motion, I pulled two apple wood stakes from my waistband. I took one vamp out by ramming the stake between his third and fourth ribs, piercing his heart through his back. Before he hit the floor, his partner came at me. The male had a hundred pounds and at least six inches on me. He grabbed me by the neck and pushed me back against the wall. He hissed as his fangs aimed right for my jugular. His elbows blocked me as I tried to angle the stake at his chest.

I managed to wriggle free enough to reach up with my left hand and jab a finger into his eyeball. He yelped and swayed for a second, but his hands tightened on my neck. He couldn't kill me this way, but if he got his fangs into my neck I was as good as dead. I crossed my arms through his and clasped my hands together. With a quick twist, I dislodged his beefy arms. I followed this with an elbow to his nose. As he staggered back, I lifted the stake and shoved it down hard behind his clavicle. His eyed widened in surprise above the bloody mess that was once his nose. He ignited and fell to the floor in a mass of ashes.

While I had been busy fending off the big guy, the faeries had their hands full with the other vampires who had been drawn out of the clinic. As I watched, Vinca took down a female a few feet away. As the titian-haired vampire combusted, Vinca smiled and held up what looked like a can of mace.

"Apple cider," she said. Her right hand held a bloody knife. "Spray 'em and slay 'em."

I didn't respond because two more workers entered the hall. I took the larger female, who resembled Attila the Hun's mother. Her meaty fists swung like battering rams at my face. I stepped to an angle and side-kicked her in the ribs. I reached for another stake, but she tackled me. My head hit the linoleum hard, but the real pain came when the female's weight settled on my ribs.

I tried to shimmy up to give myself some room, but her fleshy thighs gripped me like a vise. Her fists pummeled my face. I raised my own hands to block her blows and bucked with my hips to dislodge her. She kept coming. Vinca had jumped in and got the vamp in a choke hold. With a foot, Vinca kicked the apple mace at my hand. When Vinca ducked, I sprayed the obese vampire in her gaping mouth. She seemed shocked and I used

the advantage to kick her off me. I scrambled to get my
stake. Just as she rose to come after me again, I stabbed
her in the eye. It happened so fast she didn't have time to
scream as the wood pierced the fragile bones behind her
eye and impaled itself in her brain. As she exploded into
a bonfire, I helped Vinca up.

Her left eye was swelling into a nasty shiner and her
hands were coated in blood. "Are you okay?" I asked.

She nodded and looked around. Smoldering ash coated
the once-white linoleum floor. The two faery males
leaned against the far wall, their faces smudged with soot
and blood. As much as I'd wanted to keep Vinca away
from all this, I had to admit she was holding her own.
Plus, it was nice to have someone I trusted fighting with
me. Lilith only knew what Frank and Clovis' other goons
were up to.

A burst of sirens sounded. One of the vamps we'd just
killed must have triggered a hidden alarm. I ran to the
elevator followed by the faeries, who jumped on just before the doors closed. As we went down, we did a quick
weapons check. Lord knew what sort of scene would be
waiting for us below. We were running low on stakes, but
Vinca produced a few clips of cider bullets. We just managed to reload before the doors opened.

We clung to the sides, waiting for a spray of bullets.
When nothing happened, I carefully punched the button
to hold the doors open and poked my head around the
edge. The lab was filled with the shrill alarm mixed with
the frantic beeps of machines. Three remaining vampires
barely noticed us as they worked to unhook the mages
from their machines.

Without thinking, I ran forward, grabbing the first one

I reached. She struggled against me. Left with no choice, I used the last of my stakes to take her down. As she ignited at my feet, I looked around and saw the other two vamps being held by the male faeries.

"Vinca, check the ones they unhooked." She scrambled to plug in breathing machines. I took my gun and hit the female I held in the temple. She collapsed long enough for me to lock her and her cohorts in the supply closet. Clovis would want them questioned.

I ran back into the room to check on Vinca. She was leaning over a female mage, giving her mouth-to-mouth. She pointed with one hand to the discarded breathing tube lying on the bed. I grabbed it and handed it to her. She pulled away and I turned my back as she reinserted it. The males went to the others who had been unhooked to check on their vitals.

"They're okay," Darius said.

"We've got this, Sabina. Find Adam." Vinca shouted as she unhooked an IV from a male mage's arm, stopping the flow of blood from his body.

I went from bed to bed looking at the faces of the mages still attached to their machines, not finding Adam anywhere. At the end of the row was a blue hospital curtain. I pulled it back and saw a door. I went through it, which dumped me into a hallway. The walls were industrial cinder block and one side was lined with cabinets filled with small bottles. The heavy door thumped closed behind me, blocking out the sounds of the clinic. At the end of the hall was another door with a small barred window. I looked through the glass and saw a slumped figure huddled on the ground.

My heart spasmed. I ripped the door off its hinges,

worried when Adam didn't move despite the racket. Rushing forward, I grabbed him by the shoulders. His head fell back, revealing a bruised and bloody face.

"Adam!" I shook his shoulders. No response. I felt for a pulse and my own heart slowed to a gallop when I found it. I ran back down the hall, opened the door and yelled for Vinca. Then I ran back to Adam and continued to try to wake him. I ran my hands over him arms and legs, looking for breaks. All I found were brass manacles binding his wrists behind his back, which explained why he didn't use magic to free himself. I broke the chain connecting them just as Vinca entered.

"Is he—" she swallowed.

I shook my head. "Either passed out from pain or drugged. Can you help him?"

She moved me out of the way and lifted his eyelid. "His pupils look normal." She gently tapped his cheeks with her small hands. "Adam, wake up!" She smacked him this time. I had to hold myself back from attacking her, worried she was causing him more pain. "Sabina," she said, all business. "Check and see if they have smelling salts."

I didn't want to leave the room, but forced my feet to move. A large cabinet sat just outside the door, full of small vials and pills. I quickly scanned the shelves, looking for something that looked like smelling salts. "I can't find then," I yelled.

"Look for something labeled 'ammonia carbonate.'" Her voice was muffled.

I looked again, squinting at the small type. "Nothing!"

"Try 'hartshorn,'" she called back.

I did another quick scan, and, sure enough, the damned

bottle was right in front of me. I grabbed the brown vial and ran back to the room. She lifted the bottle to his nose and waved it back and forth.

"Come on, big guy," she said. "Take a nice big breath."

Adam's nose scrunched up and he inhaled sharply. His head twisted to the side. He winced and his eyes flew open. He squinted as he tried to focus.

"Adam?" I said, crouching down next to Vinca. "Can you hear me?"

"Sabina? What—" He tried to move. I stilled him with my hand.

"Don't. Let Vinca check you." I said, swallowing against the relief choking my throat.

"Is anything broken?" Vinca asked.

Adam swallowed and shook his head. "Just knocked me around a bit."

Vinca prodded his ribs with her fingers. He yelped and shied away. "Probably just bruised," she said. "Do you think you can stand?"

He nodded slowly. I scooted closer and got an arm behind him while Vinca took his right arm and put it around her shoulder. "On three," she said. We heaved Adam up, eliciting a low groan from deep in his chest.

"Can you do anything for his pain?" I asked Vinca as we half-carried him toward the door.

She met my eyes and nodded. "I'm sure there's some pain meds around here somewhere."

Adam's feet grounded into the floor, causing Vinca and me to jerk to a stop. "No drugs."

I looked up at him, exasperated by his typical male behavior. "Don't be ridiculous."

"No," he gasped.

I looked at Vinca, who nodded and pulled away. "You two go on, I'll do a sweep of this area."

"Okay, mancy, let's get you out of here," I said. Adam's focus was on his feet as he shuffled forward, so he didn't see Vinca head toward the medicine cabinet.

We reached the heavy door, and I managed to hold it open with my hip as I guided him through.

"Sabina," Adam said. His voice sounded strange. "Clovis—"

I leaned in to hear what he was trying to say, but another voice spoke over him. "Did I hear someone say my name?"

My head jerked up. Clovis stood in the middle of the rows of beds. Behind him stood Frank and the other vampires. Behind them, the bodies of the male faeries lay prone on the ground.

"What the—" I said. That's when I noticed the eerie silence. The breathing machines beeped no more. All the mages were dead.

29

*S*abina, my dear, I'm afraid you've outlived your usefulness." Clovis's smile didn't reach his dead eyes.

Adam stumbled back a step. I tightened my grip around him and stood my ground. Facing Clovis and his flunkies, I sent a silent prayer to Lilith that Vinca wouldn't come out the door yet.

"Sorry to disappoint you," I said to Clovis. "But I still feel quite useful."

He chuckled and crossed his arms. "Afraid not, love. In fact, I'd be a fool to let you live."

"You're already a fool." It was lame and I knew it, but I was too busy trying to figure out how to overpower Clovis and his five guards on my own. Adam was silent next to me, but I could practically feel the pain radiating off of him as he took in the bodies of his fallen kin.

"I'm the fool, Sabina? Hardly. A fool would have believed you when you said you didn't work the Dominae anymore."

I went still. "What?"

"Please. Did you really think anyone would buy that you suddenly had an urge to join your grandmother's enemy so easily? But I guess that's the irony of all this. You ended up betraying her anyway . . . with the help of my little anonymous tip about the mancy's whereabouts, of course."

If he thought he could hurt me with his words, he was wrong. Dead wrong. It wasn't Clovis who convinced me to betray her. She'd done that herself.

"Let's move this party to the warehouse, shall we?" Clovis said. He snapped his fingers and his guards came forward. Frank grabbed Adam from me, eliciting a groan from the mage. I struck out, trying in vain to protect him. Two other vamps, males that I'd thought were on my side a half hour earlier, grabbed my arms. I struggled against them. One grabbed my gun from my waistband, leaving me weaponless, except for the knife in my right boot. Fat lot of good that would do me with both arms pinned.

They dragged our motley crew—a wounded mage, two unconscious faeries, and a seriously pissed-off me—into the warehouse. They lined us up in front of a row of oak barrels. Clovis stood in front of us looking smug. I wanted to rip that smile from his face, but I had to keep my cool. If I could bide my time until the faeries regained full consciousness and Adam had time to heal, maybe Vinca, who was still M.I.A., would be able to create a diversion. I only hoped we'd all still be alive in time for that to happen.

"I don't get it," I said, trying to buy some time. "Why did you kill the mages? You could have let them live and still overthrown the Dominae's power."

Clovis started pacing in front of us. "I couldn't take

any chances. When I explain to the Hekate Council all the mages were dead when we arrived, they will have no choice but to support my bid to take over the control of the Lilim. With the Hekate Council on my side, the vampire community will withdraw their support of those bitches and follow me."

I felt Adam stiffen beside me. My eyes scanned the area for potential weapons. A long-handled broom leaned against the wall ten feet away. A pitiful weapon, but a weapon nonetheless. I needed to keep him talking.

"But why get rid of me?" I asked. "After all, I'm on your side."

Clovis came toward me. He stroked a finger down my cheek. It took every amount of willpower I possessed not to flinch away. "I'll admit I considered making you my consort. With your mage blood and my demon blood combined with our Lilim powers, we'd be a formidable team. However, you can't be trusted." He leaned in, his lips a fraction away from my own. "After all, until I handed your boyfriend here over to Lavinia, you were still loyal to the Dominae."

I lunged at him. "You bastard." He laughed as he easily held me off.

"You didn't think that when I vein-fucked you. If fact, you were practically begging for me to dominate you."

My eyes cut to Adam. He stared Clovis down with murder in his eyes. Guilt and self-loathing warred for dominance inside me. Guilt because I'd believed Clovis's story when he said the Dominae had taken Adam. I'd known something was off, but been too distracted to pursue it. Self-loathing because I'd let that demon feed from me. Even worse, he was right. I had wanted more.

"I'm growing bored. It's time to say good-bye." Clovis nodded at Frank.

Frank and the other vamps lined up in front of us. The one who'd taken my gun filled with apple-cider bullets now pointed it at me. My eyes met Frank's and I filled that gaze with every ounce of hate I possessed.

"It's nothing personal," he said with a shrug. "On three," he said to the other guards. Adam's hand grasped mine and I squeezed it.

Frank winked at me and began counting down. "One, two—"

All hell broke loose as windows overhead shattered. Glass and vampires dressed in black rained down all around us. The Dominae's force had arrived. I said a quick thanks to Lilith for the interruption even as I cursed the complication. I don't know how they'd discovered our plan to go in early, but now we'd have to fight off two forces if we wanted to get out of here alive.

A blast shook the building, rocking the foundations. I pulled Adam with me behind the barrels, grabbing the broomstick with my free hand. Shouts and pounding footsteps echoed off the concrete floors and metal walls as Clovis's men and the Dominae's guards fought.

Crouched beside me, Adam let go of my hand to peek between two barrels. "The second explosion came from near the clinic. Looks like Vinca's trying to create a diversion."

"Oh,. shit." I started to move, but Adam grabbed the back of my shirt.

"Let's see how this plays out."

"She can't defeat them on her own," I said. "We have to help her."

"What are you going to do, chase them with that stick?"

I closed my eyes for a moment and took a deep breath, trying to still the staccato beats of my heart. When I opened them I said, "It's a hell of a lot better than hiding."

Adam's color had returned and the gash on his forehead was now just a pale, thin line. His jaw was clenched as he weighed the situation. "Okay. Look, if we're going in then you're going to have to be prepared to use your magic." He held up his wrists. "With these brass cuffs on my wrists, I'm not going to be much use magically."

"Right," I said. "I'd be better off just calling them mean names."

"Sabina, look at me," he said. "You can do this. You already have the innate power—you just need to focus it."

From the sound of things, the fight seemed to be moving toward the entrance of the clinic. All I could think about was that the faeries, including Vinca, were caught in the middle of an all-out vampire brawl. Faeries were decent fighters, but vampires were ten times stronger and faster. They wouldn't last long without help.

"Fine, whatever. Let's get in there." I didn't wait for Adam to respond, just took off in the direction of the fight. He cursed and then his footfalls pounded behind me.

Finally able to see the fighting, I realized a complete melee had broken out between the Dominae's forces, Clovis's people, and the faeries. Everyone was fighting, well, everyone in an all-out brawl.

I zeroed in on a group of Dominae vamps surrounding

Vinca and the faeries. Darius had pushed Vinca behind him, but I had little hope he could protect her from the vampires. Clovis stood off to the side looking bored as he fought the Dominae's elite guard. I couldn't wait to do battle with that prick, but first I had to save my friend.

I ran straight into the fray, swinging the stick at the nearest vamp. Wood made contact with skull and the guy went down. It didn't kill him, but I moved on. My only thought was to clear a path to Vinca. I felt heat at my back and turned to see the vamp I'd taken down explode in a puff of smoke. Adam stood over him with a bloody axe he hadn't had a few second earlier. Looked like even without his magic, he was still pretty resourceful.

I reached down and grabbed the knife out of my boot. Clovis's henchman, the one who'd taken my gun earlier, came at me, pointing the muzzle at my head. I ducked and swiped the broomstick under his legs. A shot went wild, bouncing off the ceiling rafters as he fell. I straddled him across the chest. With a swift motion, I rammed the knife into his chest. His body exploded when the apple wood shaft hit him. I landed on my ass a couple of feet away.

I stood and saw Adam grappling with another vamp, one of Clovis's guards. Passing them, I ran toward Vinca, who was trying to fend off Frank. As I watched, the bastard grabbed her from behind and sank his fangs into her neck. I screamed and lunged at them. But I was too late. He ripped her jugular out just as he stabbed her in the chest.

I went totally primal. A red haze filled my vision. One second I watched Vinca fall, and the next I attacked Frank like a hellbeast. Frank's hands came up as I clawed him and went straight for his neck with my fangs. He fell back from my weight, dislodging my hold on his neck.

We rolled, punching and kicking each other. As far as fights went it wasn't my most graceful, but I was beyond caring about technique. I wanted his blood covering the floor before I killed him.

I grabbed Frank's head, ripping hair out by the roots. He slashed my face, clawing for my eyes. Somehow, I managed to flip him over. Grabbing him around the throat in a choke hold, I made him stand. He tried to twist out of the hold. I punched him in the kidneys and dragged him backward toward the gun lying on the ground. In a swift move, I reached down to scoop the gun. Spinning quickly before he could strike, I aimed it at his face. He stopped in midlunge with his hand outspread for attack.

Air stung my lungs as I heaved in great gulps of oxygen. I pulled back the hammer. "Who's changing the plan now, asshole?"

Frank opened his mouth to respond, but the sound of hands clapping interrupted. Keeping the gun pointed at him, I turned my head. My heart dipped low in my chest when I saw Clovis doing an ironic golf clap to my left. A quick scan of the area revealed the other faeries' lifeless bodies. The only other vamp had a gun pointed at Adam's temple.

"Impressive performance," Clovis mocked. "However, playtime is over. Please drop your weapon."

"Him first," I said, nodding at the vamp next to Adam.

Clovis laughed. "Your audacity knows no bounds."

"I'll kill him," I said, ramming the gun into Frank's temple.

"Be my guest."

I looked at Frank, whose face fell at his leader's betrayal. "If he's so easily beaten by a female, he deserves to die," Clovis said.

It happened fast. I swung the gun at Clovis and pulled the trigger. At the same time, Adam elbowed the other vamp in the face. I fell into a roll, grabbing the knife from the pile of ashes left over from the male I'd smoked earlier. Coming up, I turned, expecting to fight Frank. He merely stood there, his mouth agape.

I sensed movement at my back and swung around. Clovis tackled me, forcing the knife from my hand. It skittered toward Adam, who used it to take out the vamp he'd elbowed. Heat hit my face as I fell from Clovis's blow. Looming over me, the half-demon's face had changed. No longer did he look like a fallen angel. Now he looked every inch the demon that took up half his DNA. Two black horns protruded from his forehead and his face elongated into a hideous mask resembling bony red leather with black lips.

"Silly girl, you think a bullet can stop me?" His breath felt like fire and his voice had deepened several octaves. He lifted a hand casually and a ray of black light shot from his fingertips. Frank started to scream. I watched in shock as his skin melted from his bones and his body went up in flames.

Clovis grabbed me before I could recover from the sight of Frank's agony. I struggled against him, trying to free my hands. He lifted me easily, as if I were a child. My feet dangled in midair as I gasped and sputtered. With his free hand, Clovis picked up Adam, who'd been sneaking up behind him. As motes danced in my vision, I saw Adam fly backwards into a stack of crates.

"Finally, all alone," Clovis said. He shook me and my body flopped in the air like a rag doll. "Let's dance."

Before I knew what was coming, he lifted his hand again. A white-hot bolt of energy slammed into me. My back hit something hard and I crumpled into the concrete floor with a thud. Every bone in my body felt cracked as I gasped for breath. Before I could gather myself to move, he came at me again. His long, scaly fingers clawed my hair. My scalp burned as his face came into view again. His eyes blazed with the fires of Irkalla.

"Not so mouthy now, are you?" He backhanded me. My head fell back as pain radiated across my face. He dropped me and I hit the floor like a stone.

My eyes cracked open. Clovis's cloven hoof stood next to my face. Just beyond it, I saw a flash of movement.

From the shadows, my grandmother walked into the open area. I should have been surprised to see her, but if I knew my grandmother, she couldn't resist the opportunity to rub my nose in the mess I'd created.

Clovis laughed, lifted me by my hair off the floor. I dangled in his grip, my will to fight gone. Even if I managed to defeat Clovis by some miracle, I doubted I could best my grandmother.

"Lavinia Kane," Clovis said with a sneer. "Stop where you are or I'll finish her."

Lavinia didn't so much as flinch. "Don't let me stop you. She deserves to die for her treachery." She speared me with a venomous look. "Surely you didn't think you could outsmart me, girl. I knew you'd go in early. I came along with my forces to make sure the job got done properly. As usual, it appears I must do the job of killing the Dominae's enemies myself."

Clearly, she included me in that group. That was fine with me; she'd become my enemy when I found out she'd been lying to me my whole life. As for the killing part, she'd have to wait until Clovis had his turn.

Disappointed he couldn't use me as leverage, Clovis tossed me to the ground. I barely felt the impact of the cold concrete. I knew it was only a matter of time before one of them delivered a deathblow. Every part of my body ached, along with my spirit. I was tired of fighting. Tired of pain. Tired of struggling to make sense of the quagmire my life had become. Perhaps death would finally bring me some peace.

I was about to close my eyes when Adam's head appeared above the pile of boxes where he'd landed earlier. The sight of him—his face battered but determined— warmed me. He mouthed something. I blinked through the tears I hadn't noticed, trying to decipher his meaning. He repeated it and this time I recognized the word his mouth formed: "Fight."

Behind me, Clovis and my grandmother were squaring off. Shouts and grunts accompanied the occasional blast of heat and sound of fist meeting flesh. I realized then it didn't matter who won their battle. If Adam and I were going to make it out of this alive, they'd both have to be dealt with. The numb acceptance of impending death was replaced by grim resolve.

Adam was still watching me, but now he moved, ducking low as he came clear of the boxes.

He couldn't take both of them on his own, and I knew I had to do something. Without a fully formed plan, I started clawing at the floor to drag myself along. I figured if nothing else the blood oozing from the gash on my neck would create a pretty strong circle to bind one of them, if not both. Behind me, Clovis and my grandmother were so caught up trying to kill each other, they didn't notice me. Grandmother's age lent her strength and speed as she attacked with fangs and fists, but Clovis held his own with zaps of demon magic combined with his own punches and kicks.

Once I'd completed my trek, I rolled onto my back, panting. Adam nodded, showing his approval of my effort. I wasn't sure what to do next, but the mage gave me the answer. He ran at Clovis and Lavinia, waving his cuffed wrists and shouting like a berserker. The distraction surprised the pair, who stopped to gape.

I jumped into a crouch, ignoring the pain. He expected me to take advantage of the distraction he offered, but I had no idea what he wanted me to do. Adam blasted the pair with a few brass-weakened zaps of magic, but I could tell this was more distraction. Clovis and Lavinia circled Adam now, looking for an opening. I had to move soon or I'd blow the opportunity.

As I watched Clovis near the crimson circle, I knew what I had to do. My palms began to sweat even though my skin felt chilled. Left with no other choice, I scrambled to remember the spell Adam had written in the grimoire.

Clovis's foot crossed the line. Adam shouted something in Hekatian that I didn't understand, which was fine because I was trying to remember my part. Clovis's eyes widened as a flash of red light extended upward from the circle. Lavinia fell back, thrown when she made contact with the bubble created by protective barrier.

"Now!" Adam yelled, causing my stomach to leap.

"Idimmu Alka!" I shouted almost from instinct. With my right hand, I etched a simple glyph in the air.

A puff of poison-green smoke announced Giguhl's arrival. He wore a smoking jacket and held a goblet filled with neon purple liquid in his claw. He was mid-swig when he stopped and looked around, blinking rapidly. When he saw me, he stood up straighter. I sent a prayer of thanks to Lilith that he'd returned to his demon form.

"Sabina? What the—"

I pointed a bloody hand at Clovis, who stood immobile from shock a mere three feet away. Giguhl dragged his eyes from me and narrowed them at the gaping mixed-blood demon.

"Sic 'im!" I yelled.

An evil smile appeared on his lips and he tossed aside the goblet. Then he clapped his claws together and rubbed them in anticipation. "Playtime!"

He flew at Clovis and wrapped his claws around the half demon's neck before Clovis could even scream. A sickening gurgle escaped his throat as Giguhl shook him like a mongrel dog.

"Giguhl, time to go!" I yelled.

He nodded and wrapped his arms around Clovis, who scratched and clawed at Giguhl. He was no match for Giguhl's pure demon blood.

"Ready!" Giguhl shouted.

I raised my hands and sketched another glyph in the air. *"Idimmu Barra! Edin Na Zu!"*

Energy zinged out of my diaphragm to travel from my fingers. Red smoke billowed around the demons. With a thunderclap, they disappeared, leaving nothing behind but the acrid smell of brimstone.

One down, I thought. Too bad that was the easy one.

30

$\mathcal{A}$dam ran to me and he pulled me into a fierce hug. "You did it."

Over his shoulder, I stared at the empty circle formed by my blood. Lavinia's eyes widened as she looked from the spot of the demon showdown to me.

"You let him go!" she yelled. She lurched forward, ready to attack. "You betrayed your family by colluding with our enemy and using forbidden magic, and now you have let Clovis escape. I curse the day you were born."

"He didn't escape," I said, surprised my voice sounded calm. I certainly didn't feel that way. "I sent him to Irkalla. Giguhl and his friends will keep him busy for a while. Isn't that what you wanted? For him to be out of your way while you start a war?"

Her eyes narrowed. "You ungrateful little bitch."

Adam's hand squeezed my shoulder. Whether it was a warning to remain calm or a sign of support, I didn't know. I pushed him away. It was time to have this out with my grandmother.

"Ungrateful? Should I thank you for lying to me my entire life? For treating me as a second-class citizen? For blaming me for the sins of my parents?" I paused and took a menacing step toward her. "Or perhaps I should thank you for hiding the fact I have a sister."

Slowly, with great deliberation, she paced in front of Adam and me. She was like a tiger stalking her prey. "Did you know I wanted to kill you when you were born? But Persephone and Tanith thought you'd be useful to us one day." Her eyes, black with malice, met my own. "My biggest regret is that I listened to them."

Visceral pain sliced through me as I absorbed the venom of her words. Adam's hand found mine, and I borrowed from the strength he offered.

"And my only regret is that it took me so long to understand how evil you are. That I wasted so many years being brainwashed." I paused as she laughed. "Well, no more. My eyes are open now and I fully intend to make you pay—you and the Dominae. You're all going down."

She laughed, an evil cackle filled with loathing. "Such strong talk from such a weak girl. Surely you don't think you'll walk out of this room alive."

"She will," Adam said quietly. "And so will I."

She laughed again, this time there was a hysterical undertone. "How touching," she said looking at me. "I suppose it shouldn't surprise me that you'd follow in your mother's footsteps. I hope you haven't grown too fond of him, because he's going to die just like your father. Only this time, I'll do the job myself."

I didn't bother correcting her assumptions about Adam and me, but I felt him stiffen. I nudged him to keep him quiet. If I could get her angry enough, she might make a mistake.

"Actually, I'd rather you didn't," I said, matter-of-factly. "You see, I'm already carrying his child." Seeing the rage building in her eyes, I looked at Adam, imploring him to play along.

He put an arm around my shoulders and said, "Congratulations, Great-grandma."

She attacked before I saw it coming. Her white hands curled into claws, going straight for my throat. I fell back with the force of her weight. As she buffeted my body with blows, Adam struggled to pull her off me. But she had the strength of rage spurring her on. Her eyes were dilated so far they were like black pits. Finally, I managed to buck my hips at the same time Adam wrenched her off. She flew backward with a shriek. A set of keys flew from her waist as she fell. I grabbed the keys and threw them to Adam, praying one would free his wrists from the cuffs dampening his magic.

My face felt like someone had taken a meat cleaver to it, but now I was pissed. I jumped up and went after her as a lifetime of resentment and anger boiled to the surface. We collided like two freight trains. I grabbed a hunk of her hair and brought up my knee. Her nose met my kneecap with a crack. "That's for David!"

She only paused to wipe the trickle of blood from her lips. "You ungrateful little bitch." Her fist hammered into my solar plexus. The air left my lungs in a hiss.

I backhanded her, enjoying the sight of blood as it escaped her lips. Spurred on by pent-up anger, I delivered a series of punches to her midsection. She grunted with each blow, but didn't fall. When she came at me with a side-kick, I grabbed her ankle and shoved. She back-flipped and landed in a crouch.

I fell back into my fighting stance, trying to catch my breath. Trying to figure out the best way to kill her. Trying not to think about how I used to worship her.

Lavinia practically flew through the air this time. Expecting her to come in low, I shifted my weight onto the balls of my feet. But she surprised me by raising her right hand high. I saw the stake a moment before it made impact. The apple wood slammed through my chest plate. The force of the hit threw me. As I crashed into a pile of crates like a rag doll, I heard Adam yell.

"Sabina!" He sounded far away.

Pain numbed my brain, making it sluggish. My hands and feet felt cold, but the wound in my chest felt white-hot. Something tickled the edge of my brain. Something I was forgetting, but was too confused to grasp. On some level, I was aware of yelling and the smack of fist against flesh. Something bright flashed in the distance followed by a female shriek. The sound of blood pumping in my ears distracted me. My chest throbbed hotly, but no other heat came. No fire to suck away my soul.

Bit by bit, my mind shook off the shock. The sounds of fighting became more distinct. I could smell my own blood. Feeling came back to my hands. My eyes focused on the stake protruding from my chest. I lifted my hands and grasped the smooth shaft. My grip was weak and the stake was slippery with blood, but I pulled it—bit by bit—out of my chest. The pain was worse coming out than going in, but it was a blessing. It meant I was alive.

Adam's curse sounded far away, as did the crash following it. I needed to move. Using my hands to lever my body up from the boxes, I managed to get upright. Now that the stake was gone, my body was working overtime to repair the wound. I felt lightheaded and had to bend over with my arms resting on my knees. When it passed, I rose up to survey the scene.

If it was possible, the warehouse looked worse than it had earlier. Scorch marks blackened the walls and the debris of battle littered the area. In the center of it all, Adam and Lavinia squared off. I'd never seen my grandmother looking so haggard. She had a gash on her forehead and her hair stood up in weird spikes, as if she'd stuck her finger in a light socket.

Adam didn't look much better. He had scratch marks on his cheek and he'd lost a shirtsleeve, which revealed gashes on his arm. The good news is it looked like one of the keys had worked and he was able to use his magic. But he was practically swaying from exhaustion, even as he raised his arm to deliver another spell. A weak flash of energy zigzagged across the space and missed Lavinia's head by mere inches.

She laughed and started toward him, her lips pulled back to reveal her fangs.

"Stop!" I yelled without thinking.

Grandmother skidded to a halt a couple of feet from Adam. Her mouth gaped open as she stared. Adam turned his head slowly and smiled. He didn't look surprised so much as relieved. After all, he was the one who sent Giguhl to test my immunity to the forbidden fruit. How he'd thought to test me for that—and why—were questions for another time.

"About time you joined us." His voice wavered, and I have to admit I felt a little shaky myself. Our eyes met and held for a moment—an intense look shared between two beings uncomfortable with strong emotions.

"Lilith protect me." Lavinia's whisper caught Adam's attention.

Despite the sudden urge to burst into tears, I managed a shrug. "I try."

Lavinia's shrill voice broke into our little bubble. "Why aren't you dead and burning? I made sure the stake went through your heart."

I took a tentative step forward, not quite trusting my strength yet. The movement caused my grandmother to take a step back. I placed a hand over the healing wound over my heart. "Oh, you hit it, all right."

"Then how?"

"It appears I inherited more than magic from my father's people." When she still looked mystified, I said, "The forbidden fruit has no effect on me."

Her mouth gaped open, and for a moment, I reveled in my ability to shock her. Finally, she recovered enough to say, "You're an abomination!"

I shrugged. "I guess I am." I glanced at Adam, who winked at me. I had to struggle to keep a straight face. Despite the acid churning in my stomach and the weakness from my wounds, it felt good to have the upper hand with my grandmother for once in my life.

"What should we do with granny now?" An undercurrent of steel in Adam's voice contradicted the casual wording.

Lavinia's chin came up. "I'm not afraid of death."

"Oh, we're not going to kill you," I said.

"We're not?" Adam said.

Grandmother's expression turned mocking. "Some assassin you are. You always were weak."

I stepped forward and got in her face. "As much as I hate you right now, it's taking a lot of strength to not kill you."

"Talk to me, Red." Adam sounded worried.

"We're not going to kill her. She doesn't deserve an easy out." I never took my eyes off hers as I spoke. "No, we're going to let her live so she can see me destroy everything she holds sacred."

"What is this nonsense?" She sneered but the corner of her eye twitched.

I spoke slowly, so she'd not miss one word of my vow. "I will not rest until you are alone, powerless, and hunted by those you ruled."

"I'll find you," she said. Her eyes burned into mine. "And when I do, you'll regret you were ever born."

"I've wasted enough of my life doing that because of you," I said. "Instead, I think I'll return the favor."

Before she could respond, Adam chanted something in Hekatian. A flash of yellow light engulfed Lavinia. In a poof of smoke, she disappeared.

I rounded on him. "Hey!"

"Sorry, I just thought you might enjoy having the last word."

I glanced at the space where she'd stood, deciding he was right. "Where'd you send her?"

"Siberia. Lovely this time of year. A bit remote, I'm afraid. Might take her weeks to find a town and even longer to arrange transportation back to the States."

My lips quirked. I didn't feel like laughing, but the image of my half-millennium-old grandmother trudging though snow was kind of funny. "You're sick, you know that?"

"What can I say? I thought a cold-hearted bitch like her would feel at home in the tundra."

I looked around at the warehouse. Spilled wine, which spread like pools of blood among the ash of the dead, coated the concrete. A shiver passed through me as I realized tonight's battles were merely the early skirmishes in the larger war to come.

"So what now?" Adam asked. His voice had lost all traces of humor as he too surveyed the aftermath of violence.

"Let's get the hell out of here."

Adam limped over to Vinca's broken body. In death, her throat had healed and her body had taken on an iridescent cast. She looked like a wax statue instead of a corpse. Adam lifted her, cradling her body against his own.

"We'll find her family," he said. "They'll want to bury her in a sacred spot."

Gritting my teeth against the tingling of awareness threatening to rush back in the form of anger and tears, I followed him out of the warehouse. Together, we marched through the now-blackened vines, littered with bodies of winery workers. Frank and his men had obviously been busy.

When we reached the van, Adam gently laid Vinca's body on one of the rear benches. He closed the back doors of the makeshift hearse. His face was grim, but his eyes told the real tale. Through them, I could see his soul had aged.

He took his cell phone from his backpack, which he

grabbed before closing the doors. After pressing a few buttons, he lifted the phone to his ear. Without a word, I watched him talk to someone at the Hekate Council. His voice caught as he described the scene in the lab, where the bodies of his comrades lay. I walked a few feet away to give him some privacy.

I looked up at the night sky. The same stars twinkled in their constellations. The same moon hung low in the sky. Yet nothing was the same. Nothing would ever be the same.

Adam hung up behind me. "They're sending a team to retrieve the bodies. I should probably stay to help." When I turned to look at him again, I didn't know what to say. I knew I should offer to stay and help, but I knew I couldn't go back in there. Adam must have read my thoughts. "Can you handle taking Vinca to her family on your own?"

I paused, suddenly overcome with doubt. Delivering Vinca's body to her family would tear me apart, but I knew I had to do it myself. However, something else nagged at me. Adam seemed a little too quick with the offer to leave.

"You'll be okay by yourself?" I asked. Before the words left my mouth, I felt a tingle in the air. About ten feet away, a figure materialized. The male was soon joined by a handful of others, who also appeared out of thin air.

Adam sent me a smile. "When I said they were sending a team, I didn't mean by car."

"Oh," I said, watching even more mages appear. Soon, about twenty surrounded us. A male, obviously the leader of the group, came forward and shook Adam's hand.

"Lazarus," he said. "About time you called."

"Councilman Orpheus, sorry . . . things were . . . complicated."

"They always are with you," Orpheus responded. He looked at me with a curious yet distant glance, but then did a double take. "Impossible," he breathed, staring at me as if he'd seen a ghost. The other mages had all stopped too, staring at me with mixtures of curiosity and shock.

"Sir, let me introduce Sabina Kane, daughter of Tristan Graecus."

I shifted on my feet. "Hello."

"You found her?" Orpheus said to Adam, as if I wasn't standing there, even though he continued to stare. "We knew they were twins, but we didn't know if they were identical. Maisie will be ecstatic."

I cleared my throat and looked at Adam. "There's about fifty mages inside who need to be put to rest. Maybe we should hold off on the long-lost-sister issue."

The man shook his head as if to clear it. "Of course, I'm sorry, it's just I hadn't expected to meet the chos—"

Adam cleared his throat and interrupted. "Sabina, you'd better head out if you're going to make it by sunlight."

I looked at Orpheus curiously for a moment, wondering what he was about to say. Realizing I probably didn't want to know, I turned to Adam. "She told me they live in the redwood forest near Crescent City. I'll call you when I get there and let you know about the arrangements."

He nodded gravely. Orpheus, after one last thorough look at me, had walked away to shout orders at the other mages. "Please do," Adam said. "I'd like to be at the funeral."

I nodded and scuffed at the dirt with the toe of my boot. I suddenly felt self-conscious. After everything we'd been through that night, it seemed odd to part so casually. But with so many mages milling around, I didn't feel right getting all emotional. Besides, I couldn't be sure what Adam was thinking. He probably wanted to get back to New York and I had to figure out what the hell I was going to do.

"Sabina," he said, breaking into my thoughts. I looked at him and our eyes met. Unspoken emotions passed between us—sadness, regret, relief, anxiety, longing. I don't know who moved first, but I soon found myself wrapped in a fierce hug. This wasn't like the hug that started the ill-advised make-out session in the van. No, this was an embrace shared by two warriors after a battle, as well as one of two friends mourning the loss of a comrade. "Be careful," he whispered, his lips just above my ear.

I screwed my eyes shut against the sting of hot tears. I knew if I let one go, the dam would burst and I'd soon be a puddle. Instead, I sniffed and pulled back. "You too."

"Lazarus!" Orpheus' voice was a blessed interruption. Adam looked over his shoulder.

"Coming," he called. He turned back to me, his hands still on my shoulders. "Call me."

I nodded, not trusting myself to speak. With one last squeeze, Adam walked away. I watched him go for a moment. His shoulders squared, as if he'd switched into business mode. As he and the other mages disappeared over the fence to do their grisly duty, I turned to the van, ready to do mine.

The keys were in the ignition. I started the motor and adjusted the mirror and seat to my satisfaction. When I could put it off no longer, I turned to look at Vinca. Adam had covered her with a blanket he'd found in the storage compartment.

"Let's get you home," I said.

Only when I'd driven out of sight of the vineyard did I allow the tears to fall.

31

When I reached the forest, Vinca's family was waiting for me. I'd stepped out of the van ready to deliver the speech I'd practiced during the six-hour drive from Napa to Crescent City, which lay about twenty miles from the Oregon border. I was so wrapped up in getting the words right, it hadn't occurred to me to find it odd that a couple of dozen nymphs were standing in the clearing just off the parking lot of the park.

"Hello," I began. "You don't know me, but—"

A woman who appeared to be in her late twenties came forward, interrupting me. Her carriage was regal, yet her eyes were rimmed red. "Where is she?"

Shocked by the woman's greeting, I answered automatically. "In the back of the van."

The woman nodded and motioned to the males in the group. They moved forward as one, all six of them. As I watched, they opened the van and quietly removed Vinca from the van. They carried her past the now openly weeping females, and disappeared into the forest. I turned to the head female, my mouth gaping.

"Thank you for bringing her home," she said. "I am Astrid, Vinca's mother."

She offered me her hand, and, mystified, I took it gently. "I'm Sabina. Vinca was my friend."

The woman tilted her head and looked at me. Her moss-green eyes searched mine for a moment. She opened her mouth, no doubt to ask any of a myriad questions. But she thought better of it and closed her Cupid's-bow lips.

"Where are they taking her?" I asked.

"To prepare her for the rites. Come, one of my daughters will show you to your room."

I wanted to ask more questions. How had she known to expect me? Did she know how Vinca died? Those and a million others fluttered through my head like butterflies. Yet I was bone tired. The sun had risen a couple of hours earlier and I was almost dead on my feet from exhaustion. I could handle sunlight only in small doses, and the sun's rays were weighing me down. There would be time to discuss the hows and whys later.

I nodded and followed the fresh-faced nymph who came forward to show me to the house. She sniffled as she led me along a path of packed earth. The smells of the forest surrounded us—mulch and dew combined with the sharp scent of leafy things. The others followed at a slower pace, their whispers so low I couldn't make out their words.

Soon a house loomed ahead. Unlike Briallen's modest cabin in Muir Woods, this place rose two stories and I lost track counting the rounded windows that glinted in the morning sun filtering through the trees. The structure itself resembled a cluster of giant toadstools, with curving rooflines and smooth stucco walls.

My room sat on the second floor under low eaves. A simple bed with a white-and-green quilt sat under a small window, set in the slopped ceiling. The girl didn't speak much as she covered the window with a blanket. She opened a door to show me the bathroom and where to find fresh towels. "My mother said to tell you the rites will occur tomorrow night at sundown. In the meantime, you should rest. If you need anything, my room is just across the hall."

I thanked her and then she was gone. I collapsed on the bed, wondering if I'd entered some kind of bizarre fairy tale. A few minutes later, my muscles spasmed, waking me from my half-sleep. I ran a hand over my face and sat up. I needed to call Adam before I passed out.

He picked up on the third ring. His voice sounded as tired as I felt. "Lazarus."

"Adam, it's Sabina. I'm here."

"Is everything okay? How'd they take the news?"

"That's the weird part," I said. "They seemed to be expecting me. It's like they already knew everything."

"That wouldn't surprise me. Nymphs have extremely developed intuition, especially when it comes to family."

I thought briefly about Vinca's attempts at prophecy with a sad smile. "That must be it," I said. "Anyway, I'm here. They seem to already have funeral arrangements under way. Astrid, Vinca's mother, said the rites would occur tomorrow night."

"I'll be there by tomorrow morning."

"How are things there?"

His sigh carried over the lines. "As good as can be expected given the circumstances. The families of the dead have been notified."

"I'm sorry you lost so many," I said.

"I'm just thankful we will be able to bury them with the proper rites. I owe you for that."

I cringed at his praise. "If it wasn't for me, you'd have been able to save them."

"Stop it," he said. "You are the reason we found them to begin with." I heard a muted voice on the other end, as if someone had interrupted Adam. He told the person he'd be there in a minute and came back on the line. "Listen, I need to go meet with the Council. I'll be there tomorrow morning, so we can argue about this more then. Deal?"

I smiled. "Deal." After we hung up, I managed to shuck my boots before crawling under the covers. I didn't hear any sounds in the house as I drifted into a blessedly dreamless sleep.

At sundown the next night, Adam and I followed the procession from the house to a small clearing surrounded by towering redwoods. Vinca's six brothers carried her body on a litter made from bent willows interlaced with garlands of dried flowers and herbs. They'd dressed her in flowing gowns of lavender gossamer and placed a crown of purple dried heather on her head.

When we'd reached the site, we gathered in a circle. I'd never been to a funeral, much less one for a faery, so I hung back. Adam stood beside me, a soothing presence.

We watched as the brothers dug a pit in the earth at

the base of the tallest tree. The females sang dirges in a language I didn't know. The sound of their sweet, high voices singing songs of loss sent shivers through me.

Once the body had been covered, the rest fell back, offering Adam and me a chance to pay our respects. Adam moved forward first, kneeling beside the small mound. I looked away, not wanting to intrude on the private moment. When he stood, I looked back and saw tears glistening on his cheeks. He moved to the other side, motioning me to come over.

This was the moment I'd been dreading for two days. How does one say good-bye to a friend? I'd never known anyone who died while I watched. Well, not anyone I cared about. And didn't kill. Until now, death was a business, not a life-changing experience. Never had a loss cut so deep. I worried I might bleed from the pain.

I moved forward slowly, my eyes focused on the small mound. I felt disconnected from my body as I knelt. My hands reached out to touch the cold soil, as if needing to verify this was all really happening. I couldn't speak over the lump of regret in my throat. I whispered the words in my head—private words of sorrow and apology, of regret and longing, of farewell and friendship.

When I finished, Adam helped me to my feet. Astrid came forward, her face set in a mask of sorrow and resolve.

"Now we must perform the sacred rites." She did not say it, but we understood this was time for us to leave. Obviously, the faeries needed their time to mourn their loss privately, without outside intrusion.

It was as if the entire forest mourned. As Adam and I walked together from the gravesite, I marveled at the complete lack of night sounds. No birds sang, no insects buzzed, no critters scurried through underbrush. The only sounds were the periodic sobs of Vinca's family and the rhythmic beat of the funeral drums.

We did not speak as we walked further into the forest. Adam's hand found mine and we wandered to a small wooden bridge spanning a wide creek. Together, we walked to the railing and leaned against the rough wood, listening to the chatter of the water.

Adam spoke first, his voice so quiet I almost missed it. "They'll be there all night, watching over her."

I swallowed and nodded, watching a leaf dance on the surface of the water.

"It's not your fault," he said.

A tear forged a wet path down my cheek and splashed onto my hand. "I should have killed him that first night. Then she wouldn't have gotten dragged into this."

Adam took my shoulders and turned me to face him. With one hand, he tilted my chin up so I had to meet his eyes. His face wavered behind the tears gathering in my eyes. "She was a big girl. She knew the dangers."

"But—"

Adam put a finger to my lips. "Don't. Blaming yourself won't bring her back. It won't change anything."

I swiped at my cheeks with the backs of my hands and let out a breath. "You're right. I just hate this."

"I do, too. But the harsh truth is many more will die."

Startled, I looked at him. "What do you mean?"

"The Council is going to declare war against the Dominae."

My stomach dropped. "When?"

"Soon."

"But that's just what the Dominae want," I said.

He sighed and gripped the wooden bean tightly. "I know. Believe me, I tried to talk them out of it. But the Hekate Council can't let their actions go unpunished."

"It's going to be Armageddon." A sick feeling of inevitability rose in my stomach.

"Maybe not," he said. "There might be a way to avoid it."

"How? Wait, you're not talking about that prophecy BS again, are you? Get serious, Adam."

"Look, there are things I haven't told you. Things I can't tell you yet." He ran a hand through his hair. "Will you just come with me back to New York?"

His quick change of subject made me pause. "Is this about meeting my sister or the prophecy?"

"Both. Listen, you can't stay in California. The Dominae will track you down. Chances are good if you strike out on your own they'll still find you. And once the war starts, you definitely won't be safe. Your only hope is to ally yourself with the Hekate Council."

"I don't know, Adam. Not all vampires are bad just because the Dominae are. I might be able to call in a few favors."

"Yes, but once war starts, you know the Dominae will declare martial law in all the vamp communities. No one will offer you protection."

I didn't like the idea of choosing sides by default. "Maybe I'll stay here with Vinca's family."

He shook his head. "And endanger them? Sabina, be realistic. Besides, the Seelie Court will side with the Hekate Council. We've always been allies."

"It looks like I don't have much of a choice, do I?" I turned from him, feeling trapped.

He sighed behind me, a long breath filled with frustration. "I know you don't like this. And believe me, if there was any other way I'd suggest it. But look at it this way, the Hekate Council wants you. You're already a hero to them because of your help finding the mages at the vineyard. Your sister is dying to meet you." He paused. "And if that's not enough, what better way to punish your grandmother than to side with her enemy?"

I stopped and turned. "I hadn't thought of it that way." A slow smile spread on my lips as I thought of Lavinia's reaction when she found out. Once she got back to L.A. from her little arctic expedition, that is. "Okay, I'll go with you."

He smiled and started to say something, but I held up a hand. "But I have conditions. First, I am a free agent. I don't take orders from the Hekate Council or anyone else."

"But—"

"Second," I said, overriding his protest. "No more secrets. If I'm going to do this, I don't want surprises popping up left and right or things you 'forgot' to mention about this prophecy stuff."

"Okay," he said slowly. "Anything else?"

I thought about it for a minute. "Yes, that you be the one to train me. I don't want to get there and be handed off to some schoolmarm who'll rap my knuckles if I screw up a spell."

A lopsided smile appeared on his lips. "I'll see what I can do. Is that all?"

"No," I said, feeling better. "I also want Giguhl there

with me if he's willing. All mages need a familiar, right?"

"Ah, that might be a problem," Adam said. "Mages and demons aren't exactly natural allies."

"Tough," I said. "If the Council doesn't like it, they can find someone else."

Adam crossed his arms and regarded me levelly. "You drive a hard bargain, Red."

"Damn straight."

"It's a deal." He held out his hand to shake on it. Wary of his easy acceptance, I grabbed his palm in my own. I smiled at him, but inside I was freaking. If someone had told me a month earlier that I'd soon turn my back on the only family I'd ever known in favor of the one I thought had shunned me from birth, I'd have laughed and punched them in the face. Yet, here I was shaking hands with a mage to seal that very bargain. Of course, I also never thought I'd befriend a nymph, have a demon cat minion, or make out with a mancy. So maybe prophecy isn't my forte.

"We'd better get back," Adam said. "The Hekate Council wants us to report as soon as possible."

I pulled on his hand to stop him when he moved to leave. "Wait, a second. They're expecting us?"

He looked sheepish. "I told them you'd agree to come."

"Someone's pretty sure of himself."

He stopped and looked at me, his expression serious. "Honestly? I was praying you'd say yes. If you had said no, I don't know what I would have done."

I laughed out loud for the first time in days. "Lucky for you I said yes then, huh?"

He chuckled. "You ready to go meet your destiny, Sabina Kane?"

Thinking it over, I looked up. A white owl with glowing red eyes sat in a nearby tree watching us. It was the one I'd seen the night I killed David. According to Adam, it was one of Lilith's spies. I still wasn't convinced by all his talk of prophecies and underworld espionage. At that moment, however, the owl was just a reminder of the night I killed my friend. A pang of regret hit me hard. Now that I thought about it, I realized my split from the Dominae began that night. The minute they'd asked me to kill David, I should have walked away. Instead, I'd ignored my instincts in favor of misplaced loyalty. That skewed sense of honor had kept me blind as the proof of my grandmother's treachery piled up. Now the blinders were off, and I owed it to David's memory to see this thing through to the bitter end. But even more than that, I owed it to myself.

I took a deep breath and held it before exhaling loudly. "Hell, no, I'm not ready." He looked at me with a worried expression. "But I'll do it anyway."

The owl hooted and rose from the branch, its snowy wings spreading against the inky night sky as it flew east.

Acknowledgments

As much as I'd like to claim this book sprang from my head fully formed and perfect, I'd hate to start our relationship off with a lie. Truth is, without my highly skilled team of makeover specialists, it would be a mere shadow of its current awesomeness.

My infinitely patient agent, Jonathan Lyons, was this story's first fan and champion. His advice and encouragement helped me land the perfect publishing home at Orbit. Devi Pillai, editrix extraordinaire, not only loved the same things I love about this book, she also helped me take my original vision and make it even better. Also, big thanks to Bella Pagan, Jennifer Flax, Alex Lencicki, and the rest of the fabulous Orbit teams in the U.S. and the U.K. for turning my rough-hewn manuscript into a shiny and beautiful book.

Behind every author is a group of family and friends whose support is the lifeblood of perseverance. Gratitude doesn't begin to describe my debt to all of the following: To all my friends at the Dallas Area Romance Authors for your support and wisdom. To Sean Ferrell, an excellent writer and a damned fine beta reader. To Jason Evans, a good friend, great writer, and inspiring photographer. To Emily and Zivy, my cohorts and sisters by choice. To my mother, who told me early on I should be a writer and then waited patiently for me to come to that conclusion on my own.

But mostly, I have to thank the two men in my life. Thank you for teaching me about happiness. Thank you for believing I could do this even when I didn't. But most of all, thank you for loving me.

extras

orbit

www.orbitbooks.net

about the author

Raised in Texas, **Jaye Wells** grew up reading everything she could get her hands on. Her penchant for daydreaming was often noted by frustrated teachers. Later, she embarked on a series of random career paths before taking a job as a magazine editor. Jaye eventually realized that while she loved writing, she found reporting facts boring. So she left all that behind to indulge her overactive imagination and make stuff up for a living. Besides writing, she enjoys travel, art, history, and researching weird and arcane subjects. She lives in Texas with her saintly husband and devilish son. Jaye Wells has her own website at www.jayewells.com.

Find out more about Jaye Wells and other Orbit authors by registering for the free monthly newsletter at www.orbitbooks.net

interview

Did you always know that you wanted to be a writer?

I didn't, but my mother did. She told me early on I should pursue writing, but I never considered it as a career. Later, after I'd tried other paths, I finally gave in to the inevitable and took a job writing for a magazine. It took a few years after that to finally get the courage to take my first fiction-writing class. Once I got the bug, though, I looked back and realized that I'd been headed in this direction for a long time. Like a lot of authors, I have boxes of scribbled scenes and angsty poems from my youth. I've also always been a voracious reader, which is critical to writing good fiction. Plus, I was that annoying kid who always preferred essay questions on tests. These days, I can't believe I didn't try my hand at fiction sooner. I guess it just took me a while to admit mom really is always right. But don't tell her I told you.

As a writer of urban fantasy, are there any writers in the genre that you've been particularly influenced by?

Kim Harrison, without a doubt. When I picked up *Dead Witch Walking,* I remember just being blown away. I'd never read anything like it. That was my first exposure to the genre and I loved the mixture of elements. I also loved the rebelliousness of it. There are no sacred cows in urban fantasy. Harrison isn't the only one pushing boundaries, but she was the first one I saw doing it.

Another favorite is Christopher Moore. I'm not ashamed to admit I have a major creative crush on that guy. He's just brilliantly funny.

Red-Headed Stepchild *is such a unique take on the genre, combining a highly original mythology with some very comical elements (a certain demon cat comes to mind). How did you come up with this concept?*

It all started with a piece of flash fiction. My friend hosted contests on his blog, and I always played along. We'd have to come up with a 250-word story using the picture he posted as inspiration. This particular time it was a lovely picture of a full moon.

The idea came to me as I was driving down the road one day. I had been racking my brain to think of a unique take on the picture when all of a sudden the first line came to me: "Digging graves is hell on a manicure." I almost got into a wreck in my haste to pull over and write it down. The rest of the story came easily after that. The original title was "I Can Dig It."

After the story got a lot of encouraging comments on the blog, I decided to expand it. I started with the world building because I felt a lot of the vampire mythos had been done to death and I wanted to push some boundaries. I've always been fascinated with the folklore and mythology surrounding Lilith, so I started there with my research. The rest was basically me asking "what if."

Most of the comedic elements were included to amuse myself. However, it was important to me to find a balance. I didn't want it to be too slapstick because that would diminish the gravity of Sabina's situation. On the other hand, I felt the comedy was needed because real life is both horrifying and hilarious.

Which character was the most enjoyable to write? Is this character your favorite, or do you have another?

Giguhl. Hands down. I knew from the get-go that I had to have a hairless cat demon in this book. I'm fascinated by hairless cats. I defy anyone to look at one and tell me they don't look demonic.

He was probably the easiest to write because he was so clear to me from the beginning. I had to be careful with him, though, because he threatened to steal the show. Plus, he makes me laugh. I have no idea where he comes up with that stuff.

After the trilogy, will you be writing more novels featuring Sabina Kane?

Let's just say, I have some surprises in store over the next two books that could lend themselves to further exploration.

When you aren't writing, how do you like to spend your time?

Like most authors, I lead a life filled with excitement and glamour. When I'm not chained to my laptop, I'm doing the mom thing. Luckily, my son is hilarious and keeps me on my toes. Otherwise, I spend way too much time online, read every chance I can get, and watch a lot of bad reality TV. My hobbies include sloth, gluttony, and sarcasm.

As a first-time author, what have you found to be the most exciting part of the publishing process?

The whole experience has been exciting. What could be better than being paid to play make-believe all day? But I'd have to say getting "The Call" was the most exciting. It's surprising my agent isn't deaf given all the screaming and crying that followed the announcement that Orbit wanted to buy my books. I'll never forget anything about that day.

if you enjoyed
RED-HEADED STEPCHILD

look out for

THE MAGE IN BLACK

by

Jaye Wells

Thus far, the food in New York left a lot to be desired. Back in California, none of my meals ever bit back.

"Ouch!" I reared back and checked to be sure my ear was still attached. My meal stared back with glittering eyes, black in the dim light. He had a few days' worth of scruff and a diamond stud glinted from beneath greasy black hair.

"Fuck you, bitch." His attitude–and his blood—left a bitter taste in my mouth. Frustrated and too tired to deal with this shit, I pushed him away. Instead of running like a normal person, he had the nerve to pull a gun on me.

"Seriously?" I said. If I hadn't been so annoyed, I probably would have laughed. "I think you better hand over the gun before you hurt yourself—or I do it for you."

He pulled the trigger. The bullet ripped through the flesh just below my right collarbone. I might be immune to the damage, but it fucking hurt.

"Dammit!" I yelled, pressing a hand to my chest. "Gimme that thing." I jerked the gun out of his hands and threw it into the wooded area off the trail. His eyes widened and he stumbled back, mumbling prayers to the Virgin Mary.

"She can't help you now," I said menacingly. He tripped over his feet and ran off into the night. I briefly considered giving chase, but decided it wasn't worth the effort.

Despite the empty trails this time of night, Central Park still hummed with energy. Occasionally I'd get the sense of dark shadows shifting in my peripheral vision. The chill October air held the promise of rain. In the park, the city scents of trash, exhaust, and humanity were muted and mixed with smoky aroma of fallen leaves. I slowed my pace and took a deep lungful of air. I winced and pressed a hand against the wound in my chest. The hole was already closing, entombing the bullet lodged there—a morbid souvenir of my first visit to the Big Apple.

A twig snapped behind me. Another. Someone or something wasn't worried about me knowing they were there. I didn't change pace. They'd reveal themselves when they were ready—and I'd be ready for them.

"You picked the wrong woods tonight, Little Red Riding Hood." The voice came from behind.

I turned slowly, silently cursing myself for not bringing more weapons with me. Three vampire males stood on the path. From the corner of my eye, I saw two others come from the tree line to stand behind me. Five-to-one odds. Not too bad, I thought.

"Can I help you?" I asked, keeping my tone conversational.

The leader laughed. He was young, judging from his light coppery hair. His flunkies chuckled, while casting uncertain looks at him. He strolled forward with the others getting his back. His laugh cut off as quickly as it started. "You're poaching on our territory."

"I'm sure I don't know what you mean." I crossed my arms, reaching inside my jacket for the knife hidden there.

"This here's the official hunting ground of the Lone Wolves."

I shifted my weight onto my back foot. "The what?"

"Lone Wolves. It's the name of our gang." He turned to show me the back of his raggedy jacket. Sure enough, a snarling wolf face stared back at me from the leather.

"Wait a second," I said. "You're vampires, not werewolves. Plus, isn't it supposed to be 'Lone Wolf,' as in, you know, one? If there's more than one of you, then it kind of defeats the purpose of being 'lone,' doesn't it?"

He squinted hard, as if trying to follow my logic and getting lost. "Shut up, bitch. Hold her, boys."

Rough hands grabbed me from behind. I allowed them to do so. "You don't know who you're messing with." I said calmly.

"Oh, this should be good," the leader said.

"My name is Sabina Kane." I said this a tad more dramatically than I'd intended.

The leader blinked. "Is that supposed to mean something to me?"

I opened my mouth to tell him— What? That I used to be an assassin on the Dominae's payroll? That I was the granddaughter of the Alpha Domina? What good would it do me now? Even if that information meant something to them, it wouldn't do me any favors. Hell, it might even convince them to turn me over to the Dominae. They'd probably put a hefty price on my head by now.

"No, I guess it shouldn't," I said instead. The realization that my old life was gone hit me hard in the gut. Looked like I was the lone wolf now. But if these assholes thought I was going to lower my neck in submission, they had a nasty surprise coming.

"Look, I'm new to town. I didn't know this was your territory."

"Well, you're in New York now, bitch. And we're gonna show you what we do to poachers." He nodded at the guys behind me, and their arms tightened on mine.

The leader flashed his fangs, which were sorely in need of a good brushing. He started to lean in as one of his buddies forced my neck to the side. The problem with this type of macho group was they always assumed a female would automatically submit.

Not this chick.

I delivered a swift knee jab to his crotch. He yelped and fell down into the fetal position with his hands covering his groin. His friends seemed unnerved to see their leader whimpering on the ground. I took advantage of the distraction to free myself from the two holding my arms. Easy work given their haste to cover their own testicles.

I grabbed the knife from my coat and dispatched the one on the right. He ignited into a pile of cinders immediately. I spun and kicked the other in the chest with the heel of my boot. As he fell, I removed an apple wood chopstick from my hair and stabbed it into his chest. Three down, two to go. Only the other two were already running. I took off after them.

The problem was I didn't know Central Park nearly as well as they did. They disappeared like rabbits into the brush. After giving chase for a few minutes, I was winded, hungry, and my feet hurt. So I gave up and hobbled back toward the entrance of the park where I was supposed to meet Adam.

Needing a minute, I sat on a bench near a sign that read "Strawberry Fields." The famous Imagine mosaic memorializing John Lennon lay a few feet away. Someone had left an offering of red roses in the center of the circle. All around me, trees reached up toward the inky night sky, and just beyond them the lights in New York's looming towers glowed like stars.

What the fuck was I doing here?

I'm not sure how long I sat there before I heard footsteps. I looked to my left, expecting more trouble. Possibly the cops who enforced the park's curfew. Adam had warned me about them before I left him at the park's entrance to go feed.

Instead, Adam's familiar silhouette approached. He must have grown impatient waiting for me.

He stopped a few feet from the bench. "All set?"

I looked down at my hands, which felt sweaty despite the cool night. With a thumb, I rubbed at the moisture on my palm.

"Sabina?" He sat next to me, his thigh touching mine. "You okay?"

I turned my head, surprised at the sympathy I heard in his voice. "I'm not nervous."

"I know."

"How far is this place?"

"Not far. About twenty minutes."

"Great," I said without much enthusiasm. It's not that I didn't want to meet my sister. It's just everything was happening so fast. But like it or not, I didn't have a choice. With the war looming and the Dominae after my ass, it's not like I had the luxury of self-pity.

Adam stood and grabbed my hand. I resisted for a moment before allowing him to pull me up. He stared at me for a moment, as if making sure I wasn't about to run the other direction. Honestly, it had crossed my mind.

"Um, Sabina?"

"I'm fine—let's go," I snapped. Maybe it would be like ripping off a Band-Aid, I thought. Just do it fast. It'll be uncomfortable for a moment and then be fine. I hoped.

"Wait," he said, pulling me to a stop when I tried to march off toward my destiny. "Is there something you want to tell me?"

I looked at him, trying to think of anything I'd done recently that I needed to admit to. When nothing came to mind other than the usual, I shook my head. "Not really. Why?"

He reached out and touched my leather jacket. "Is that a bullet hole?"

Freaking great.

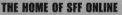